Charles John Cornish, C. J. (Charles John) Cornish

Animals at Work and Play

their activities and emotions

Charles John Cornish, C. J. (Charles John) Cornish

Animals at Work and Play
their activities and emotions

ISBN/EAN: 9783337816131

Printed in Europe, USA, Canada, Australia, Japan

Cover: Foto ©Raphael Reischuk / pixelio.de

More available books at **www.hansebooks.com**

ANIMALS
AT WORK AND PLAY

THEIR ACTIVITIES AND EMOTIONS

BY

C. J. CORNISH

Author of 'Life at the Zoo,' 'Wild England of To-Day,'
'The New Forest' and 'The Isle of Wight'

With Illustrations

LONDON
SEELEY AND CO. LIMITED
ESSEX STREET, STRAND
1896

PREFACE

In a previous book, 'Life at the Zoo,' the writer gave the result of some experiments showing the tastes and preferences of animals for colour, music, and perfumes. The following notes deal with some of the more general activities and emotions of their every-day life. Routine, as M. George Leroy remarked in his '*Lettres sur Les Animaux*,' is the main feature in their existence; but this routine embraces a very wide range of practical effort. Considering the difference of their equipment contrasted with that of man, they secure a large share of happiness and comfort, judged from the animal point of view. Most of the papers were originally contributed to the *Spectator*, to whose Editors the Author has to offer his renewed thanks for permission to publish them consecutive form.

C. J. CORNISH,
Orford House, Chiswick Mall.

CONTENTS

CONTENTS

CONTENTS ix

LIST OF ILLUSTRATIONS

ANIMALS AT WORK AND PLAY

ANIMALS' BEDS

BIRDS which make such elaborate nests for their young, seldom seem to think of making beds for themselves to sleep in on winter nights.* This contradiction is the more surprising because many animals do make, or own, or appropriate beds. Some, like the prairie-dogs, make a fresh one every night ; and almost all that possess a bed at all, are vastly fussy, important, jealous, and particular about this their only article of household furniture.

Prairie-dogs ought to take the place of the stupid guinea-pigs as pets, if only because they throw away their old bed every day, and make a new one. The sight of the prairie-dogs making up their beds on winter afternoons is the funniest scene in

* Wrens are an exception to the rule. They habitually sleep, during the winter, in the unlined 'spare' nests built in spring.

the Zoo. There are several sets of these genial little fellows in the Gardens, two or three in a cage, each of which is supplied with a sleeping-box in one corner, while every other day a few handfuls of fresh straw are put in. In the morning, the prairie-dogs carry every bit of their last night's bed out of the box, and throw it out into the cage. They then eat their breakfast, and spend the day in playing about, staring visitors out of countenance, cramming long pieces of straw into their mouths and pouches, and nibbling carrots. About three o'clock, when the days are short, they suddenly recollect that they have not made their beds, and at once set to work in a hurry to get it done before dark. As the closing-bell rings at dusk, and that is the moment at which the prairie-dogs earnestly desire to be in bed, it almost seems, to anyone who watches them, as if they knew the time and were waiting for the 'curfew' before turning in. But bed-making with them is a very serious matter. Common straw, dragged in just as it is, does not suit them at all. It has all to be cut up to a certain length, and then carried in in bundles and 'made up' inside. Each prairie-dog sits up on end, and crams straw into its mouth in a most dreadful hurry, holding the straws across and breaking them off on each side with its paws, exactly as sewing-maids indulge in the bad habit of breaking cotton with their teeth.* As soon as the prairie-dog has filled its mouth till it cannot hold any more, it drops on all-fours and gallops off into the sleeping-box, arranges the cut straw, and rushes out again for a fresh supply. Each seems to watch the others severely, as they sit up straw-cutting, to see that they do not shirk. From time to time they all jump into the air and bark, as if suddenly projected upwards by a spring in the boards of the floor. Dormice also make beds, though they are not so particular as the prairie-dogs about a change of blankets. When wild, they often fit a roof to an old bird's nest, and fill the inside with moss and wool, in which they curl up and sleep through the winter. But when kept in a warm house, only the bed needs to be provided. The best selection of bedding by a dormouse which the writer has known was made by one which had escaped, and remained for some weeks in the house before being recaptured. When winter wraps were once more coming into season, some jackets were taken out of a drawer, and under the astrachan collar of one of these the dormouse was found fast

---

* In the spring of 1896, Mr Jannach kindly presented the writer's wife with a prairie-dog. It preferred sleeping under some heavy piece of furniture to using its own bed. If any pieces of paper or string had fallen behind a bureau or chest of drawers, it carefully carried them out and laid them on the carpet, treating them as 'old bedding.' It burrowed into a sofa among the springs, where it would bark when anyone sat down. Two others, the writer hears, burrowed into a chest of drawers in a house, and tore up dresses to make beds.

asleep, in a bed which it had nibbled out in the cloth, with the fur on the top for a blanket. Another and much larger hibernating animal—the badger—takes a quantity of grass in to make its bed in the winter, and removes this when it comes out more freely in the spring. But the oddest fancy of the badger in bed is that it actually sleeps on its head. This is true, in any case, of one of the Zoo badgers. Twice, when the straw in which he buries himself has been moved, the writer has seen him, not curled up on his side, but with the top of his flat head on the ground, and the rest of its body curled over it, as if it had fallen asleep in the middle of turning head over heels.

No one can have failed to notice how particular children are about their beds—how much they object to have them altered, how they insist on their being 'made' in their own way, and how they carry their newest and most valued possessions up to bed with them, and poke them away under the blankets and pillows. Animals do exactly the same, and a pet dog which is on the friendliest terms with master and servants, often makes the most ridiculous fuss if anyone touches the box or basket in which it sleeps. Like children, or the old women who hide sovereigns and bank notes in the mattresses, the dogs have nearly always a small hoard of very old, dry bones hidden away in their bed, in the straw or under a rug, as the case may be, and think it necessary to make a show of the fiercest displeasure if anyone comes near who might carry their savings away.

As a rule it is only petted domestic animals that are 'faddy' about their beds. Many of these are as particular about their arrangement as the old 'nabob' at St Roman's Well, who drilled the housemaid into adjusting his matresses to the proper angle of inclination. The writer has seen a little dachshund which would not go to her basket until the blanket had been held to the hall-stove. This she required to be done in summer as well as winter, though the stove was not lighted. A spaniel, kept in a stable, used always to leave its kennel to sleep with the horse. Hounds make a joint bed on the bench after a long run, lying back to back, and so supporting one another. But sporting dogs should have proper beds made like shallow boxes with sloping sides. They are far more rested in the morning than if simply left to lie on straw. This was noted by a clever old Devonshire clergyman, a great sportsman, who observed that his best retrieving spaniel used always to get into an empty wheelbarrow to sleep when tired. The dog's bed should be a rough reproduction of a navvy's barrow standing on short legs. Foxes are very careful to find a comfortable bed by day. Their round 'forms' in the long grass are made well sheltered from the wind, often in the bottom of a pit or hollow, unlike those of the hares, which are oval, and on a hill-side. The crown of a pollard-tree they like even better. The prettiest fox's bed the writer has ever seen was under a dog-rose bush, which grew on a little circle of sound ground in a rushy marsh. Two foxes were curled up under it, enjoying the winter sun; and as all the rushes and the rose bush were white with hoar-frost, the momentary glimpse of the foxes in bed was as pretty as it was unexpected. The poet Cowper's cat was not alone in her taste for making a bed in such odd places as watering-pots and open drawers. Cats are the most obstinately capricious, in their fancies about their beds, of any domestic creature. They will follow a particular rug or shawl from room to room, if it be removed, in order to sleep on it, or insist on the use of one chair, until they get their way, and then for some reason take a fancy to another. The cleanliest of all animals, anything newly washed or very fresh and bright, strikes them as just the thing for a bed. A nicely-aired newspaper lying on the floor or in a chair, or linen fresh from the wash, is almost irresistible. Outdoor cats seek a warm as well as a tidy bed. The writer was once much surprised, when passing through Mr Thornycroft's shipbuilding yard at Chiswick, to see a cat fast asleep, lying, it seemed, on a muddy path.

But the spot which the cat had selected for its couch, was one at which a hot steam-pipe passed under the road, and the mud was there baked into a warm, dry cake, which made not only a clean but an artificially-heated sleeping-place. But the oddest taste in beds developed by a cat, was that entertained by a very highly-bred grey Angora, which was justly petted and admired by the family in which it lived. For some months it would only sleep in or upon a hat, if such could be found, ladies' hats being preferred. If it could discover one with the inside uppermost, it would lie inside it. If not, such was its love for this form of couch, it would curl itself round the brim, and with its long, furry tail and pliant body, made a fine winter trimming to a summer hat, though gentlemen who found it cuddled round their tall hats regarded its taste with less admiration. By some accident, a drawer in which all the 'summer' hats had been disposed for the winter was left open for some days, after which it was discovered that all the hats had been tried in turn, the cat having finally selected one adorned with white laburnum flowers, which never recovered from the 'ironing' to which it had been subjected. Even the animals of the farm have certain preferences in their sleeping arrangements. Cattle and sheep, when left out to 'lie rough,' always sleep under trees to avoid the dew; and sheep, if there is no such cover available, lie on the highest, and consequently the driest ground. Horses seem less particular, though they have curious fancies as to their bed-litter in stables. It would be interesting to know what is the horse's point of view as to the substitution of 'moss-litter' for straw, which the rise in the price of the latter has brought into such general use. But perhaps the hardier animals are right. A rise in the 'standard of comfort' is not an un-mixed blessing even to their owners

ANIMAL SLEEP

THOUGH many animals look on sleep as a luxury, and make comfortable beds for its enjoyment, others sleep but little ; and their slumbers are so light, that they seem to have the power of becoming instantaneously awake, however soundly they may have been sleeping. It is commonly said of some creatures that they 'sleep with one eye open.' The instantaneous transition by which, when wakened, they pass into action, such as flight and escape, with full possession of their faculties, almost suggests that they have some additional sense, which takes the form of vigilance in sleep, and remains conscious when all other consciousness is lost. This is an easy, but not a satisfactory, explanation of this quick recovery of sense by sleeping animals ; for it attributes to them a faculty not possessed by man, under conditions in which the life of men and animals would naturally be supposed to differ least—that is, when the use of their higher faculties is for a time partially suspended.

There is good reason to believe that the broken
and timid form of animal sleep in the greater
number of species, is not such as they would
naturally choose, but is the result of habits acquired
and transmitted in centuries of danger and avoid-
ance of their enemies; and that the same causes
which have modified the hours of sleep, have also
modified its character. Of the animals which, when
wild, now sleep by day, snatching broken periods
of unrestful slumber as and where they can, not a
twentieth part are night-feeders by nature or choice.
The true nocturnal animals are those which can only
find their food at night. With the exception of the
owls and opossums, which are only partly insectiv-
orous, they are nearly all insect-eaters, bats, lemurs,
lorises and nightjars; and though the last, like the
owls, do move with rapidity and some precision
when once disturbed, the others might be distinguished from those creatures which are only
nocturnal by necessity, by the absence of that wakefulness in sleep which the latter possess in such a
marked degree. The bats, lemurs and lorises are,
during the day, steeped and drugged with slumber.
If once discovered, they make no effort to escape;
like the opossums, which let the 'black fellows'
chop them out of their holes in the hollow trees
without moving from their sleeping-places, it does

not seem possible for them to awaken. Light benumbs their faculties like freezing cold, and they seek darkness with the same instinct that a human being, with senses benumbed by sickness, demands more light. Bats, the only purely nocturnal animals in this country, show this characteristic in its completest form. Their daylight sleep paralyses them, though not because they are unable to see and fly with safety in the sunlight, for they can do both. But if handled and disturbed, they make no effort even to spread their wings, and seem unable to shake off the drowsy influence. Not even the great night-flying moths are so completely the slaves of this unyielding habit of diurnal sleep. Contrasted with this deep repose, the slumber of the great body of herbivorous animals is so light and broken that it may be doubted whether their senses are ever so completely at rest as to deserve the name of sleep at all. In human sleep the sense of hearing is that which remains awake longest, and to which the brain most readily responds. But in sound and heavy sleep, the ear often suggests a long train of thought in dreams before the brain awakens to a sense of reality. In most sleeping animals, its warning is instantaneous, and the faculties obey the call for action with no apparent interval of inertia. A sleeping fox will rise, gallop off, and dodge the hounds with as much coolness and knowledge of the ground as if it had been surprised on the prowl with all its wits awake. It may have allowed the pack to approach fatally near; but when once roused, it is wholly awake—not drowsy, bewildered or confused.

Hares seem never to sleep; however closely they may lie in their forms, the eye is alert and vigilant. Stags sleep soundly when watched by their hinds. But a solitary stag, sleeping on a hill-side, retains the two senses of hearing and scent in full vigour. Deerstalkers have discovered by experiment that the *sleeping senses* of the stag are sensitive up to a distance of at least two hundred yards on the wind-ward side. Between the drowsy sleep of the nocturnal animals and the hyper-sensitive sleep of those which spend their lives in constant fear of their enemies, a place must be found for the form of slumber enjoyed by the large carnivora, and that of domestic animals. The former have no enemies to fear, except man, and the latter, protected by man, enjoy to the full the blessing of natural rest. Tigers are frequently found fast asleep in the daytime. Native hunters have been known to track them after a 'kill' to the place in which they were lying fast asleep and gorged with food, and to shoot them as they lie. When taking its mid-day repose in districts where it is little disturbed, the tiger does not always retire to a place

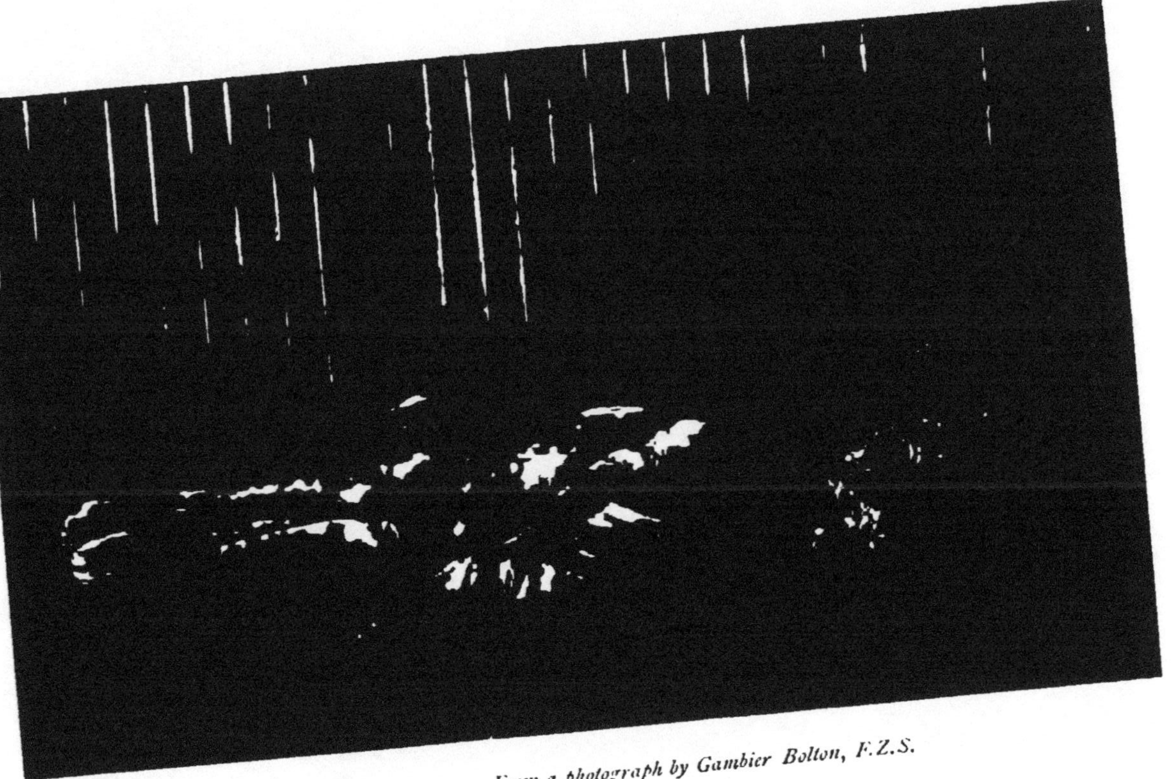

A Sleeping Lion. *From a photograph by Gambier Bolton, F.Z.S.*

of security, like the bear, or even the leopard, which usually sleeps on the branch of a tree. It just lies down in some convenient spot, either shady or warm, according to the weather, and there sleeps, almost regardless of danger. They have been found lying in dry nullahs, under trees, and even in the grass of the hill-sides, unobserved, until their disturber came within a few yards of them. General Douglas Hamilton, when shooting in the Dandilly Forest, came upon a tigress and two cubs lying fast asleep on their backs, with their paws sticking up in the air, under a clump of bamboos. When he was within a few yards of the group, one raised its head and without moving its body quietly looked at him along the line of its body between its paws. Tigers kept in captivity awaken gradually, stretching and yawning like a dog. Yet, like the dog, they possess the power of vigilance in sleep, which they can use if required. Those at the Zoo will spring to their feet in a second, when apparently in deep sleep, if they hear the keepers moving at the back of the cages, near the store where their food is kept; and in parts of India where they are much disturbed by hunters, they sleep as lightly as deer. Dogs, which are at once the drowsiest and most wakeful of domestic animals, according to their state of mind and circumstances, seem to sleep lightly or heavily at will. Nothing can be more slow, reluctant and leisurely than the enforced waking of a petted house-dog when it does not wish to be disturbed. It will remain deaf to a call, twitch its feet if tickled, but not unclose its eyes, and finally stretch and yawn like a sleepy child. But mention something interesting to the same dog when sleeping, such as the word 'walk,' or click the lock of a gun, and it is on its feet in an instant, and ready for enterprise. Thus animals seem capable of three forms or degrees of sleep—one, the deep stupor of the nocturnal creatures ; a second, the semi-human slumber of carnivorous and domesticated animals, which have a power of vigilance at command ; and lastly, the vigilant sleep of the persecuted ruminant and rodent tribes. The highly-sensitive sleep of the last is probably a development from natural causes. Even human sleep can be made vigilant by solicitude or previous resolve. It is a common experience that persons who are heavy sleepers can awaken at a certain hour by resolving to do so, or, if roused by a sound previously agreed on, recognise it as a call to awaken and do awaken instantly. In cases of sickness the least movement of the patient will arouse an anxious nurse who sleeps ; and in sleep itself the brain often exercises a curious vigilance, for it recognises in dreams forgotten sensations which have only been experienced by the sleeper in previous dreams. The experiments by which M. Jouffroy conceived that he had proved that the brain was always dreaming, because persons awakened at various times all said they were then dreaming, are not conclusive. The extraordinary quickness with which the association of ideas follows a sound and produces dreams might account for the dream at the time of awakening, even if the interval between the sound made to rouse the sleeper and that of consciousness were only momentary. But some functions of the brain can be kept alert in sleep; and the animal which passes all day in the constant apprehension of danger, naturally preserves its vigilant faculties during sleep in a very high degree. Such sleep can hardly be restful, and it is not improbable that this want of complete and secure repose accounts in a measure for the shortness of animal life, even when aided by the healthy influence of their free and open-air existence.

ANIMALS' TOILETTES*

THE sailor's fancy that pictured the mermaid sitting on a rock with 'a glass and a comb' in her hand was not quite the myth it seems. Weary of male companionship, he painted the bright-eyed seals as sea-maidens. But if for 'glass' we read 'fan,' we may take it as a true account of the seal's toilette. These harmless and affectionate creatures, have, fixed to their front flipper, a neat little comb, with which, when resting on the rocks, they carefully arrange and smooth the fur on their faces. But the Northern fur-seals are very sensitive to heat ; and when assembled in the rookeries on the Pribilov Islands, both old and young may be seen in thousands, lying on their sides, and fanning themselves with their fore-flippers. The writer noticed that Barnum's showman had taken advan-

* This chapter, almost in its present form, was originally written for the *Spectator* in 1893. It was quoted at length in various American papers, without reference to the source from which it came, and the writer found a portion of it quoted in Mrs Brightwen's book, *More About Wild Nature*, and attributed to an American Journal.

THE WOODCOCK'S TOILET.
From a Japanese woodcut.

tage of this habit to teach his seals to beat a tambourine! On one occasion a tambourine was missing, but this made no difference to the seal, who *fanned* himself instead, though anxiously looking round for his instrument.

But fans are hardly needed for the toilette. Brushes and combs most animals carry with them. 'Brilliantine' also is carried in a small and handy reservoir by all ducks and divers. Mud serves for cold cream and vaseline; dust for Fuller's earth and pearl powder; and water, as with us, is perhaps the most important necessary. But birds especially are mighty particular about the quality of their 'toilette-dust,' and equally nice as to the water in which they prefer to wash. Some use water only, some water or dust, others dust and no water. Partridges are a good example of the dusting birds, and are most careful in the selection of their dust-baths. Dry loam suits them best. But perhaps their favourite place is a meadow where a few turfs have been removed. There they scratch out the loam, and shuffle *backwards* under the grass roots till their feathers are full of the cool earth. In wet weather they find, if possible, a heap of burnt ashes on the site of a weed-fire, and dust there. Sparrows, on the contrary, always choose road-dust, the driest and finest possible. Larks also are fond of the road, and dust there in the early morning. But they too have their fancy, and choose the dry, gritty part, where the horses' hoofs tread. Wild ducks, though feeding by the salt water, prefer to wash in fresh-water pools, and will fly long distances inland to running brooks and ponds, where they preen and wash themselves in the early morning. But though passing so much time on the water, ducks seem to prefer a shower-bath to any other; and in heavy rain they may be seen opening their feathers and allowing the rain to soak in, after which they dress the whole surface with oil from the reservoir which we mentioned above. Swallows and martins are as nice in their choice of bath-water as any 'professional beauty;' nothing but newly-fallen rain-water thoroughly pleases them, and if tempted to bathe, it is generally by some shallow pool in the road which an hour's sun will evaporate.

The writer has never seen hawks or falcons bathing when wild. Trained birds in good health, bathe almost daily, and the bath of a peregrine falcon is a very careful performance. But no nymph could be more jealous of a witness than these shy birds, and it is not until after many careful glances in every direction that the falcon descends from her block and wades into the shallow bath. Then, after more suspicious glances, she thrusts her broad head under the water and flings it on to her back, at the same time raising the feathers and letting the drops thoroughly soak them. After bathing head and back, she spreads her wings and tail fan-like on the water, and rapidly opens and shuts them, after which she stoops down and splashes the drops in every direction. The bath over, she flies once more to the block, and turning her back to the sun, spreads every feather of the wing and tail, raises those on the body, and assists the process of drying by a tremulous motion imparted to every quill, looking more like an old cormorant on a buoy than a peregrine. Sparrows, chaffinches, robins, and, in the very early morning, rooks and wood-pigeons, bathe often. One robin we knew always took *his* bath in the falcon's bath, after the hawk had finished. The unfortunate London sparrow has few shallow places in which he can bathe, and a pie-dish on the leads delights him. If the dish be white, his grimy little body soon leaves evidence that his ablutions have been genuine.

No doubt the cats, large and small, make the most careful toilette of any class of animal, with the exception of some of the opossums. The lions and tigers wash themselves in exactly the same manner as the cat, wetting the dark, india-rubber-like ball of the fore-foot and the inner toe, and passing it over the face and behind the ears. The foot is thus at the same time a face - sponge and brush, and the rough tongue combs the rest of the body. Hares also use their feet to wash their faces, and the hare's foot is so suitable for a brush that it is always used to apply the 'paint' to the face for the stage. One of the most charming pets we have kept, and the most particular as to washing and brushing its feet and fur, was a lovely brown opossum from Tasmania. 'Sooty phalanger' was, we believe, its scientific name; it was covered with deep rich brown fur, had a face something like a fox, a pink nose, hands with a nailless thumb, and long claws on the fingers. It washed its feet every two or three minutes, and would pay the same attention to the ear, hair, or hands of anyone on whose shoulder it was allowed to sit. Once having upset a bottle of turpentine over its hands, it almost fretted to death because it could not remove the scent. Oddly enough, it would, if possible, retire during the day to a chimney, which it perhaps took for a hollow tree, and did not object to the soot in its fur, perhaps considering it 'clean dirt,' as children do earth. Water-rats are very clean animals, and wash and brush their faces with the greatest care.' We saw one this summer on a pond at Welling, in Kent, swim out to pick up the blossoms of an acacia blossom, which were falling on the water. After daintily eating each flower on the bank, he licked his hands, wiped his moustaches, and swam off for another. We also tried an acacia blossom, but except a slightly sweet flavour, could find nothing to account for the rat's taste for them. Sporting dogs, which are used in mud, snow, and wet, are strangely clever and quick in cleaning and drying their coats ; and it is a sure sign that a dog has been over-tired if he shows any trace of mud or dirt next morning. Most of their toilette is done with the tongue, but they are very clever at using a thick box bush or the side of a haystack as a rough towel.* One small spaniel which we allowed to live in the house was well aware that if he returned dirty, he would not be admitted indoors. About an hour before the close of the day's shooting, he used to strike work and begin to clean himself; and if urged to do more, would slip off home and present himself neat and clean in the dining-room. One day the dog had been left at home, and his master returned and seated himself, wet, and with half-frozen drops of ice sticking to his gaiters, by the fire.

* When shooting on the famous 'Scoresby Leas,' where the army of the Pilgrimage of Grace encamped, near Doncaster, I saw a curious example of the importance some animals attach to having a ' clean up ' the moment work is over. As soon as we sat down to luncheon, a small retriever bitch, belonging to my host's keeper, began at once to pull off with her teeth all the burrs that had stuck to our gaiters and knickerbockers. This was her constant habit.

'Pan' ran up and carefully licked off the frozen ice and snow, stopping every now and then to give an anxious look, which said as plainly as possible: 'Dear me, if I don't get him clean quickly, he will be sent to lie in the stable.'

Horses and cattle not only wash and clean their own coats, but also assist at each others' toilets. The greatest difficulty which most animals find in the pursuit of cleanliness and neatness is to wash their own necks. A cat does this by licking its fur as far as its tongue will bend upwards and backwards, and finishing by wetting its feet and rubbing the parts behind its ears and the back of its neck. But cattle and horses can use no such expedient. Consequently they wash for each other such parts of their coats as they cannot reach themselves. If a horse and a cow are alone in the same field, they will perform these good offices mutually, though, as the horse cleans its own or the cow's coat usually with its teeth, while the cow uses its tongue, the process is not quite satisfactory to either. But they are ever so much better off than the solitary giraffe at the Zoo. After its arrival it soon made all its coat bright and clean *except its neck*. This could only be washed by another giraffe; and as it has no companion, its neck is several shades darker than its body, and clearly needs washing.

ANIMALS IN SOCIETY

Mr Kipling in his *Jungle Book*, has amused himself and delighted his readers by constructing a wild-beast society living in the woods, true in habits to the instincts each of its kind, but recognising a sort of social obligation, laws, and customs which are inherited, discussed, enforced, or remitted by the collective wisdom of the creatures themselves. The effect is perfectly convincing, and there is no sense of incongruity or make-believe in reading these chapters, partly because of the art with which they are written, but partly because the real life of the jungle creatures is itself so intelligent and intelligible that it seems perfectly rational to find that they have progressed a step further, and formed themselves into a society whose members play parts subordinate to some generally understood law. The wonder is not that they should do so, but that they should not. Yet it is on the whole true of the higher individual intelligences among animals, that, properly

speaking, they do not live in society at all. They
live in association ; but that is a different matter,
often the result of chance—such as travelling on
the same lines of migration, or meeting where food
is present in unusual abundance. But that is quite
a different matter from society as we understand
society, which is association for reciprocal benefit,
and nearly always results in some form of division
of labour and separation of classes. The appearance
of social life in the case of all the ruminant animals,
deer, wild cattle, antelopes, and wild sheep, is somewhat misleading. They are nearly always seen together in herds, and the association is voluntary. But
through the ages that they have thus associated they
have made no progress in their manner of life, and
have not developed the least tendency towards forming the rudiments of 'community.' The explanation
of this is probably to be found in the motive which
makes them gregarious. Apart from a liking for
'company' which they all share, the main motive
for their assembling together is fear, *sentiment peu
fécond en progrès*, as M. George Leroy remarks in
his *Lettres Sur les Animaux*. Among these animals
it has developed one social device, the habitual placing of sentinels, whose place is taken in turn by
members of the herd. It is division of labour, and
shows that the idea is understood by them. But it

has not led to any further progress. On the other hand it may be doubted whether the large gregarious animals have any sufficient motive for progress at all. Their life consists in the daily repetition of a few actions which satisfy all their wants ; they develop no new ones ; and for them life may perhaps have reached perfection. One rather curious exception to this extreme simplicity and incompleteness of the 'society' of the deer tribe is noted by Lord Lovat, in his essays on 'The Highland Deer' in the 'Badminton Library.' Large stags are often attended by a smaller stag, who acts as a kind of servant and humble companion to the big beast. 'In sheep-ground, or where there are few deer,' writes Lord Lovat, 'a big stag is seldom found quite alone ; he has a small one as his slave. This little fellow has to do all the dirty work—in fact, fag for his master. The old gentleman lies snug in a hole out of the wind, or sheltered from the flies ; the slave has to lie out on the hillock, where he can see ; and if, trusting to the old fellow being asleep, he looks out for a snug corner for himself, woe betide him if his master catches him. In an instant he rushes out upon his fag, and drives him back to his post. Then if there is any doubt as to the safety of the road, the little stag has to go on in front, driven on by the horns or fore-feet of the big one.'

Slavery is one of the early developments of the social instincts in man, so the 'fagging' instinct in the Highland stag must be credited to it as a sign of progress. On the other hand, the same high authority who has recorded this selfish instinct in the stag, hastens to add an anecdote of another character, which shows that deer have a sense of obligation in society which is probably more common among animals than is believed. 'Sometimes an old stag takes compassion upon a youngster. The writer saw a pretty instance of this on the West coast in the season of 1885. Three stags had been moved in a young plantation. The two best jumped the three-foot wire fence, but a third, a two-year-old stag, got frightened, and refused. The two waited for him for some time, while he walked and ran up and down; at last the larger of the two—a good royal—came back to the fence. The little one ran towards him, and the royal trotted away; but no, the little one could not make up his mind to jump. Back came the royal over the fence, went close up to the little fellow, and actually *kissed him* several times. With the glass, not five hundred yards away, we could see them rub their noses together. Then the royal led down to the fence, but still the little stag would not have it. At last the royal tossed his head in the air, and seeming to say " Well, you are a fool," went off up the hill to join his companion. When out of sight the little one took courage, got over the fence with a scramble, and followed.' An animal which has the slave-using instinct, and the instinct of sympathy, and desires to give practical aid to another, evidently possesses the necessary intelligence for developing a more complex form of society than that in which deer now live. The probable reason that it does not do so is that which has been already suggested—that their life is already perfect, for them, and needs no improvements. This is partly corroborated by the greater development of common organisation in creatures of far lower intelligence—the common wild rabbits. Experience seems to have taught them that they are far safer when avoiding their enemies underground than on the surface, and that the chances of escape from a stoat or weazel are greater when numbers of burrows are combined into a labyrinth of passages, than if each had a separate and disconnected burrow. It is evident that the food supply would be larger and more lasting if they lived apart ; yet they always prefer to unite in colonies, and the combined dwellings of the rabbit must be looked upon as the result of a genuine social instinct. Most rodents are singularly stupid creatures individually, yet in another of the class, the beaver, the social instinct is seen in by far the most complete development known among the higher animals. The work of the beaver colony, apart from the astonishing engineering skill and knowledge of the use of different material it displays, their employment of water transport, and their control and retention, as a means of protection, of streams and ponds, is alike in motive and purpose as perfect an example of common and organised labour for a common good, as the associated labour by which the population of Holland maintain the dykes and dams. . The whole beaver village works at the dam, and the equally wonderful, though less known, engineering device of the beaver canal, to which logs are rolled, and then towed up to the 'lodges,' is the joint work of the colony. When this is made, and the requisite area of deep water secured by the dam, the families work separately at private house-building. Thus the distinction between public and private duties is recognised and maintained.

Yet this single instance of a highly-organised society among creatures of high development is so far exceeded by the social life of insects, that the problem of instinct seems for the moment beyond solution. If deer and antelopes do not make ·progress because their wants are already satisfied, on what theory can we account for the divisions and subdivisions of social functions in nests of crawling ants? Take, for example, the Amazon ants. Their homes are filled with slaves, and the master-ant has lost not only the desire to work, but even the habit of feeding itself, so that it would die of hunger beside a pile of sugar if a grey ant were not there to put it into its mouth. 'Among the Amazons the slaves undertake every labour; it is they who build, and who carry the young for their masters. They bring them food, clean them, and carry them from place to place, if there is need to emigrate. The masters, by losing interest in work, lose also their votes when it is a question of taking a resolution concerning the whole colony. The servants act on their own initiative and their own responsibility, and even in grave concerns, such as emigration, the idle masters do not seem to be consulted.' The divisions of insects into castes of fighters and workers seems in some instances due to sexual difference, as in the case of bees and hornets. But this does not explain the subsequent apportioning of the tasks of each in the common interests of the society. Who directs that one set of bees shall go abroad to fetch honey, another set wait to receive and clean them on the platform at the mouth of the hive, and a third body guard the entrance against robbers? Yet the working of this organised system can be watched wherever a bee-hive is inhabited in an English garden. The 'gardening ants,' which collect pieces of vegetable, and pile them up to rot in the dark interior of their nests until they are covered with a kind of fungus, on which the ants live, make a walled street, partly roofed, up to the plant whose leaves they propose to cut, and divide the labour according to the size of the workers. The largest act as road-menders, and repair the 'permanent way' when it becomes injured by traffic. The next in size cut the leaves and carry them, and the very small ants fuss around, and being unable to cut leaves, get in the way, and are sometimes carried themselves on a leaf in whose transportation they are anxious to assist. The mechanical societies of these insects are wholly beyond explanation. The analogies of reason which hold good in the case of the higher animals must fail when applied to any theory of rational development in the ant and bee. Their instinct is born fully developed, whereas in the higher animals there is at least the rational attribute, that though they do not progress as a class, individuals do occasionally develop social tendencies which are analogous with our own.

THE ANIMAL DISLIKE OF SOLITUDE

MOST animals have such a dislike of solitude that
nothing less than some form of social banishment
enforced by their species can ever induce them to
seek loneliness and seclusion. When they do fall
under any such social ban pronounced by their companions, they not unusually revenge themselves on
the world by 'keeping a pike,' as proposed by Mr
Weller, senior, with the important difference that they
seek satisfaction from travelling humanity by taking
toll of persons instead of purses ; and the wayfarer
pays the penalty of animal exclusiveness by being
eaten by some mangey and ostracised tiger, or knocked
down and stamped in the mud by an elephant or
buffalo crossed in love.

Voluntary recluses are almost unknown in the
animal world. Perhaps the one consistently unsociable
creature in Europe is the hamster, an ill-tempered, sulky
little rodent. As the squirrel was said, by the old
Norsemen, to bring all the news of the animals to Thor,

because he was the merriest and most sociable of beasts, so, in the talk of the Russian peasants, the hamster is the synonym for all that is sullen, avaricious, solitary and morose. Even in colour he is unlike most other animals, being light above and dark below. This gives the hamster somewhat the same incongruous appearance that a pair of black trousers and a light coat lend a man ; in other respects he is like a large shaggy guinea-pig, with very large teeth and puffy cheeks, into which he can cram a vast quantity of rye or beans for transport. Each hamster lives in a large roomy burrow all by himself, in defence of which he will fight like a badger against any other hamster who may try to enter. Family life he wholly avoids, never allowing a female inside his burrow, but keeping her at a good distance, and making her find her own living for herself and family. The last burden is, however, not a serious one, for by the time the young ones are three weeks old, each discovers that family life is a great mistake and sets off to make a bachelor burrow for itself and save up beans for the winter. For, in addition to its other amiable qualities, the hamster has that of avarice in a marked degree, and heaps up treasures of corn, rye and horse-beans far in excess of his own private wants for the winter. His favourite plan is to dig a number of treasure-chambers, all communicat-

ing with a central guard-room, in which the owner
eats and grows fat until the hardest frosts begin,
when he curls himself up to sleep until the spring.
But this life of leisure does not begin until the
harvest has been gathered.   While the crops are
ripening the hamsters work incessantly to increase
their hoards, and as much as three hundredweight of
grain and beans have been taken from a single burrow.
After harvest, the peasants often search with probes
for the treasure-chambers of the robbers, and no doubt
exact a heavy tribute from the hamster's stores.
But these hoarding propensities are not enough to
account for the anti-social disposition of the hamster.
The sociable squirrels also make a hoard, though
in a careless, slap-dash fashion suited to their mercurial
character.   (It is certain that they often forget where
they have buried their treasures, for during a wet
summer, young hazels and horse-chestnuts sprout in
all sorts of strange sites in the writer's garden, between
the roots of rose bushes and in flower borders, where
the squirrels must have hidden them in the autumn.)
There is another little rodent, the *pika* or calling-
hare, which is obliged, like the hamster, to make
some provision for the winter, but lives, like the
marmots of the Alps, in sociable colonies.

The *pikas* inhabit the desolate steppes which
stretch from the Crimea across Central Asia, and

in preparation for the long winter, each makes a stack of hay over one of the entrances to its burrow. In the bitter cold of the Central Asian winter, when the steppes are covered with snow, these haystacks are the only source of food left to them, and are gradually drawn into the burrow from below. Its position gives a certain security that, if all goes well with its neighbours, only the owner of the stack will eat the store so carefully collected. But these poor little stacks of hay are often taken by the Kirghiz for their fires, or as food for their camels, a source of danger probably unknown in the distant ages when *pikas* first turned haymakers. The question naturally arises as to how the ruined owners of the store are to save themselves from starvation. Clearly the only resource left is to borrow from a neighbour's stack. But animal sense of private property in food is very strong, and in the *pikas'* colonies there is no attempt at making a common stock. Consequently the price paid for society is the liability to support at a personal loss any suddenly pauperised neighbour. The hamsters avoid any such possibility by living alone ; but the loss of society is apparently too great a sacrifice to be made by the *pikas*, even to secure the sole and safe enjoyment of their winter's food. The social instinct, so apparent in the case of the calling-hares, exists in many creatures which are wrongly supposed to prefer solitary lives. Hawks and other predatory birds do not, as a rule, flock together, because they require a large area from which to obtain their food. But in confinement they suffer from solitude in a marked degree. Tame hawks and falcons, if kept alone in a room, mope and lose condition, and in some species a suicidal instinct is developed. Willoughby noticed that merlins kept in solitary confinement destroyed their claws and toes, and the writer has himself seen one instance in which this had happened. The lively, gregarious birds of the tropics cannot endure to miss the society of their fellows. Wilson, the American naturalist, took with him in his travels in South America, one of the green Carolina parrots which he had tamed. This bird was a most affectionate creature, but whenever a flock of its own species passed by, showed a strong desire to join them. Wilson soon caught a companion for his pet, but by an accident it was killed, and the survivor was inconsolable. He then tried the experiment of showing the parrot a small looking-glass. As soon as the bird saw its image in the mirror, it seemed quite contented with its shadowy companion, and would sit for hours cuddled up against the glass with great satisfaction. The flocking of the non-migratory birds after the nesting season is mainly due, not to the pressure of hunger, or the pressure of food in particular places, but to their love of society. In late summer and harvest time, when the face of the country is one broad table of food for the birds, they flock together solely for the sake of company. Recently the writer watched a vast flock of jackdaws, rooks and starlings, feeding on one of a long line of fields of newly - cut wheat. It was late in the afternoon, and another flock of starlings soon passed overhead, on their way to a distant roosting-place. As the sound of rushing wings reached them, the starlings on the ground rose at once, and flew up to meet the travellers. Some invitation was evidently given, for both flocks descended to the ungrudged feast. In a few minutes the strangers resumed their journey, but not for want of a welcome. It is the same with the human gleaners in the fields. The love of society keeps the wives and little ones of the hamlet in a flock, and a solitary gleaner is never seen, though the harvest of ears so gathered might be heavier.

Domestic animals are still more affected by solitude than the wilder natures; for in addition to their original liking for their own kind, they are rarely satisfied to remain long shut out from intercourse with man. No dog can long endure

SOCIAL SPARROWS.   *From a Japanese woodcut.*

to be alone ; but there is little doubt that, so long as it can secure the society of its master, it can dispense with the company of other dogs. Cattle, on the other hand, have a strong liking for the company of their own kind. Waterton, who was never tired of promoting the happiness of all animals tame and wild, was for some time exercised by the difficulty of allowing his cattle to lean over the gates which separated the grazing-fields on his estate, and at the same time preserving the gates from being strained and broken by the pushing and jostling which generally takes place when the cattle in one meadow are making the acquaintance of those in the next. He met the difficulty by stretching an iron chain across from one post to the other on the opposite side to that on which the gate was hung, and so providing a more substantial barrier for the broad chests of the cattle to lean against. Waterton was in all probability no loser by his thoughtful provision for the social amenities of animal life. Society is almost as necessary to the well-being of animals as of men. When wild and free, they can, and do in most cases, secure its enjoyment for themselves. When confined, or in the semi-restraint of domesticity, a wise master will see that this factor of animal happiness is secured. Fortunately, they are, as a rule, neither exclusive nor exacting in their liking for companionship. A carriage horse will find comfort in the company of a kitten, just as a caged lion has attached itself to a dog. And we knew a solitary pigeon which was very much attached to its owner's horses, and spent most of its time in the stable perched on their backs or heads, apparently quite satisfied so long as it had the society of other creatures, though not of its own kind.

ANIMAL ETIQUETTE

It has been noted that the etiquette of high life is by no means the only form of its observance among men. There is such a thing as professional etiquette —the etiquette of sport, and even the etiquette of labour. This sometimes takes the form, not only of prescribing who shall do what, but how things shall be done. It would be very bad form, for instance, for a bricklayer to use more than one hand to work with, or for his 'labourer' to carry up bricks or mortar in anything but the traditional hod, though it might be far quicker and easier to haul them up in a lift. Animals seem to share this feeling for the etiquette of labour; only, as they do not belong to a Trade-Union, it often works entirely to their disadvantage. Take, for instance, the following case of the otter at the Zoo, which, on the Saturday on which the great frost of 1895 began, had just been provided with material for a new bed. It was freezing hard; half its pond was

covered with ice; and the nice, warm, dry straw
was pushed partly into its house, while part of the
bundle lay on the bridge, and some in the water.
In order to make itself comfortable, all the otter
had to do was to step out of its house on to
the bridge and pull the dry straw in. There was
plenty for a bed without meddling with that in the
water at all. But it is not permitted by otter
etiquette to do any work on dry ground which can
possibly be done in the water. Like most of the
etiquette of labour, this is based, partly on prejudice,
but partly on sound principles. A waterman, for
instance, prefers to push a plank into the water,
make it fast to his boat, and tow it, rather than
carry it on his shoulder, even if the way by land is
shorter than that by water. In the first place, it
would be unprofessional, just like a 'docker's job,'
to carry it; and in the next, the water supports the
plank, and he really incurs less labour in towing it.
So has an otter less labour in transporting material
it can drag when floating. Unfortunately, in this
case the material was one in which weight made no
matter, and in which dryness was essential for it to
be of any use, that is, for a bed on a frosty night.
This did not weigh with the otter in the least. Instead of pulling the straw in dry, it plunged into
the icy water, dived and came up on the side of the

bridge on which some of the straw was dipping into the water. It swam along and collected as many of the hanging ends as it could in its mouth; then dived back *under* the bridge, and dragged all the dry part of the straw into the water, having considerable difficulty in doing so, because it was hitched over the edge of the bridge-plank. It then pulled all the dripping straw into its bed, rushed out, took another plunge, and collected another mouthful, which it pulled into the water, and swam off with it as before. After several visits it had collected the whole of what was lying on the plank, had wetted it all thoroughly, and was preparing to go to sleep on it inside its house — a proceeding which almost induced rheumatism at sight among the spectators. But the otter was quite satisfied. It had acted according to rule, and been true to amphibious etiquette, down to soaking what were to be its bedclothes for the coldest night of the year.

The common American ''coon' is a slave to an unusual form of etiquette, which in its case has grown almost beyond the forms of conventional observance, and become a kind of conscience to it. It will *wash* everything which it eats if there is any water near. The fact seems to have been questioned by some writers, but it is certainly the habit of racoons when kept in captivity with access to water. They are very fussy, particular creatures, much given to picking up and carrying off anything odd which takes their fancy. And this, whatever it may be, is duly taken to the water and well 'rinsed out,' whether vegetables or bits of cloth, or even solid hard things, like shells and shiny stones. No 'social pressure' can have been put upon the racoons at the Zoo to make them conform to the laws of the 'coon etiquette; but they do so all the same, and it is a fact that, last spring, one which had a litter of young ones, to which she was much attached, was suddenly seized with a desire to wash them, and carrying them down one by one to her little stone-bath, paddled and washed the poor little creatures as if she had been washing cabbages. It may be doubted whether the kittens did not owe their death to this perverted feeling of social duty in their parent, for they did not long survive their immersion.

Those who have watched the Thames swans in the courting season will have noticed that, as might be expected, these grave and stately birds have certain rules for behaviour which no temptation can make them break. When approaching a lady-swan, or pursuing a rival which has intruded into its particular reach of the river, the cock swan has certain set movements which it goes through. It

is said that the word of command for action in the
Chinese drill is first, 'Prepare to look fierce;' next,
'Look fierce;' and, thirdly, 'Approach the enemy.'
The swan does all this, and something more. He
sets up his wings like plumes, and draws his head
very far back, which corresponds with the first and
second words of command; but for his mode of
approach he always uses a special stroke in swimming which is kept for grand occasions. He strikes
the water with both feet together, which sends him
forward with a rush, the water rippling from his
chest as from the prow of a ship. Then he strikes
again, as his 'way' gets less, and in this manner will
swim very long distances, either in pursuit of his
enemy or of some coy female swan. If he chose
to swim in the ordinary manner, or to fly, or even
to get out on to the bank and run, he would have
no difficulty in overtaking the other. But etiquette
prescribes that this slow and stately stroke shall be
used on such occasions, and swans are too conservative to break the rule.

Conventional rules are most useful in intercourse
with strangers, and this feeling, the result of deliberate
reflection among men, seems quite as well understood
by animals. The number of steps which a Prince
or Ambassador might advance to meet the other
without derogating from his dignity, and the frequent

halts and bows, find a parallel in the amusing form of canine etiquette when one dog 'spies a stranger' at a distance. The first dog stops short, then trots on a little, then crouches, and finally lies flat down, with its nose on its paws, like a skirmisher ordered to open fire on the enemy. The other dog which was less quick-sighted, sometimes lies down too, but more usually trots slowly up, with occasional halts. The action of the first seems clearly to be a survival of a time when a dog naturally crouched in order to conceal itself the moment it saw any other creature which might hurt it, or which, on the contrary, it might want to stalk. The sudden drop is something like that of a setter when 'creeping' up to the birds, but more like the crouch of a fox when it sees a hare, or wants to conceal itself from persons whom it sees while it is still unseen. But now it is observed as pure convention, one which is obviously mere show, but to omit which would be a breach of canine etiquette, which might, and sometimes does, lead to a fight. It is not polite for one dog to omit the form of pretending that the other is a big, strong, important person, against whom he must take precautions. The etiquette of combat is apparently among the most artificial of human observances. It does not seem to take form except in states of society in which public and private war has been recognised as one of the conditions of life, in which fighting becomes not only a fine art, but an agreeable pastime for persons of quality. Hence the elaborate salutations of the duello, and the punctilio of the fencing school. 'Shall I begin with a "damme?" asks Bob Acres, when writing his challenge. And his demur to the plain 'Dear sir,' on the ground that he was not asking his rival to breakfast, seems to plain people rather natural. Yet some of the creatures which are fighters by instinct go through formal preliminaries not unlike those of the set duels of the Middle Ages. The early phases of the cock-fight were so well known as to provide materials for series of illustrations, in which the birds appeared as acting by rules well known and recognised by the 'fancy;' and even a single combat between a ferret and a rat is conducted in its early stages with curious reticence and a recognition of rule. The rat, always on the defensive, sits up on guard while the ferret runs to and fro, often approaching so near as almost to touch the rat. Both parties then draw back most politely, as if they begged each other's pardon for the accident; and this is repeated several times, each appearing to ignore the other's presence, until the ferret makes its spring and the two engage in a furious wrestle, in which the rat is not unfrequently the victim. This is quite different from the conduct of the lobster in 'The

Water Babies,' who held on to the otter's nose 'because it was a point of honour with lobsters never to let go.' That there is an etiquette of demeanour among different species of birds will have been noticed by all who have fed them during the hard weather. Some are always assertive and forward, like the robins and sparrows; others, which are equally familiar with man, are as diffident and reserved, the hedge-sparrows being perhaps the most noticeable examples. Why this rule of behaviour should be constant in a single species is difficult to conjecture. The late Mr Booth reaffirmed from his own observation the truth of the old belief that every bird, such as the crows and ravens, withdraws from its meal at the approach of the eagle, just as the carrion birds do before the king vulture. But the strangest instance of etiquette in dealing with royalty is that observed by bees when a strange queen is introduced into the hive. Sometimes the first queen is allowed to fight the rival. If not, the other bees will kill the intruding queen, not by stinging it, but by suffocation—a death only reserved for royalty.

MILITARY TACTICS OF ANIMALS

THE training of dogs to act as messengers and sentries in war reminds us that many animals are themselves in the habit of using methods and means to secure their own safety against surprise, or the success of attacks on the lives or property of others, which in some cases exhibit a high degree of military training and organisation.

Regular sentries, duly relieved at intervals, are employed by so many of the gregarious quadrupeds and larger birds, that their use seems to be rather the rule than the exception. Chamois, wild sheep, ibex, and other mountain antelopes, as well as the guanacos of South America, always post a sentinel. So do seals when sleeping on the rocks; and the peccaries, the small wild pigs of South America, which are fond of lying in the hollow trunks of fallen trees, are said to leave a guard at the entrance, whose place, if he be shot, is occupied almost mechanically by the next in order within the trunk.   This instinct survives even with animals in captivity.   When the prairie-dogs at the Zoo occupied a small paddock, instead of the cages which are now their home, they always kept a sentinel on duty, though he seldom uttered his warning whistle, having learnt, probably, that the visitors would not come inside the railings.   The prairie-dogs at the Jardin d'Acclimatation at Paris observe the same precaution.   Wild geese and wild swans take turns at 'sentry-go,' the former when feeding on land, the latter on the water.   Of the former birds, St John says : 'They seem to act in so *organised* and cautious a manner when feeding or roosting as to defy all danger.   When a flock of wild geese has fixed on a field of newly-sown grain to feed in, before alighting they make numerous circling flights, and the least suspicious object prevents them from pitching.   Supposing that all is right and they do alight, the whole flock for the space of a minute or two remains motionless, with erect head and neck, reconnoitring the country round. . . . They now appear to have made up their minds that all is safe, and are contented to leave one sentry, who either stands on some elevated part of the field, or walks slowly with the rest— never, however, venturing to pick up a single grain of corn, his whole energies being employed in watching.'   After describing the march of the geese across the field with 'a firm, active, light-infantry step,' St John says : 'When the sentry thinks that he has performed a fair share of duty, he gives the nearest bird to him a sharp peck. I have seen him sometimes pull out a bunch of feathers if the first hint is not immediately attended to, and at the same time uttering a querulous kind of cry.' St John was constantly baulked of a shot by these sentinel geese, and when stalking wild swans on a loch, he noticed that the whole flock would sometimes have their heads under water except a sentry, who was relieved from time to time. The Port Meadow geese near Oxford prefer to roost, except in floods, on a mud-bank in the river, where they are perfectly safe from attack. It is necessary that the sentry should be able to give a *signal* of danger which shall be universally understood, and it will be found that most of the animals named have a special alarm-note. Ibex, marmots, and mountain-sheep whistle, prairie-dogs bark, elephants trumpet, wild geese and swans have a kind of bugle-call, rabbits stamp on the ground, sheep do the same, and wild ducks, as the writer has noticed, utter a very low, cautious quack to signal 'The enemy in sight.' Tactics of offence are rare among the larger gregarious animals. Deer, antelopes, sheep, and even wild horses are generally peaceable creatures, and if a dispute arises between two herds, the leaders fight a duel, and the conqueror annexes the rival's following. When Lady Florence Dixie's horses were attacked by a wild drove the biggest of the tame animals fought the wild leader and was beaten. None of the others attempted resistance, and their owners could with difficulty prevent their being driven off by the conqueror. But horses have a natural taste for drill. The riderless chargers at Balaclava ranged themselves in line with the surviving troopers ; and Byron's fine lines in ' Mazeppa ' :

> ' In one vast squadron they advance,
>   A thousand horse, the wild, the free,
>   Like waves that follow o'er the sea.
>
>   .   .   .   .
>
>   They stop, they start, they snuff the air,
>   Gallop a moment here and there,
>   Approach, retire, wheel round, and round.'

do not seem to exaggerate the natural military instinct of the horse. The writer remembers to have read of a number of cavalry horses abandoned on the coast in a retreat, ranging themselves in squadrons and fighting a battle on the sands. The stories of their forming a ring to resist the attacks of wolves may be true ; but it is difficult to find any reliable account of such combination. Indian wolves have been seen to leave some of their number in ambush at points on the edge of the jungle, while others drove in antelopes feeding in the open ground beyond. But wolves, as a rule, hunt alone or in families, except when pressed by hunger. Wild dogs, however, habitually combine to hunt; and Baldwin, in his 'Game of Bengal,' mentions a case of four or five martens hunting a fawn of the 'muntjac,' or barking deer. But in real military organisation and strategy, monkeys are far ahead of all other animals, and notably the different kinds of baboon. Mansfield Parkins gives an excellent account of the tactics of the dog-faced Hamadryads, that lived in large colonies in the cracks in the cliffs of the Abyssinian Mountains. These creatures used occasionally to plan a foraging expedition into the plain below, and the order of attack was most carefully organised, the old males marching in front and on the flanks, with a few to close up the rear and keep the rest in order. They had a code of signals, halting or advancing according to the barks of the scouts. When they reached the corn-fields the main body plundered while the old males watched on all sides, but took nothing for themselves. The others stowed the corn in their cheek-pouches and under their armpits. They are also said to dig wells with their hands, and work in relays. The Gelada baboons sometimes have battles with the Hamadryads, especially when the two species have a mind to rob the same field, and if fighting in the hills, will roll stones on to their enemies. Not long ago, a colony of Gelada baboons, which had been fired at by some black soldiers attending a Duke of Coburg-Gotha on a hunting expedition on the borders of Abyssinia, blocked a pass for some days by rolling rocks on all comers. This seems to give some support to a curious objection raised by a Chinese local Governor in a report to his superior on the difficulties in the way of opening to steamers the waters of the Upper Yangtze, which was quoted in the *Times*. The report, after noting that the inhabitants on the upper waters were ignorant men who might quarrel with strangers, went on to allege that monkeys inhabited the banks which would roll down stones on the steamers. 'The two last facts,' the report added, 'would lead to complaint from the English, and embroil the Celestials with them, especially if the men or the monkeys kill any English.'

The facility with which large herds of animals or flocks of birds travel for great distances in close array without crowding, confusion, or delay, has always struck the writer as the necessary result of some system and method well understood by them, though in many cases not yet ascertained by us.

There are some exceptions to the general smoothness which marks the evolutions of these animal regiments and army corps; the blind rush of the migrating bison has been known to force thousands into the bottomless mud of American rivers, and the swarms of lemmings are said to march into the sea. But, as a rule, herds of antelopes, of deer, or even flocks of mountain sheep, will travel for days without disaster, arriving simultaneously at the point desired, and 'keeping distance,' that great difficulty ot the march, throughout the journey. A large herd of deer will gather in column, or break into file, and disappear through a mountain pass in less time than the same number of trained troopers would take to 'form fours;' and a flock of half-wild sheep on a Yorkshire moor will assemble, descend into the valley, cross a river in single file, and form upon the opposite bank without a false movement by any one of their number. The military precision with which flocks of birds wheel or advance is even more remarkable, because, in the case of some birds at least, a regular geometrical formation is always observed. Wild geese, wild ducks, and their relations adopt the V formation; and not only adhere to this, with certain modifications to suit circumstances, but also to a regular scale of distances between the different birds in the flock, so closely, that we are forced to infer that they have some strong motive for observing such an order. The old-fashioned explanation, that by advancing in a wedge the front bird acted as a kind of pioneer, to break the force of the wind, is, however, probably the exact reverse of the truth. Wind, in moderation, is almost a necessity to the sustained flight of birds, and the probable object of the wedge-formation when advancing against the wind is, that each bird *avoids* the 'wake' of its neighbour, while at the same time the flock has a leader. When the wind blows on the side of the V, it has been noticed that one limb is generally much longer than the other, or that the birds forming one limb occupy positions which coincide with the spaces between the birds on the windward side, and are thus exposed to the wind current. But often with a strong side wind the wedge formation is abandoned altogether, and the ducks fly in single file, though the 'distances' are always accurately kept. If these distances could be measured, they would probably be found to bear some relation to the space required by the particular species to make a turn, more or less complete, to either side. The sudden changes in the method of flight, from steady beats of the wing to gliding or sailing, which takes place with such wonderful uniformity of time and action in the flight of flocks of starlings or plovers, are probably due to corresponding changes in the force or direction of the wind, affecting simultaneously all the birds of the flock. But for determining the causes of these ordered changes in the aerial tactics of birds, a body of observation has yet to be obtained, for which London, with its parks and lakes and wild fowl, offers unusual facilities.

ANIMAL COURAGE

Nothing in his inimitable series of pictures of the wild life of India, from the animals' point of view, is more thrilling or better told than the triumph of Mowgli over the red dogs of the Deccan, which Mr Rudyard Kipling has reserved for the climax of his epic of the Jungle. Nothing could be more vivid than the words in which he depicts the terrors of all the beasts at the tidings of the invasion of the 'Dhole,' the stratagem which brings them into the stronghold of the 'busy, furious, black wild bees — the "Little People of the Rocks"' — or their destruction by the awakening of the 'clotted millions' of the sleeping insects. But it is not the climax which might have been expected by those less familiar than the writer with the natural history and native lore of the Indian peninsula. That the most courageous creatures of the jungle should be dogs, and these of no great size or very formidable appearance, seems at first hardly creditable; yet there is abundant evidence to prove that, from the animals' point of view, Mr Rudyard Kipling is right. The story has this additional attraction, that of all the commoner animals of Asia, none is so little known and is the subject of so little detailed information as the wild dog, though none has left a stronger impression on the fancy and fears of the natives. It has been extinct in Europe for centuries. Yet alone, of all vanished creatures, it still survives in legend, and there is no wild district of the forests of Central and Northern Europe where tales of the ghostly pack of wild hounds, intent and unremitting in the chase, are not part of the tradition of the woodman's hut.*

The place of the wild dogs in the imagination of the jungle dwellers may be gathered from Mr Kipling's story. But they have always had a curious fascination for naturalists, and this attraction is largely due to the habits and mental qualities of the creatures themselves. They are the only fierce carnivorous animals which *always* live in society. Even wolves hunt in packs largely by accident, or for convenience, or when driven to associate in severe weather. But the wild dog is by choice and habit a social animal, and one which, unlike any other race except the baboons, has made a real

---

* The story of the 'Gabriel Hounds' current on Dartmoor and on the Yorkshire Wold, seems an indication that the wild dogs once existed in England.

advance in the scale of animal well-being by its inherited instinct of combination. Its courage, which is not exaggerated by any of the traditions current, is probably as much due to the survival of the fittest in their combined hunting, as the endurance of a foxhound to a century of careful selection by owners of packs. It was this disciplined, hound-like habit, and a certain fearless confidence shown by the red-dogs on the rare occasions on which they were encountered by Europeans that suggested the idea that they must be the 'original dog.' Indian naturalists, struck by their unlikeness to the sneaking wolves, jackals, and foxes, classed them as the natural 'hound,' and distinguished the race by the honourable title of '$\kappa\acute{\upsilon}\omega\nu$,' the word '*canis*' being appropriated to the less noble wolves and their allies. There is a slight, though real, difference in the structure of the Asiatic hunting dogs, which have only forty-two teeth, in place of the forty-four of the dogs; but the habits of the wild dogs are so distinct in character from the wild ancestors of the domestic breeds, that, though Professor Huxley pronounced, from the evidence of structure only, that they were 'nothing but a large and slightly modified form of the jackal type, which seems to have become specialised in the Eastern extremity of its area of distribution,' the impression of the earlier

naturalists survives the tendency to simplify classification.

One species of the hunting dog is found north
of the Central Asian plateau, in the Siberian
forests. It is thickly furred, with a mane, and
rough coat like a collie; but its habits are, so
far as can be gathered, identical with those of the
'dhole.' It hunts in packs, and one curious fact
has been preserved among the doubtful tales of
Siberian hunters. It 'clears out' the whole neighbourhood in which the pack has settled. In 1859,
all the deer were driven from the valley of the
Irkut by these dogs, which hunted under the leader-
ship of old male hounds, as they have been observed
to do in India. The 'woolly-coated' wild dog does
not cross the Central Asian Plateau. But the rough-
haired, bushy-tailed Indian species holds its own,
from the barren uplands of Eastern Thibet to the
Malay Peninsula. It can live everywhere, though
it seems common nowhere. The packs are found
hunting wild sheep and ibexes on the uplands of
Eastern Thibet, killing sambur and spotted deer in
the Himalayas from Cashmere to Assam (its puppies
have been taken close to Simla), and it haunts all
the large forests of India, the Annamully Hills, the
Ghats, and the uplands of the Deccan, those 'grassy
downs' where Mowgli had 'often watched the fear-

less dholes sleeping and playing and scratching themselves among the little hollows and tussocks they
use for lairs.' This quotation sounds like an original
observation of the habits of the 'dhole,' though it
may not be Mr Kipling's own experience.

The 'field naturalist' does not seem to exist
in India; and though the chroniclers of big-game
shooting occasionally meet the wild dogs, and have
described their method of hunting, the presence
of a pack is almost sufficient inducement to the
sportsman to leave a district where they appear.
'They become a regular pest to the sportsman,
as well as to the natives,' writes General Douglas
Hamilton, in his *Sport in Southern India*, 'as they
drive away all the deer from the district; the
sambur has the most intense dread of these poach-
ing rascals, and will leave a locality for months,
after being hunted by them.' General Hamilton
disturbed a small pack, and shot one dog as it
was 'leisurely walking up the slope of a hill.' This
dog 'had a wound all along its back, some days
old. It was seven inches long, and had opened
out two or three inches wide, and was evidently
a gore from a deer's antler.' This dog was exactly
four feet long, the tail being one foot. They were
constantly seen hunting sambur deer on the Annamully
hills. The country was open, but studded with

small woods, and the packs, which varied from five or six to much larger numbers, used to drive the deer from the woods, and work them into the open ground. The deer were then pressed until they 'took soil,' like a hunted Exmoor stag, and were soon pulled down. In the low country the wild dogs were even more plentiful; and it was noticed that they always attacked a large deer on the flank, and endeavoured to disembowel it. The big sambur deer were almost as terrified by the pursuit of the 'dhole,' as a rabbit when chased by a stoat. They rushed past the human hunter with their coats standing on end in an extremity of fear; and their sole chance of throwing off the pack was by reaching the thick woods, where the wild hounds were compelled to hunt by scent, while the strong stags rushed on and gained on them. There is a persistent tradition that the 'dhole' hunt and kill the tiger. Mr Kipling is evidently not convinced that this is true. But he notes that the tiger 'will surrender a new kill to the "dhole."' Such a scene was once witnessed by a friend of General Hamilton's. He was going round his coffee plantation when he heard a noise in the forest bordering on the clearing, and went into the wood to ascertain the cause. 'On going round the corner of a thick bush he almost trod upon the tail of a tiger standing with his back towards him ; he silently retreated ; but as he did so, he saw there was a pack of wild dogs in front of the tiger, yelping at him, and making the peculiar noise which had previously attracted his attention. Having procured his rifle, he returned with some of his men to the spot ; the tiger was gone, but a large pack of wild dogs was feeding upon the body of a stag, which upon examination was found to have been killed by the tiger, for there were marks of its teeth upon the stag's neck. The dogs had evidently driven him from his prey.' But the general belief of the wild tribes of India is borne out by two stories told by Colonel Baldwin of their attacking the bear and the tiger, which put the fact beyond doubt. A bear was found by an English officer standing at bay before the dogs. He had killed one ; but his hide and body were torn in strips by the bites of the pack. In the other case, the fresh bones of a tiger were found, from which the flesh had been eaten ; one paw still remained whole, and close by lay the freshly-killed bodies of three wild dogs which had fallen in the fight. Remembering not only the strength and activity of the tiger, but the astonishing pluck with which, even when wounded, it will constantly charge a line of elephants, and endeavour to scale the howdah—which is, in fact, a fort with an armed garrison—it is difficult to over-estimate the courage of the wild dogs in meeting and destroying such an antagonist. It is extremely probable that future observations of the courage of the wild dog may justify a statement once made, perhaps without sufficient evidence, that they have 'an inherent hostility to the larger *felinæ*, and are incessantly on the watch to destroy their whelps, so that the species are the instrument by which Nature keeps down the super-abundant increase of the great *felinæ* of the wilderness.' It seems as if the tiger's dislike of the 'dhole' has engendered in it a nervousness which extends to all dogs. An anecdote given by Captain Williamson illustrates this, as well as the extreme courage of the domestic dog. He was shooting in India with a spaniel, which apparently found some game which his master guessed to be a hare. 'The dog came to a stand over a bank, wagging its tail, with ears up, and his whole frame in a state of ecstasy. I expected that he had got a hare under the bank, and, as the situation was in favour of getting a shot, I ran towards him with more speed than I should have done had I known that I should find a tiger sitting up and staring "Paris" in the face ; they were not three yards asunder. As soon as the dog found me at his side, he barked, and, giving a spring, dashed at the tiger.' His owner admits that his own alarm was so extreme that he did not observe the further demeanour of either till he saw the tiger cantering away followed by the little dog barking. It is, of course, just possible that the tiger was 'nervous,' and that the little dog merely exhibited the impudence habitual to little dogs who know that they can worry a horse or a bullock into beating a retreat when quietly lying down in a field. Extreme nervousness is often the accompaniment of great courage in certain animals, especially of the larger kinds. Indian rhinoceroses, kept by a Rajah for fighting in the arena, where they would exhibit the most obstinate courage when matched with elephant or buffalo, would tremble and lie down at the unusual sight of a horse outside their pen ; and the elephant is more liable to sudden panics and alarm than any other animal. It is strange to think of the same animal advancing boldly to face a wounded tiger and receiving its charge upon its tusks, and running away in uncontrollable panic from a piece of newspaper blown by the wind across the road.

It is said that the scent or roar of a bear in the jungle will often scare elephants beyond control ; and they have the same intense nervousness shown by the horse at the sight of things unusual or out of place. · A big elephant which was employed to drag away the carcase of a dead bullock, and had allowed the burden to be attached by ropes without observing what it was, happened to look round, and instantly bolted, its fright increasing every moment as the unknown object jumped and bumped at its heels. After running some miles, like a dog with a tin can tied to its tail, the elephant stopped, and allowed itself to be turned round, and drew the bullock back again without protest. Yet an elephant, *with a good mahout*, gives, perhaps, the best instance of disciplined courage—courage, that is, which persists, in the face of knowledge and disinclination—to be seen in the animal world. They will submit, day after day, to have painful wounds dressed in obedience to their keeper, and meet danger in obedience to orders, though their intelligence is sufficient to understand the peril, and far too great for man to trick them into a belief that it is non-existent. No animal will face danger more readily at man's bidding. As an instance, take the following incident, which recently occurred in India, and was communicated to the writer. A small female elephant was charged by a buffalo, in high grass, and her rider, in the hurry of the moment, and perhaps owing to the sudden stopping of the elephant, fired an explosive shell from his rifle, not into the buffalo, but into the elephant's shoulder. The wound was so severe, that it had not healed a year later. Yet

the elephant stood firm, although it was gored by
the buffalo, which was then killed by another gun.
What is even more strange is that the elephant was
not 'gun-shy' afterwards. Indian hunters, who have
experience of most wild animals of the Old World,
do not concede the highest claim for courage either
to the elephant, the rhinoceros, or the tiger; we
have said enough to show the title of the wild dog
to respect; but of the animals best known to the
hunter, the wild boar is by common agreement at
once the most fearless and the most collected in
danger. He will attack any creature that molests
him, and many, including men, that intend no harm.
When hunted on horseback he always fights to the
last, and though distressed by the long chase, often
conducts his defence with a skill and vigour which
enlist the reader's sympathy for the hunted rather
than the hunter. An old boar is said to be the only
animal which beats off the wild dogs, setting his
back against a tree and killing them until the pack
retire. The quality of the courage exhibited by the
boar is clearly different to the blind fury or insensi-
bility of the peccaries of South America, or the
ferocity of creatures like the hamsters, though it is
doubtful if any wild animal has equalled the 'game-
ness' of the bull dog, which, when ordered by its
master, pinned a wild American bull bison by the

nose, and held it down until the bison brought its feet forward and stamped the dog to death, without inducing it to relax its hold. It is in the association of man and animal that the nearest approach to human courage is developed, enabling the creature to face what it fears, and conquer natural shrinking by the desire to please or to obey. So recently as the gales of November 1894, an account appeared of two attempts made by a retriever dog to swim to shore with a line from a stranded ship. Very probably neither the object with which he was sent or the the danger was very clearly present to the dog's mind; but the task imposed must have caused some reluctance, and called for the exhibition of disciplined courage. When the self-sacrifice takes the form of obedience to the notion of duty; when no one is present to issue a command; then the act becomes as purely moral as any similarly prompted exhibition of human courage. The story of the dog 'Gelert,' which defended its master's infant from the wolf when the house was empty, could probably be supported by many instances in which the motive was similar, though the circumstances were less picturesque than those with which the legend has invested the death of the dog of Wales.

THE ANIMAL SENSE OF HUMOUR

So many of the higher forms of human pleasure
are shared by the other vertebrates, that it seems
difficult to deny positively the faculty for any of
the simple mental and æsthetic pleasures to animal
understanding. Colour and music, scents and sounds,
and the various 'cosmetics' of a simple toilet, are
all within the scope of their enjoyment; and
in many forms of play, sometimes of a rather
elaborate nature, animals find a pleasure similar to
that which the same amusements arouse in mankind.
There are no limits to their enjoyment of that kind
of 'fun' which romps and make-believes of all sorts,
especially mock-fighting and serio-comic farce, excite
in their minds. But the sense of fun, which may be
defined as the merriment which takes form in play,
is, we think, in some few animals, capable of a
further development. That refined sense of the incongruous or the odd, which we call 'humour,' is
probably possessed in a large degree by a few

animals ; while in others some of its elements are so often present, that it would be difficult to deny to them a share in it. We fancy, however, that humour in its most developed form is possessed by dogs alone among the animals ; and that they have acquired the faculty partly from man. The power of laughter is peculiar to man, and the sense of humour may be said, speaking generally, to be also his special property. In seeking to disentangle the 'manifestations' of humour in the animal mind, we must carefully distinguish between the instances of the conscious appreciation and enjoyment of what is comical, and the extreme but involuntary comicality of many animals themselves. There are at least a dozen species whose form and actions are so absurdly humorous that it is next to impossible not to read into an interpretation of their thoughts something of the feeling which they excite in ourselves. A polar bear in the ordinary enjoyment of his tub, or an eagle-owl holding a young rabbit in one claw and a duckling in the other, and making alternate efforts to swallow each whole, while his eyes wink in time to the gulps, look as if they were consciously performing for the public amusement, though neither is the least aware that it is doing anything odd, or would hesitate for a moment to leave off and claw the spectator the instant he appeared on the wrong side of the bars. We recollect a perfect instance of apparently intentional humour performed by an intelligent and serio-comic raven, the property of a river keeper, which always accompanied its master when engaged in assisting his employers in catching a basket of trout. The raven soon comprehended that the object of the rest of the party was to get things to eat out of the stream. That he knew, first, because he saw it; and, secondly, because he was often given a small trout. So he went off fishing on his own account, and returned with a small drowned kitten, which he poked into the hole in the top of the basket among the fish. Now this, in a human being, would be humour of a nasty, low kind, only fit for horrid schoolboys; but still it would be humour. Whereas the raven was in sober earnest, and very pleased with himself for his success. Mark Twain's imaginary description of the efforts of the blue jay to fill up a hole with nuts, when the 'hole' was a crack in the roof of a house, is hardly more comical than the reality of some instances of animal stupidity; yet we never saw the slightest approach to amusement in one animal at the mistakes of another, though dogs, so far as we can venture to interpret their thoughts, do really feel amusement at the mistakes of men.

Yet many animals have a keen appreciation of the

peculiar and unpleasant form of humour which consists in inflicting annoyance and mortification on
others. Instances of this indulgence in its crudest
form must be familiar to most observers. Given a
cow lying down and comfortably chewing the cud,
there is hardly a fox-terrier living which can resist
the temptation of rushing up and barking at its nose,
until the persecuted animal forsakes comfort and
repose, and rises awkwardly to its feet to drive off
the tormenter. 'Monkey tricks' have passed into
a proverb for the description of this side of humour,
though not every monkey is so clever as the ape
which was seen to pass its hand behind the back of
a friend in order to tweak the tail of a third, whose
resentment naturally fell upon its nearest neighbour.
But all the cleverest species of birds and animals
seem to share the unholy amusement which the
light annoyance—not the permanent injury—of others
affords. A jackdaw of the writer's acquaintance had
an ingenious method of tormenting the numerous
dogs of the establishment, which was most comic to
behold, and which owed something of its finish to a
more artistic conception of the humorous side of
teasing than most jackdaws are credited with. It
was an extremely hot summer, and the dogs, of
which there were three, spent the greater part of the
day dozing peacefully on the lawn. Being all either

Clumber spaniels or setters, they had fine silky coats which extended to their feet, little tufts of flossy fur sticking out between their toes. When a dog was comfortably asleep, with its feet stretched out, dreaming of partridges, the jackdaw would hop gently round, and then make a sudden dive at these fluffy tassels between its toes, which never failed to wake the dog up with a quick sense of discomfort, which a tug at the hair anywhere else on its body would never have provoked. At another house, a tame magpie was kept in a stable-yard with a couple of kestrels. The kestrels were in the habit of sitting on the sides of the water-pails set to warm in the sun outside the stable doors. The magpie, being in want of amusement, hit on the following plan. He cautiously approached a kestrel from behind, and, seizing the bird's long tail in his beak, gave it one or two violent pulls and pushes, and having worked the kestrel quite off its balance, with a good forward push, pitched it into the pail, or so far in as its flapping wings allowed. The magpie then 'saved itself' with great haste in the hay-rack above the manger. In this case the joke was paid for ; one of the kestrels, more wide-awake than usual, caught the magpie as it was approaching and drove its claws into the practical joker's legs until his screams brought help. Sometimes the animal practical joke takes a more refined form. We recently heard of a young cat which conceived a great dislike for a peacock which was fed from the windows of the house, and took the following method of expressing its aversion. When the peacock was anxious to display its charms, and had spread its tail and was moving slowly backwards and forwards, the cat used to rush out on to the lawn and *jump through the peacock's tail.* The effect of this was to entirely disconcert the peacock's swagger, and leave the cat a moral victory. Even this, though the effects were hardly such as the human sense of humour interprets with satisfaction, may have been due to another feeling. The cat, for instance, may have taken the peacock's movements as an invitation to play, and the humour may be only due to the incongruity of the peacock's frame of mind and the cat's interpretation. But we have no doubt whatever that the dog does really possess a sense of humour of a kind not very much different from our own. It is by no means universal, or even common. But then humour, or even a slight sense of the comical, is by no means equally distributed among men. There are prosaic men and women, and there are matter-of-fact dogs. These have their good qualities, like matter-of-fact people. For purely business purposes they are often the best. We once owned, for instance, an excellent retrieving spaniel of the simple order of mind, without a grain of humour. This dog accompanied us unasked when we wanted to shoot a bullfinch in the garden to stuff. The gun went off, and the poor bullfinch dropped. Now, this dog had been accustomed, when the gun was fired, to go and look for a dead or wounded rabbit. So, instead of looking under the apple tree, he disappeared into the hedge, and in a few minutes he returned with *a rabbit in his mouth.* So much for the value of a matter-of-fact dog. The serious business of a dog's life—if we except collies, and the Dutch cartdogs—is sport; and it is in matters connected with sport that the development of humour is most often seen. The first and most amusing step is to see the grave and serious dog unbend to suit the humour of his master. The spectacle of a carefully-educated setter's demeanour at a stack-threshing, should his master take a share in hunting mice, can never be forgotten. At first he sits down and looks on. Then, after a little encouragement, he joins in the fun, with a look which clearly says, ' Well, if you *will* do it, I don't mind, just for once.' Then all his dignity goes. He curls his tail, jumps about, and enjoys the joke, but never loses his sense of the impropriety of the whole thing. St John had a dog which always joined in the rat-catcher's work, but cut him and his curs if he saw his master. Our own dog never took a part unless he saw his master engaged also, except when he went to bed at night in the stable. Then his whole demeanour changed. He would wag his tail like a cur, and sit waiting till the corn bin was opened to give the horse his last feed, and try to catch the mice that rushed out when the lid was raised. His appreciation of the ludicrous grew with his knowledge of the world ; and though he never showed the slightest inclination to indulge it by annoying other creatures, and never even chased a cat unless he were told to, he was always immensely amused when we did anything which struck him as incorrect. His behaviour on the first occasion on which he saw a wild duck shot was unmistakable. The bird—a teal—fell in a pond, and the setter, who was an excellent water dog, swam in, and brought it to land. The bird was alive, and as soon as he had reached the bank, the dog set it down and danced round it, and then came back and looked up doubtfully, wagging his tail just as he did when mouse-hunting, evidently meaning to say : ' Here's a lark, you've shot a duck.' As he had left it on the other side of a ditch, we told him to go and fetch it. But ' Jack,' like Sally Harowwell in *Tom Brown*, would have nothing more to do with it, and though we endeavoured to persuade him that it was all right, like a true-born Suffolker, as he was, he 'knowed better,' and we had to fetch it ourselves. He behaved in exactly the same way when we shot a black rabbit. Nothing would persuade him that it was not a cat ; and he would do no serious work for the rest of the day. Like many other dogs, this one had the greatest dislike to being laughed at—a fact which, in itself, goes far to show that, with the sense of humour, animals possess its frequent concomitant, a dislike of ridicule. But in no case have we seen the least approach to the sense of humour, in its developed form, in wholly wild creatures. In animals, as in man, humour is the result of civilisation, and not, as we understand it, a natural and spontaneous development.

THE EMOTION OF GRIEF IN ANIMALS

GREEK fancy personified grief lasting and unconsolable in the metamorphosis of Philomel into the night-ingale, bewailing the loss of Itys through ages of midnight melody. Keats, in a more modern, though no less classical, vein, sees in the nightingale's note nothing more suggestive of sorrow than Shelley did in that of the skylark. But fancy and allusion apart, there is a strong balance of popular belief in favour of the theory that many animals do feel an emotion more lasting than momentary chagrin or inconvenience in the loss or absence of those for whom they entertain a regard, and that in some cases this is so marked as to rank with the degrees of regret, sorrow and lasting grief, felt by human beings in similar conditions.

The intellectual factors which play a part, and a necessary part, in the emotion of sorrow, are possessed by most animals. Memory, without which lasting regret cannot exist unless excited by some concrete visible reminder of loss, is undoubtedly part of the animal faculties. Their affections do not go to sleep the moment the loved object is removed, only to awaken automatically at its reappearance. In one respect the animal indulgenee in sorrow is superior, by its sense of reserve and discrimination, to that in man. They keep their sense of proportion, and if in many cases they show indifference where we should expect emotion, they never make sorrow cheap by wasting it on trifles. Animal grief, when it is shown, is always respectable, never morbid. That is why, in the cases where it is noted and authentic, it has always awakened the interest and commanded the sympathy of thoughtful mankind. There is nothing more encouraging than unexpected testimony to a cause. One of the earliest, and at the same time one of the freshest, of English records of this form of animal emotion, comes from a source which, judged by the other work of the writer's life, is certainly unexpected. Dr Caius, 'a most shining light of the University of Cambridge, its jewel, its glory,' according to his translator, in 1576, Abraham Fleming, 'wrote an epitome concerning British dogs, not so concise as elegant and useful, an epitome compact of the various arguments and experiences of many minds,' for the use of Conrad Gesner, the Swiss naturalist. Dr Caius was a very strong as well as a very learned man—

not only the author of a defence of the Continental pronunciation of the classics against the Erasmian change, but a skilful physician, and rigorous head of the college which he founded. Gesner probably expected from such a quarter a learned dissertation on the anatomy and history of the dog. But his correspondent was so wholly and so quaintly absorbed in the moral and mental qualities of the animals, with the present merits and ancient history of which he shows a most minute acquaintance, that he supplied Gesner with a series of character sketches of English dogs, as a supplement to a scientific list of the British fauna and flora, which he had previously placed at his disposal. This is his estimate of the emotion of grief, or, as he calls it, 'love' in the dog :—'This kind of dogges, called "defending dogges," hath principall property engrafted in them, that they love their masters liberally, and hate strangers despight-fully . . . . . . if it chaunce that their master be op-pressed, either by a multitude, or by the greater violence, and so be beaten downe that he be grovelling on the ground, it is proved true by experience that this Dogge forsaketh not his master, no, not when he is starcke dead ; but induring the force of famishment, and the outrageous tempests of the weather, most vigilantly watcheth, and carefully keepeth the dead carkasse many dayes, endeavouring, furthermore, to kil the murtherer of his master, if he may get any advantage. Or else by barcking, by howling, by furious jarring and snarring, and suchlike means, betrayeth the malefactour, as desirous to have the death of his aforesaid master rigorouslye revenged.' The desire of 'revenge' or 'justice' is a very human accompaniment of grief for a loss so incurred, and looks like an overstatement of the case. But Dr Caius probably thought that the constant association of good and evil doing with reward and punishment in the canine mind, worked as it does in the human understanding. Such an instance, 'fortuned within the compass of his memory' in the case of 'the dogge of a certain wayfaring man, travelling from the City of London to the towne of Kingstone, who passing over a good portion of his journey, was assualted and set upon by certaine confederate theefes, lying in waight for the spoyle in *Come parcke* (Coombe Park), a perillous bottom, compassed about wyth woddes;' and also a dog whose sire was English, and whose master was murdered near Paris, which, 'manifestly perceiving that his master was murthered, did both betray the bloudy butcher, and attempted to tear out the villons throate, if he had not soughte meanes to avoyde the revenging rage of the dogge.'

Wordsworth bears out to the letter the statements of the old Cambridge scholar, that 'the dogge forsaketh

not his master, no, not when he is starcke dead.'
The story of the 'Dog of Helvellyn' is given with
sufficient detail in Wordsworth's verses. For three
months it remained the only mourner by the body
of its master, until it was found by a shepherd, who
recognised it as the dog which he had seen with the
lost man on the high passes late one summer evening.
A shepherd gave the following account of the incident
some years afterwards. 'The unfortunate man,' he
said, ' was a resident of Manchester, who was in the
habit of visiting the Lakes, and, trusting in his
knowledge of the country, had ventured to cross one
of the passes of Helvellyn late in the afternoon
accompanied only by his dog. In the dusk he
wandered from the track, fell over the rocks, and
perished. After many weeks of fruitless search the
dog was discovered guarding his master's body.' The
shepherd had never heard the poem, but concluded
his story with exactly the same sentiment, if not
the same words, 'God knows,' he said, 'how the poor
beast was supported so long.' The ' Dog of Helvellyn '
gained a monument in Wordsworth's verse. Another
dog mourner has been honoured by a monument of
stone. This is the Edinburgh dog, 'Greyfriars'
Bobby,' which followed its master's body to the
funeral, and, after the burial, lay so constantly by
the grave that the keepers of the graveyard gave it

F

a small kennel in which to lie. Its master's grave became from that time its home, and on its death it was honoured with a monument recording its devotion. In the case of the dog the strongest forms of the emotions of affection, jealousy, and grief centre round human beings. They are shown in a very minor degree in their relation to each other. Perhaps the most curious instance is that of a female which mated for life with a handsome male dog, for which she reserved her entire affections, and after his death would associate with no other—an instance both of grief and constancy. But the minor forms of sorrow are very readily evoked in their dealings with men. 'Why should I leave the dog at home?' asks the sportsman in Mr Oswald Crawfurd's witty account of a Portuguese 'cacada.' 'If I leave him at home, he will howl all day, and my wife will wish herself dead.' Their sensitiveness under temporary disgrace or neglect is no less obvious; but canine sorrow is in its strongest form reserved to deplore the loss of human friends or masters. In no other domestic animal is the emotion so constantly exhibited, or in so strong a form, although Mr Rudyard Kipling's story of *My Lord the Elephant* (if founded on fact) shows that that animal is sometimes capable of devotion as great as that of the dog.

Horses and cattle, though attached to individuals,

do not usually exhibit emotion at their loss. In all the ruminant animals the expression of emotion is very limited, and not easily recognised. Cows certainly are much distressed at the loss of a calf, and deer by that of a fawn. On the other hand, the former are so inexplicably dull of comprehension, that in India it is the custom to stuff the skin of a calf which has been turned into veal, and set it in the cow stable, which at once induces the cow to continue giving milk. Cats, when in distress, seem moved by exactly opposite causes to those which induce sorrow in the dog. They are infinitely miserable at the loss of their kittens, and frequently adopt some other creature in their place, but they seem little moved by the death or sickness of human friends. But this is not always the case. During the last influenza epidemic a lady who was attacked was moved into a different room from that which she usually occupied. Her cat, a grey Angora, at once discovered this, and came and sat outside for some days, but was not admitted for fear it might also catch the universal plague. When it did contrive to enter, it sprang on the bed, purring and showing as much pleasure as it had previously shown dejection. Wild animals naturally limit both their affections and regrets to each other's society. In the social life of most animals there is so little difference between the individuals, that the loss of one is easily replaced. It leaves no gap in the daily life as the loss of a human being may in that of a domestic animal. But Lord Lovat has given a sufficient number of instances of the grief felt by wild deer at the death or wounding of their companions to supplement the lesson of Sir E. Landseer's picture entitled 'Highland Nurses,' in which the hinds are watching by a wounded stag. Birds, which since the days when Æschylus described the hurried and anxious flight of the vultures robbed of their young, have always shown the utmost distress and grief at the loss of their nestlings, seem seldom affected to sorrow by any other circumstance, though Miss Benson, in her book, *Subject to Vanity*, has lately given an account of the 'inhuman' indifference of a hen Budjerigar parrakeet when its mate was ill, and of the obvious dejection which this indifference caused in the sick bird. But it is now doubted whether 'love birds' die of grief after the loss of their mate, though the fact that one usually dies very soon, often only a few hours after the other, is not disputed. But they are delicate birds, and the same unsuitable food or sudden draught which kills one usually affects the other. They are probably victims, not of sorrow, but of errors in 'domestic hygiene.'

ANIMALS AT PLAY

OUR estimate of the sense of pleasure possessed by animals has suffered from a double set of errors. The older ethical writers were leagued against them and declared that the only pleasures which they shared with ourselves were those of touch and taste, and that they had no enjoyment of the senses of hearing, scent, or sight, but such as suggested the presence of their prey, or of their own species. Modern feeling, on the other hand, has inclined to go to the other extreme, by attributing an excess of human emotion and sentimentality to these very simple natures. It will not, however, be difficult to show that, so far from the sense of pleasure in animals being limited to touch and taste, or the love of fighting so generously conceded by Dr Watts, they do, in fact, share with ourselves many of the pleasant emotions excited by sweet scents and sounds,*

* The writer's experiments on the animal liking for perfumes and music are described in *Life at the Zoo.*

not for what they may suggest, but for their own sake, and enjoy amusements, exercise and emulation, imagination, love of beauty, pride in accomplishments, 'hobbies'—such as the mania for collecting art treasures—love of society, family pride, and personal affection. A logical order in which to consider some of these powers of enjoyment is that of their development as the animal itself grows up. In them as in our own case, the faculty of amusement comes early. Many animals are so well aware of this that they make it part of their maternal duties to *amuse* their young. Even a ferret will play with her ferocious little kittens, just as a cat will with hers, or an old spaniel with her puppies. A mare will play with her foal, though the writer has never seen a cow try to amuse her calf, nor any birds their young. If their mothers do not amuse them, the young ones invent games of their own. Near Bembridge, in the Isle of Wight, a flock of ewes and lambs were in adjoining fields, separated by a fence with several gaps in it. 'Follow my leader' was the game most in favour with this flock, the biggest lamb leading round the field and then jumping the gap, with all the others following in single file ; any lamb that took the leap unusually well would give two or three more enthusiastic jumps out of sheer exuberant happiness when it reached the other side. Near the same place we have seen lambs play the game which children call 'I'm the King of the Castle.' This flock was in a field in which seaweed was piled in heaps ready to be spread on the field. A lamb would jump on to a heap of seaweed and half-a-dozen others would attack the position and try to drive him from it. Occasionally no one would appear to dispute the possession of the 'castle' and in that case the lamb playing 'king' jumped, capered and performed the most ridiculous antics as if inviting competitors to 'come on.'

Another flock of lambs, confined in a straw-yard, had steeplechases over a row of feeding-troughs stuffed with hay, right down the yard and back again. On a Yorkshire moor they have been seen to race for a quarter of a mile, round a spring and back to the ewes. Fawns play a kind of cross-touch from one side to the other, the 'touch' in each case being given by the nose. This game was played for an hour in the glades of Haddon Chase. Little pigs are also great at combined play, which generally takes the form of races. 'Emulation' seems to form part of their amusement, for their races seem always to have the winning of the first place as the object, and are quite different from those combined rushes for food or causeless stampedes in which little pigs are wont to indulge.

Racing is an amusement which is natural to some animals, and is very soon learnt by others, and becomes one of their most exciting pastimes. Many horses, and all racing dogs, soon learn to be as keen on winning as public schoolboys in a half-mile handicap. It is a common impulse with horses to pass, or at least to keep up with, any other horse in their company, and this instinct, developed by training, makes the professional racehorse eager to win. He at least is no partner in the frauds of owners or jockeys. The year that the Duke of Portland's celebrated horse 'St Simon' won his first race—a nursery stakes for untried colts—there were a dozen or more other colts at the starting-post, near the Red House on Doncaster Town Moor. Many of them were ridden by small boys, who had the geatest difficulty in controlling the efforts of the young horses to break away, and the eagerness of the colts to get a good start was quite equal to that of their riders. Those horses which refuse to start, or sulk when running, have usually been the victims of whip and spur in some race in which their powers were overtaxed; and the memory of such experience, which prompted one horse, when at walking exercise in a string at Newmarket, to turn and bite Archer, who was passing them in review, causes some others to shrink from the start. But this is the exception. More often defeat causes an exhibition of temper ; and the public have not forgotten the performance of the savage 'Surefoot' in the Derby of 1891, who, instead of responding, to the jockey's efforts to overtake the leading horses, did his best to bite not only them but their riders. But animal enthusiasm for racing is best seen in a dog race ; and, except on the high-road from some Dutch town after market, when the dogs that have brought in the vegetable carts race back to their farms, this kind of contest is never seen in perfection outside the colliery districts. For those who are not privileged to live on the 'coal-measures,' Mr Barnum's show provided an excellent dog race of its kind. Those who saw the way in which his dogs scoured round the great oval at Olympia, not so much barking as shrieking with excitement, felt that it was one of the most genuine of the performances exhibited. * On one occasion the writer happened to be close to the starting-point, and saw a curious instance of dog 'jockeying.' The race was a handicap, distances of from one to three yards separating the dogs competing, each of which was held by a man who placed one hand on the dog's chest, the other on its shoulder. They were

* In the summer of 1895, at a show of ladies' dogs held at the Ranelagh Club, dog races were part of the entertainment, which was watched by the Princess of Wales.

already barking with excitement, when one, a dwarf greyhound, twisted its head round and looked at the dog next behind it. Apparently it thought that its rival was too near, for it began to whine and bark in the most persuasive way, licking the man's hand, and making earnest requests of some kind. Apparently he understood, for he patted the dog, and moved it on about a yard. This satisfied the dog, which then began to bark in a very confident manner, and on the signal being given, rushed away with the rest. It was leading when they passed the second time ; but the distance of the finish was too great for the writer to see if it won in the end. In any case it was a clear instance of manœuvering for a start, and showed genuine keenness to win. It is this spirit of rivalry which distinguishes the racing tastes of animals from their very strong enjoyment of feats of speed and activity for their own sake. The *motive*, when a greyhound like 'Fullerton' is galloping over the Downs for exercise, or running the last desperate course against his rival for the Waterloo Cup, is quite different. Yet animals keenly enjoy the vigorous exercise of their powers of speed. Birds especially delight in the free and fanciful use of their wings. There is all the difference possible between the flight of birds for 'business' and pleasure. In the fine days of spring our sparrowhawks and kestrels, and even rooks, will soar for long periods without a flap of the wing for pleasure alone ; and the herons will do the same, circling to vast altitudes. The writer once had the pleasure of seeing the first flight of two young kestrels, which had been kept in confinement in a large room until their feathers were perfectly grown. For days they had hovered before the window of the house anxious to try the almost unknown power. When released, they at once soared, sweeping ever upwards in opposing circles, until it seemed as if the sky itself could set no limits to their airy climb.

In any comparison of the games and sports of animals with our own enjoyment of the same amusements, it must not be forgotten that imagination, the 'make-believe' which enter so much into the play of children, is also the basis of much of the play of young animals. Watch a kitten, while you tap your fingers on the other side of a curtain or tablecloth, imitating the movements of a mouse running up and down. She knows it is not a mouse, but she enters into the spirit of the game, and goes through all the movements proper to the chase. Or perhaps she has a ball. If you set it in motion so much the better. That helps the 'make-believe.' The ball is 'alive' and she catches it, claws it, and half-kills it, taking care all the while to keep it moving herself. The beautiful young lion which was given by the Sultan of Sokoto to the Queen would play in exactly the same way with a large wooden ball, growling and setting up its crest and pursuing the ball across the cage. Indeed, play of some kind is so necessary to the health of these big 'kittens' that they are always supplied with a wooden ball to amuse them. These playthings are evidently greatly appreciated, and the distress of one very tame tiger, 'Jack,' and his mute appeals for help when his ball slipped down under the bars, where he could no longer reach it, were quite pathetic.

This 'make-believe' sport, in which half the interest is supplied by the imagination, is by no means confined to quadrupeds. Tame rooks often go through an elaborate performance of 'killing' a biscuit before eating it, and tame seagulls play a game with stones and sticks, throwing them into the air and catching them in their beaks just as they would a fish.

It is perhaps a doubtful gain to find a philosophical basis for the wide category of children's naughtiness which comes under the head of 'mischief.' But is not the motive which prompts boys to smash windows, crack open the nice tight tops of jam pots, 'pop' fuchsia buds, poke sticks through pictures, muddy clean doorsteps, burn holes in carpets with hot pokers, light whole match-boxes at once, and even upset trains by putting stones on the line, due to a wish for that satisfaction which is derived by getting a maximum of result from a minimum of effort? Rightly directed that is the object of most mechanical invention, wrongly applied it is 'mischief.' Apart from consequences, such acts are hugely productive of pleasure to boys, and young animals share the feeling. We once watched the united efforts of a litter of setter puppies to enjoy the satisfaction which is derived from such activity, the particular object being the destruction of a fine bed of geraniums, an enterprise which promised a 'maximum of result' with a set-off of a mere trifle of effort, if once a protecting fence of wire-netting could be surmounted. One after another the puppies charged the fence, only to fall back baffled, but not discouraged. Failure only made them more determined. With savage barks and growls they returned again to the attack, until, after a desperate leap and scramble, the biggest puppy rolled over among the geraniums. For a moment he was almost awed by his success. He squeaked and sat down, but only for a moment. Then he hurled himself into the thickest part of the bed and tore the geraniums to pieces. But this is a side of animal enjoyment which it is not advisable to dwell upon. It is too human. But even in their amusements, it may be granted that they do share to a large degree the love of innocent sport and emulation which is not the least rational and healthy side of the pastimes enjoyed by mankind.

ANIMALS IN PAGEANTS

THE taste for pageants has grown in London, and promises to increase. With this comes an increased demand for large and stately animals to make part of these shows and processions. At the Indian Exhibition, held at Earl's Court in 1895, the whole of the elephants and camels used to be taken twice a-day to do duty in Kiralfy's pageant, and the scene would have been improved by the introduction of twice the number available.

With a reformed Corporation, we shall perhaps be treated to an improved Lord Mayor's Show. In that case, the art of pageantry will need to be studied from the ancient models, as well as from modern survivals.

Rightly ordered, a great procession needs three elements for spectacular success. It must contain a series of striking subjects, except in the case of a Royal procession or State funeral, where the attention must not be too far distracted from the central personal element; and the grand chain of ideas suggested must be linked together by living chains as gorgeous as they can be made, yet with as much variety of form as the necessity for movement allows. General consent agrees to group the central subjects in some form of triumphal car. Whether any of these devices have been wholly satisfactory may be doubted. There was a rude success of symbolism in one of the most striking of 'one man' triumphs of the sombre kind—the burial of Nelson. The funeral car was a model of the bows of the 'Victory.' But the emblematic or allegorical car will always give the leading ideas of the great pageant. Between these, bands of men, on foot or on horseback, but always uniformly clad, each company or squadron in contrast to the next, are the natural and necessary links. The unity of movement of disciplined men, able to suggest the leading emotion of the moment by their tread and bearing, has set the time of the piece, from the tramp of the legionaries in the triumph, to the slow march of the modern military funeral. But while unity of impression makes the success of a pageant, nothing causes failure sooner than uniformity; and sameness of movement is as dangerous as repetition of form. A break and variety in both are needed; and animal movement, as well as animal forms, are essential to the success of a great procession. Pompey, who for all his 'frigidity,' which Cicero lamented, had correct views on the subject of popular shows, wished to be drawn in triumph, after his African war, by four elephants, instead of the white horses usually harnessed to the car of the victorious general. Not till the third century of our era was this innovation permitted in the conservative traditions of the triumph. But the effect must have justified the change. The motion of great beasts is so leisurely, deliberate and withal so silent, that they are the 'making' of a procession. Nothing gives the needed break, in form and motion, between the mechanical progress of the cars, and the 'staccato' trip of the most dignfied biped, so well as the noiseless progress of the velvet-footed camel, and the solemn gait of the elephants, as they keep their places, with the dignity of a century's experience of great occasions. Motion without sound, and the appearance of vast, whole-coloured, and un-familiar forms, are their contribution to the pageants of the West. Indian taste decorates the State elephant with arabesques and colour. We prefer him 'plain.' But the effect of an elephant column in an English pageant has not yet been tried.

In the four triumphs represented in the Hampton Court tapestries, perhaps the most splendid pageant ever designed, the cars of victory are drawn by four white horses, four elephants, four camels, and four brown-skinned buffaloes with enormous horns. Other elephants walk by themselves, a reminiscence perhaps of the part taken in a procession at Rome by an elephant presented by the King of Portugal to Leo X., which knelt at the Pope's feet. But animals produce a finer effect when led, or allowed to walk alone in a pageant, than when harnessed to cars. Connoisseurs say that when led, it should always be by black men or brown men — African, for choice—with bare arms holding the leading reins. The organiser of the next Lord Mayor's Show might do worse than break up the columns of cars and uniformed processionists by teams of all the beasts of burden used in the British Empire. Bactrian camels, white Indian draught oxen, reindeer cars, Indian elephants, water buffaloes, and Egyptian dromedaries, with their native drivers and equipments, would give the spectacular effect required, with just that amount of symbolism which the sentiment of pageants demands.

Horses regarded as material for State processions, occupy a different place from that assigned to other animals by European custom. In the East, led horses, richly caparisoned, always form part of the show on State occasions, and in princely stables many animals are kept solely for processional

The Rajah's Dromedaries, at Jeypore. *From a photograph by Gambier Bolton, F.Z.S.*

purposes. In modern Europe, except in military funerals, horses are always ridden or driven in pageants, of which they have been an indispensable part since the four white steeds drew the Roman general in his triumph. Those best remembered in England are the Queen's cream-coloured State horses. With their manes plaited with purple, and each led by a broad purple ribbon, they were a most striking object in the Jubilee procession. In England, the military funeral is the only pageant in which the horse appears without its rider. The custom is probably ancient beyond record, the horse having been led to the tomb and there killed for the use of its rider in the next world. In the tomb of Childeric, father of Clovis, the skeleton of his war-horse was found, with hundreds of small gold ornaments which had decorated its harness in the funeral procession. But the impressive custom now in use at the military funeral, when the charger follows the body to the grave, with the boots hanging reversed on either side, seems to be a modern revival of an ancient custom. In Tudor times, the horse, or horses, of the dead soldier followed the body, but without the silent appeal of the empty saddle. At the funeral of Sir Philip Sidney, for example, immediately following the car, came his 'horse for the field,' or charger, led by an esquire and ridden by one of his pages, who trailed a broken lance. His 'barbed horse,' for State occasions, covered with cloth of gold, also followed, led by a second esquire, and ridden by a page in full dress, who carried in his hand a battle-axe reversed. Here is, perhaps, the origin of the curious custom of reversing the boots, unless both are associated with the old classical symbol of death, the inverted torch. In the funeral procession of the Duke of Wellington twelve horses drew the car; these were covered from eyes to fetlocks in housings of black velvet, with black ostrich plumes upon their heads. The Duke's funeral was modelled upon the precedent of that of John Monk, first Duke of Albemarle, the only change in the trappings of the horses being that the animals were only plumed on the head, instead of carrying a second plume on the crupper, which, as the tail was hidden by the velvet clothing, had rather a ludicrous appearance. But in the funeral of the Duke of Albemarle, led horses formed an important part of the procession. 'Mourning horses,' as they were called, draped in black cloth and plumed, were distributed at intervals in the *cortège*. The 'chief mourning horse' followed the Standard of England. The funeral car was also followed by a cream-coloured 'horse of honour,' with crimson caparisons, in the Duke of Wellington's funeral procession. The only led horse was his charger, not 'Copenhagen,' but the animal which he was in the habit of riding in his last years. Yet the riderless steed, pacing behind its master's bier, awakened the emotions of the gazing thousands with an appeal more potent and direct than that of all the accumulated pomp which preceded it.

THE SOARING OF BIRDS

THE soaring of birds is probably the highest form of pleasure derived by living creatures from the use of physical gifts. In it the power of flight reaches its perfect development. To float in air with no effort of the beating wing must be a form of physical beatitude like no other sensation, and birds evidently regard it as such, for, except in the case of those birds which soar mainly to watch for prey from vast heights, it is as a rule reserved by birds as a form of pleasure, many species only soaring in weather which strikes them as inviting them to soar, much as the owner of a boat finds that certain days are particularly inviting for a sail. Other birds only soar at certain hours in the day, and when work is over, and especially before sunset. Mr J. G. Millais when in South Africa noticed that the storks chose the hour before dinner to finish the day by 'drifting spirals' in the clouds. In his 'Breath from the Veldt' he gives an exquisite drawing of the soaring storks, and thus describes their movements : 'The whole of the Jabiru storks in the place had mounted high in the air above the river, and were soaring like eagles, drifting slowly down the wind in three huge spirals, each of which for the moment was composed of thirty or forty birds. The effect of the sun on the snowy backs and wings of the birds was very beautiful, whilst the constantly moving spirals, as the individuals kept changing from one line to the other, had an exceedingly pleasant effect on the eye. The *wings were never beaten*, but every bird in turn, with stationary pinions, commenced a spiral descent of each pillar, and then passed on to the next, returning to the summit of the first one on reaching the lowest position of the third one.' It is not necessary to go as far as South Africa to see this power of soaring without beats of the wing. 'The finest exhibition of flight I ever saw,' writes the Rev. J. G. Cornish of Lockinge, Berks, 'was that of a pair of kites. We were standing on the bridge of boats, across the Rhine at Mayence, when we saw the two birds come cricling up far above the river. They came steadily onwards against the wind, and passed on overhead towards the Taunus Hills. We watched them for more than a mile, and saw *not a single beat of the* wing as they swung on in great circles till they were lost to sight. It was an instance, if such were wanted, establishing beyond doubt the power of birds to sail without flapping their wings or gradual loss of height for long periods against the wind.' Until recently, however, instances establishing this fact *were* very much wanted. Because they would not understand how it could be done, many people denied that it could be done, and like the Professor in the *Water Babies*, who called Tom a holothurian and a cephalopod because he would not admit that he was wrong, they invented all sorts of ingenious theories to account for the 'appearance' of soaring, or to show that though birds did float in air it was not soaring but something else. One, that soaring birds 'imparted a vibratory movement to their feathers,' which they can do, but only use it to dry them after washing or when they are frightened; another, that the air in the bird's bones and air vessels expanded and kept them up like a balloon; and a third and more probable one, that they only soared when there were upward draughts of air, on which they floated like burnt paper over a chimney-pot. This was quite satisfactory so far as it went, and where the existence of an upward current could be proved. A good example was seen by the writer in the playing fields at Eton in an autumn gale.

The strong wind struck the tall front of Windsor Castle and the terrace scarp, and caused a strong up-draught, carrying the dead leaves of the trees high up above the battlements of the towers. On this up-current the rooks were floating and sailing with motionless wings, and up among and between the black rooks floated the yellow leaves. In the same way we have watched the sea-gulls soaring in the strong upward current of air near the top of a cliff against which a high wind was blowing. But these were exceptional conditions; and there are many birds, such as the kite, the condor and the vultures, with whom this wonderful and effortless soaring is the normal way of flight. Darwin thus describes the soaring of the condors: 'When the condors are wheeling in a flock round and round any spot, their flight is very beautiful. *Except when rising from the ground, I do not recollect ever having seen one of these birds flap its wings.* I watched several for nearly half-an-hour without once taking off my eyes. They moved in large curves, sweeping in circles' [as did the kites at Mayence], 'descending and ascending without giving a single flap. As they glided close over my head, I intently watched from an oblique position the outline of the separate and great terminal feathers of each wing ; and these separate feathers, if there had been the slightest vibratory motion' [as by the theory which we have mentioned], 'must have appeared blended together. But they were seen distinct against the clear blue sky.'

Soaring in such perfection is not an accomplishment possessed by many of our English birds; or, rather, it is seldom exercised. But the writer has seen a trained peregrine falcon soar at a vast height exactly like the condors, and so much did the bird enjoy the newly-discovered power—for it was a young one that had only been allowed to fly occasionally—that it was long before she would return to the lure. Rooks will also soar, and kestrels late in March and early in April. But this feat of the kestrels must not be confused with their *hovering*, which is accomplished by very rapid and partial beats of the wings. Gulls also 'sail' grandly, though not, as a rule, in such wide circles as the birds we have mentioned. But in face of facts, doubts were constantly thrown on the power of birds to find in the force of the wind a power to 'move against the wind itself. It was, some said, as absurd as to expect that a log thrown into a river could find in its currents a force able to make it float against the stream. D'Esterno made careful observations, and saw that they did sail without beating the wings, but admitted that he could not account for what he saw. M. J. Marey, the author of *Animal Mechanism*, after watching flocks of pelicans on the coasts of the Mediterranean mount up to a great height, and there soar for hours with no beat of the wing, proposed to discover the way in which this was done, and published the results of his labour in a most fascinating book, entitled *Le Vol des Oiseaux.* Amongst a mass of interesting facts and information about the general phenomena of flight the following is briefly the result of his inquiry into the *soaring* power of birds. The soaring of the kites, condors, vultures and peilcans has three points in common. In the first place, the progress made, even if very slight is *against* the wind. Secondly, they fly in circles or ellipses, which are not parallel with the line of the horizon, but oblique,* though to the observer who stands below they appear horizontal. This last fact was discovered by Bakounine, who, seeing a pair of eagles soaring in the Carpathian Mountains, climbed up to a point level with the tract of air in which they were flying, and saw at once that the circles were not horizontal—a fact which Darwin also noted in the soaring of the condors. Lastly, wind, however light, is a necessary condition. From these data, M. Marey concludes that the soaring of a bird is to

* Compare Mr Millais's accurate observation of the method of soaring on spirals quoted at the beginning of this chapter.

be accounted for by the action of the same laws as the flying of a kite. The wind, striking the inclined face of the kite, divides into two forces, one parallel, the other at right angles to the face. The last is again resolved into two forces, one of which acts vertically, the other horizontally. The horizontal force, would cause it to *drift*, but it is checked by the action of the string. The other is an upward force and drives the kite aloft. So, when the bird sets its wings at an angle to the wind, the horizontal force of the wind current should make it drift to windward. But the bird resists this drift by its inertia, and only yields to it gradually, and at a uniform rate of increase. Moreover, by the form of its body and the angle at which it presents its wings to the blast, it offers very little surface for this horizontal force to act upon ; at the same time, it presents all the surface possible to the second, or upward, force of the wind. Its tendency then is to rise much, and to drift backward little and gradually. The bird thus gains greatly in height, and loses a little in progress, until the wind drops somewhat— variations in the force of the wind are a postulate of the theory which most people who have flown a kite will be disposed to grant. The bird then changes the angle of its wings, and glides forward and downwards with all the added force gained by its ascent, and is so carried *against* the wind far beyond its starting-point. The next gust carries it up again; and thus the sailing and circling against the wind are repeated. This is the theory by which M. Marey accounts for the soaring of birds. But they also seem to have the power of modifying the action of the wind, even if it is not intermittent, by shifting the angle at which their wings are presented to it, and thus have the power of 'sailing' against a steady breeze. Gulls do this frequently, and rooks in a less degree; but in all such cases there is the series of ascents and descents, though greatly modified, which characterise the soaring of the condors and kites. This masterful flight, made without effort and at vast heights, seems to us the perfection of movement. Strange as is the power of the beating wing, this soaring on the wind of the condors and pelicans, kites and cranes, is stranger and yet more wonderful. 'Oh for the wings of a dove!' cried the Psalmist—for he sought for rest on *earth*—'then would I wander afar off, and be at rest in the wilderness.' But for the picture of these mightier feats, we must look to the vision of the prophet: 'The *wind was in their wings*, for they had wings like the wings of a stork; and they carried the ephah up between earth and heaven!'

ANIMALS IN RAIN

' When a blanket wraps the day,
   When the rotten woodland drips,
And the leaf is stamped in clay.'

THE signs and warnings of rain given by birds and
animals have for ages been among the commonplace
of rustic poets and their more cultivated imitators.
But these have, for the most part, been contented
to interpret the warnings of animal foreboding and
discontent for the benefit of man, without dwelling
on the obvious relation which this extreme sensitiveness to the approach of wet weather bears to the
sufferings inflicted by it on what we rightly call the
' beasts of the field.' If anyone doubts the danger
and discomfort which most wild animals in England
undergo in great rains, their effect upon inanimate
nature may give some measure of the necessary result
to warm-blooded, sensitive, and, for the most part,
unsheltered creatures. Take, for instance, a district
in which, as sometimes happens, the measured rain-

fall for two days exceeds two inches of water. The whole surface of the arable fields is 'patted' flat by the pelting rain—for the drops which 'hollow the stone' flatten the earth. Wherever the surface is steep or concave, it is carried away, or scooped out often to depth of several inches. In the autumn rains all the willows, plane trees, alders, limes, and other trees whose leaves are heavy in comparison with the attaching stalk, are stripped bare, and where soft ground lies beneath, the leaves are beaten into it. On the open fallows and stubbles every stone stands out clear like a miniature cromlech from the ground. The entrances of the burrows of the field mice and moles are washed open, the hedge bottoms are cleared of leaves, which have been carried into the ditches, and lie piled in sodden heaps at the mouths of the conduits beneath the gateways; every watershoot leading from the deep subsoil drains is spouting yellow water, and the field ponds, which before showed a strange, unnatural transparency—due to the decay of the larger water weeds, and the cold, which kills the summer growth of algæ, and precipitates all alike to the bottom—are brimful, turbid and discoloured. Weather which lowers the land-level by the inch and raises the water-level by the foot cannot fail to cause a corresponding disturbance in animate life; the difference between April showers and Autumn rains is as great as that

between a fire and a furnace. The first stimulate
life and love ; the last bring decay and death, and
if the time of their coming were not coincident
with the period of the greatest vitality of wild
creatures, after the genial months of late summer
and early autumn, the last days of a wet October
would claim more victims among the birds and
beasts of our fields than the heaviest snows of winter.
There is scarcely any English animal or bird that
can remain healthy during a week's rain—even young
ducks die in a wet summer. The danger from snow,
even to the weaker creatures, bears no comparison,
either at the time or in view of the after-mischief
caused by it, to the effects of cold and pitiless rain.
It is the cutting off of the food supply, caused by
the long continuance of frost, that kills the birds
and starves the hares and rabbits, not the snow itself.
Animals, which would be sick and ailing after three
days' rain, seem to enjoy a week's snow. You may
see where, after a moonlight night, hares and rabbits
have been rolling in the snow, just as dogs roll and
romp in the powdery white. But neither man nor
beast can face the rain. It was not snow, but famine,
that destroyed the *grande armée* in the retreat from
Moscow, though Generals *Janvier* and *Février* completed what hunger had begun. But the incessant
rains of the following autumn, lasting from August

till October, wasted the new conscript army almost as fast in the fertile plains of Saxony, and even arrested the veterans of the Peninsular War whom the Pyrenees had failed to stop.

The reluctance with which most human beings face any voluntary exposure to such weather will account for our very limited knowledge of the shifts and devices by which our wild animals endeavour to avoid the worst discomforts which it brings. But those who are bold enough to go forth in all weathers know by experience that in all but the most open countries there are generally to be found some cosy corners to which the rain does not penetrate, or which, even if not dry, are sheltered from the direct access of the driving drops. Animals, birds especially, while showing the utmost dislike to endure the storm, are by no means so clever in the use of such natural shelters as might be supposed. Hares, as a rule, leave the open country, and seek shelter in the woods ; and stupid as they are in circumstances new to their experience, as when suddenly chased, or in avoiding snares and traps, they show considerable ingenuity in securing their comfort. They nearly always make a form near, but not touching, the trunk of some large tree. Thus, while securing the shelter of the stem and overhanging limbs, they avoid the water which drains downs the main column, and forms, as any one may see by looking at the foot of a large timber tree in a meadow, a tiny canal at the base of the trunk. The writer has sometimes seen hares not lying in their form, but sitting up in such places, just as a labourer shelters himself behind a haystack. Where there are no woodlands, they creep under the irregular overhanging cornice made by the crumbling away of the mould beneath the roots in the hedge-banks, and there scratch out a snug and dry retreat. Rabbits usually keep underground in their burrows, only coming out to feed, unless their holes are flooded, as often happens after a long course of wet. They then leave the warren altogether, and lie out among the turnips, or even on the open stubbles, huddled up into the smallest possible space, as if they had lost all faith in the possibility of finding further shelter.

Rats have the strongest possible dislike to damp, and on the first approach of settled wet swarm into the stacks and farm buildings. Those which spend their lives along the banks of rivers and brooks—a semi-aquatic breed of land-rats which resemble the true water-rats in all but their vegetarian diet—have a simple and clever resource for wet weather. They leave their holes in the banks, and go up into the crowns of the pollard willows which fringe the streams and line the hedges ;

in these they find warm, dry and well-drained winter lodgings, safe even in flood-time; for their powers of swimming enable them to shift from tree to tree, and the swarms of snails and insects which shelter in the hollow trunks provide them with food for a 'rainy day.' Foxes often lie in these large hollow pollards during very wet weather; and the writer has seen an otter slip from the crown of one of them into the Cherwell during an autumn flood. But foxes more often prefer to lie still for hours curled up in the high grass and brambles in some thick double-fence, or dry furze-brake. Sometimes, in heavy rain, they are so reluctant to leave their dry quarters that they do not move until their disturber is close upon them; and the comical, half-reluctant, and wholly sulky look of an old dog-fox as he stands hesitating between prudence and comfort should appeal to the most unsympathetic sportsman. Horses and cattle never look so miserable as when standing exposed to cold and driving rain. Every field in which cattle are turned loose should have some rude shelter pro-vided, however rough and hardy the stock. If left to themselves in a state of nature, they would travel miles to some well-known bank or thicket, which would at least give cover against the wind. Shut up between four hedges they are denied alike the aid of human forethought and of their own instinct.

Bewick's vignettes of old horses, or unhappy donkeys, huddled together in driving showers on some bleak common, express a vast amount of animal misery in an inch of wood-cut. It seems strange that no animal, unless it be the squirrel, seems to build itself a shelter with the express object of keeping off the rain, which all so much dislike. Monkeys are miserable in wet, and could easily build shelters if they had the sense to do so. 'As the creatures hop disconsolately along in the rain,' writes Mr Kipling in his *Beast and Man in India*, 'or crouch on branches, with dripping backs set against the tree-trunk as shelter from a driving storm, they have the air of being very sorry for themselves.' But even the ourang-outang, which builds a small platform in the trees on which to sleep at night, never seems to think of a roof, though the Dyaks say that when it is very wet it covers itself with the leaves of tree ferns. Birds, some of which carefully roof in the nests in which they rear their young, and even, as in the case of the swallow, choose some existing roof, such as the eaves of a house or a projecting cliff, to cover the nest, when built of materials which wet would destroy, seem incapable of making a waterproof house for themselves. Grouse and all the fowl of the open moorlands go to the most open and exposed spots in rain, avoiding the thick heather and even the 'peat-hags,' in whose hollows they might find shelter. Partridges huddle under the fences, or lie on the driest and barest places on the fallows, apparently caring less for shelter above than for dry soil beneath them. Rooks often flock into thick fir trees, or in summer take refuge in the old and close-growing oaks which line the roadsides. But the small and helpless birds, yellow-hammers, buntings, chaffinches and linnets, seem quite bewildered by the beating storms. They creep into cart ruts or behind tufts of grass; often they take refuge under the big swede turnips round the edges of the fields, where they are so numbed and cramped by cold and wet that they may be caught by the hand, or are picked up by stoats and rats, humble and unconsidered victims of the 'plague of rain and waters.'

BIRDS LOST IN STORMS

THE possible existence of a 'sense of locality' to guide birds when migrating is not contradicted by the fact that birds are constantly 'lost,' and wander over enormous distances of land and sea, not knowing how to return to their familiar haunts. 'Lost' birds are nearly always the victims of severe gales which carry them completely out of their reckoning. After storms of exceptional violence in the Atlantic accounts are certain to appear in the papers of ocean-birds which have been driven from distant seas, and even from other continents, or the New World itself, and have drifted to the rain-soaked fields of England. No doubt all shore-birds are liable to be driven inland during a gale; but these are rarely, if ever, *lost* in a storm. Every seagull and cormorant, puffin or razor-bill, has its own home, the particular shelf or ledge of cliff on which it sleeps every night, and from which it launches itself over the sea when the first streak of dawn appears upon the waters. But these are only 'long-shore' birds that can lie snug in harbour, like their rivals the fishermen, in a gale of wind, and suffer, like them, mainly from the interruption of their fishing.

When the true ocean birds, like the petrels, are found scattered inland, dead or dying, we may safely infer that the weather from side to side of the Atlantic has borne hardly, not only on the ships, but on the friendly birds that love to follow them. Numbers of these, of at least two different kinds, one of which, as a rule, makes the Azores the eastern limit of its ocean range, appeared on our coasts or inland during the gales of October 1892. Wilson's petrel was seen in Ireland, in County Down, and a second is said to have been shot on Lough Erne. The fork-tailed petrel, another ocean species, appeared in far greater numbers. These birds were seen in Donegal, and in Argyllshire, in Westmoreland, and in the Cleveland district in Yorkshire. As the last appeared after a strong north-westerly gale, it seems that it must not only have come in from the Atlantic, but have flown over England before falling exhausted to the ground. They were also seen in Mayo, in Tipperary, at Limerick, Dumfries and Northampton. From an account given of these petrels in Argyllshire, it is clear that they retained after their long journey all that misplaced confidence in man which marks their behaviour when accompanying ships in mid-ocean. After five had been shot by the owner of a yacht in Loch Melfort, they settled on the vessel, and one allowed itself to be caught under the sou'-wester hat of a sailor.

As we have said, the petrels are true ocean-birds, living by choice far from land, in the 'uttermost parts of the sea.' Perhaps their favourite haunt is the great Southern Ocean beyond the Tropics. There, at any-rate, is the main nesting-place of Wilson's petrel, on the Island of Kerguelen. They also lay their eggs at the southern points of Nova Scotia; but though they join and accompany the ships in the mid-passage to and from Europe, they say 'Good-bye!' at the Azores, as the stormy petrels did to Tom the Water Baby when he reached the ice-pack, and nothing but the extremity of distress could force them to the English shore.

Perhaps the strangest instance of the forced wandering of a petrel was that which brought one of the last-known members of an extinct, or at any-rate a lost species, the capped petrel, whose only home appears to have been the islands of St Domingo and Guadaloupe, from the West India seas to a Norfolk heath. In March or April 1850, a bird was seen by a boy on a heath at Southacre, in Norfolk, flapping from one furze-bush to another, until it crept into one, and was there caught by him. Exhausted as it was, it violently bit his hand, and he thereupon killed it. A Mr Newcome, one of a race of falconers, happened to be hawking in the neighbourhood, and his falconer, seeing the boy with the dead bird, brought it to his master, by whom it was skinned and stuffed, and placed in the Newcome collection, where it still remains. It was a large bird, about 16 in. in length, with the long curved wings characteristic of all the petrels, and a black head, as its name indicates.

Only two other instances of the capped petrel's appearance in Europe are known. One was shot near Boulogne, and one in Hungary in 1870, which is in the Museum of Buda-Pesth. Two others have been taken in the United States. But the strangest part of the story is that the capped petrels are now either extinct, or lost to the knowledge of man. 'It is certain,' says Mr Southwell, the editor of the last and unfinished volume of Stevenson's *Birds of Norfolk*, 'that the true home of this very rare species is, or *was*, in the islands of Guadaloupe and Dominica, in the West Indies, where it was formerly very abundant ; but one of its old breeding-places in the last-named of these islands was explored, without finding a single bird, in February 1889, by Colonel Feilden.' It appears that ten years before, not only Dominica but also Guadaloupe was searched in vain for the 'Diablotins,' the name by which these petrels were known to the old voyagers. It is believed that they were possibly destroyed by a South American opossum which was introduced to the island ; but as the young and even the old birds were constantly caught by the islanders for food in the holes in which they nested, their destruction may be due, like that of the great auk, to human greediness.

At first it seems difficult to believe that the petrels, gifted with powers of flight so great that, like their first cousins the albatrosses, they make the central ocean their chosen home, should so far succumb to the Atlantic storms as to fall wholly under the dominion of the wind, and drift for thousands of miles to unknown and inhospitable shores. But any one who has watched the flight of a 'lost' bird in a gale on land may form some idea of the danger to which the petrels are exposed when a hurricane bursts in the Atlantic. Take, for instance, this scene near Oxford, when a gale was at its height, and the 'centre boards' were rushing up and down over the floods on Port Meadow, with a strong current and the wind on their quarter ; the geese were flying over the flood to avoid the canoes and small craft ; and the wind was blowing a full gale from the south-west, with a brilliant sun, occa-

sionally hidden by a white, drifting cloud. Far away
to the north was a long-winged bird, beating up
against the wind. At one time it rose high in the
air, facing the gale ; then it descended with a rapid
swoop progressing westwards, but at the same time
' falling off' still further to the north. It was a
young herring - gull, its chequered grey - and-white
plumage showing clearly in the bright light as it
approached. It was easy to conjecture from the
gull's flight the power of storms to drive birds from
the course which they aim at. The bird's point was
clearly westward. It used every shelter and every
lull of the wind to make it ; but the gale was too
powerful, and it appeared that it must either stay on
the inhospitable land until the wind dropped, work
its way slowly to the west with a rapid drift to the
north, or abandon its struggle and drift with the wind.
But all birds seem to have an instinctive knowledge
that if they once surrender to the force of the wind,
and allow themselves to drift like leaves, there are
unknown dangers in store for them. They will
hardly ever do so unless to escape pursuit, and then
only for a few minutes, when their pace is so marvel-
lously rapid that, in the case of land-birds, a few
minutes is sufficient to carry them out of the district
they know into others from which they will perhaps
never find their way back to the fields which are

their native home.   In a gale on September 1st,
the writer saw a successful effort made by partridges to avoid the consequences of thus abandoning
themselves to the wind.   A covey of very strong
birds, which had been hatched on the highest part
of the Berkshire Downs, was flushed down wind,
and, rising high in the air, the whole brood were
carried in a few seconds to the extreme edge of the
hill, below which was a sudden fall of some 300 ft.
into a country quite unknown to these hill-birds.   As
they approached the limit of their own district, the
partridges made an extraordinary effort to release
themselves from the power of the wind, and to avoid
being forced over the hill-top.   Closing their wings,
they sank almost to the ground, and so gained the
slight shelter of a low bank.   This enabled them to
wheel, and so to face the gale.   Even then they
might not have achieved their object, had not a small
thorn-bush broken the force of the wind just on the
edge of the down.   The whole covey used the respite
so given, and skimming up almost in single file, they
alighted one by one behind the bush, on the extreme
limit of their native ground.   But recent instances
are not wanting in which partridges have been carried
out to sea, when drifting on the wind.   At Sizewell,
in Suffolk, nine partridges were blown out to sea,
and dropped in the water some 400 yards from

the shore ; and in another case thirteen of the 'red-legged' variety attempted the flight across the estuary of the Stour, and falling exhausted, were picked up by some boatmen fishing for 'dabs,' a welcome and unlooked-for haul. But perhaps the most remarkable instance of land-birds being carried to sea by the wind, just as the ocean-dwelling petrels are drifted over the land, is that recorded in the last century of a flight of woodcocks, which drifted over England, and dropped in hundreds into the sea beyond Cornwall and the Scilly islands. Probably they had started from Norway against a gentle southerly wind, and had then been caught in mid-air by a gale from the east. But mishaps of this kind indicate no such stress of storm as the appearance on our shores of the ocean-loving petrels, to whom, rather than to the 'cormorants, ducks, and gulls,' Clough's appeal to the sea-birds more nearly applies :—

> 'Ye over stormy seas leading long and dreary processions,
>   Ye, too, brood of the wind, whose coming is whence we discern
>   not,
>   Making your nest on the wave, and your home on the crested
>   billow,
>   .   .   .   . fill ye my imagination!
> Let us not talk of Growth ! We are still in our Aqueous Ages !'

WHAT ANIMALS SEE

Writing in *Land and Water* on the sleep of fish, Mr Matthias Dunn accounts for the transition state between sleep and waking observed in fish by the existence of a dual nervous system, and a double use of the eye—'the under eye being closed, while they watch their enemies with the outside eye.' The first supposition would account for the power which most animals have of passing instantaneously from sleep to wakefulness—or of 'sleeping with one eye open,' as the phrase is. The second is somewhat misleading, supposing, as it does, that the eye of the fish, which is flatter and less perfectly fitted as an organ of sight, can perform functions which, even in the eye of the higher vertebrate, are mechanically impossible. What animals see, and what they do not, is by no means easily discovered. The compound eyes of insects present an image pieced together like mosaic, each portion being conveyed by a separate facet of the eye. But a much more interesting question is that of the vision of quadrupeds and birds, which have 'simple eyes' constructed like our own, though differing greatly from ours in positive size, as well as in size compared with the animal which uses them. Tradition and general consent have made current a certain amount of very uncertain 'data' as to animal sight. But these are mainly limited to the range or accuracy of vision possessed by animals, and hardly touch the question whether objects appear to them as they do to us, whether their eyes readily suggest to them the ideas of solidity, transparency, roundness, or squareness, how far they recognise colours, or whether to many creatures of considerable development the world is not all black and white, or a 'harmony in green and grey.'

If they do not readily distinguish solid form and colour, their ideas of things must present themselves to the animal in a very different form from that in which we suppose them to appear to the animal brain. But though the eyes of the horse, or of the dog, are adapted for presenting the image on the retina coloured as we see it coloured, it does not follow that the animal sees it as we do, or that by seeing a mere black-and-white picture it would be at any disadvantage in the life which it naturally leads. The sense of colour, which is the perception and distinction of colours and shades of colours by our brain, depends, not only on the organ which makes the picture, but on the mind which interprets it. It is largely the result of education, even in those whose eyes are perfect, and who are not colour-blind to any particular shade or tint. It is possible that the animal eye, provided with all the requisite apparatus for producing a coloured picture, may be so ill-interpreted by the uneducated animal brain that the creature sees mainly, though probably not entirely, in monochrome. An evidence of the latent and inert character of colour-vision is that the human eye, which is trained to distinguish colours, may also, by want of use, forget how to distinguish colours. No human being would probably be found so reckless of self in the pursuit of knowledge as voluntarily to submit to forego the use of his eyes, and be blind for a season, to establish this fact, that colour can be forgotten, as well as learnt, by human sight. But the unique experience of Dr George Harley, F.R.S., who, in order to save the sight of one, perhaps of both eyes, when one was injured, voluntarily immured himself in a room made totally dark for nine months, shows that this is the case. The fortitude which enabled him to adopt this course, and the ingenuity by which he preserved his health and faculties in this, the most mentally and physically depressing of all forms of imprisonment, are sufficiently remarkable; but Dr Harley also kept an accurate record of his impressions when he at last looked again upon the light, after the supreme moment at which he satisfied himself that he was not blind, but could see. He found that in the nine months' darkness his eyes had lost all sense of colour. The world was black, white, and grey. They had also lost the sense of distance. His brain interpreted the picture wrongly. His hand did not touch the object meant to be grasped. Practice soon remedied the last induced defect of sight. Experiment with skeins of various-coloured wool, in the presence of one who had the normal powers of colour-vision, restored the first.

From this personal record, it may be gathered that as the trained human eye has to learn, and might lose, the sense of colour, so the animal brain, which receives little or no training of this kind, may in many cases be unaware of the colours which the eye presents for recognition. We have no power of determining this by simple tests, as in the case of human beings. But there is little positive evidence that the larger quadrupeds, oxen, deer, the felidæ, or dogs, have much sense of colour; and their power of vision in its wider sense varies so greatly in different species as to suggest that the mental factor in sight is often so little exerted for the main purpose of discerning objects, as to leave its more specialised use for distinguishing colour very imperfectly developed. Domestic animals, which see bright colours other than green in large masses more frequently than wild ones, might be supposed to exhibit the consciousness of such differences in the most pronounced way. Yet it is next to impossible to cite an instance in which a dog exhibits curiosity as to colour, or identifies an object by its hue. The writer has seen a setter refuse to retrieve a black rabbit because it apparently thought its master had shot a black cat. But a house-living dog shows no preference for a red carpet or rug over a blue or variegated one, and expresses no surprise or curiosity whether its master wears a red uniform or a black evening suit. Domestic cattle are so far affected by violent contrast of white and dark that the presence of a black, white, or very clearly-spotted animal in the herd sometimes results in calves being thrown of the same colour or markings. But though red is said to irritate a bull, and to excite hunters by association of ideas, the latter statement rests partly on surmise. They are equally excited by the sound or sight of hounds, or of a number of riders, whatever the colour of their coats. None or the cats, whether wild or tame, show any partiality for bright hues ; and among all the stratagems used from time immemorial by hunters, the use of colour as a lure for quadrupeds is notably absent. Many birds, on the other hand, have a marked preference for bright colours, and exhibit strong curiosity when unusual tints are shown to them. Among the less known examples is that of the red-legged partridge. These birds abound in the lower spurs of the Lesghian Mountains, near the Caspian, and the native hunters use a device for killing them based on this æsthetic preference of the partridges. By the door of nearly every house stands a wooden frame, on which canvas is stretched, covered with daubs of brilliant colours. This the shooter carries with him, and sets up in front of him as soon as he has discovered a covey. As soon as their attention is attracted he waits behind the screen, until the whole covey run up to within shot, and then fires through a loop-hole in the centre of the screen. The Russian Government has now forbidden the use of these coloured lures, as the birds were being exterminated. It is probable that the idea of their use was first suggested by the interest the birds took in the carpet frames set up outside the houses for weaving the brightly-coloured Shushak rugs.

Birds are commonly credited with an extraordinary *range* of vision. Circumstances lend aid to the development of the mental factors in their case. The usual distance at which terrestrial species use their eyes is limited by the ground horizon. But in the case of the soaring birds, such as vultures and eagles, the horizon, the natural limit of sight, is enormously extended. Macgillivray early noted that though birds of prey have orbits of great size—the eyeball of the common buzzard being $1\frac{1}{8}$ in. in diameter—they do not, as a rule, soar when seeking their prey. The eagle, when hunting, flies low, just as do the sparrow-hawk and the hen-harrier. Yet the vultures and condors, birds which admittedly do soar when seeking food, have been proved to find carrion by sight. A carcase was covered with canvas, and some offal placed upon it. The vultures saw this, descended and ate it, and then sat on the covered portion within a few inches of a putrid carcase. When a hole was made in the covering they saw and attacked the food below. But the rapid congregation of vultures from a distance to a carcase, is probably due to their watching their neighbours, each of which is surveying a limited area; Charles Darwin pointed out that in a level country the height of sky commonly noticed by a mounted man is not more than fifteen degrees above the horizon; and a vulture on the wing at the height of between 3000 ft. and 4000 ft. would probably be two miles distant, and invisible. Those which descend rapidly and appear to have come from beyond the range of human sight, were perhaps hovering vertically over the hunter when he killed his game. There remains one undoubted instance in which bird-vision is far keener than that of man. The great grey shrike, *Lanius excubitor*, is habitually used by the men who catch falcons at Valhenswaard to give notice of the approach of a hawk. The bird sees it far sooner than the men, and at once gives notice of its approach. This is a single instance in which the specialised acuteness of sight may be due to the fact that the bird in question much resembles in colour the pigeons, which are the falcon's favourite food. But long-sight does not seem a common property of bird-vision. The gannets, which catch fish at sea, descend from a considerable height, but they kill their prey on the surface of the water or near it. Nocturnal birds and animals, though able to see with little light, have no enhanced powers when the light is more powerful ; and those animals which, like deer, feed by night or day indifferently, have only developed a keenness of vision from constant fear and vigilance. Horses and cattle, which have the same power of sight by night, have never increased their visual range. Dogs habitually rely on another sense, that of scent, in preference to their eyes, and will walk over a dead bird while their brain is intent on discovering its place by scent alone. Weasels, when hunting, will run up to a human being who imitates the squeak of a rabbit and peer up at him to discover where the sound comes from. The smallness of the eye limits its powers ; just as the best telescope has usually the largest object-glass, so the largest eye will probably be the best organ of sight ; and in the absence of any extraordinary developments in the size of the organ itself in animals, their power of vision must, in the absence of evidence to the contrary, be supposed to be proportionately limited.

ANIMAL INDUSTRIES

A RECENT and interesting contribution to the sum of popular knowledge of animal instinct is M. Frederic Houssay's work on *The Industries of Animals*, published in the 'Contemporary Science Series' by Mr Walter Scott. It is an ingenious attempt to bring man and animals into line on the common ground of their provision by industry of the necessities of life. ~ The arts of collecting provisions, storing and preserving food, domesticating and managing flocks, and capturing slaves, are quite as well understood by animals and insects as by man in the earlier stages of his civilisation, and show a curious analogy in their development in the case of the more backward among human communities. Ants of the same species both have, and have not, learnt to keep 'cattle.' Lespè found a tribe of black ants which had a flock of 'cows' which they milked daily. But he also discovered a nest of the same species which had no flocks. These he presented with some of the aphides used by their cow-keeping relations. The ants instantly attacked, killed, and ate them, behaving in exactly the same improvident manner as a tribe of Australian 'black-fellows' when presented with a flock of sheep. A little known and striking instance of foresight and industry exhibited by a bird is that of the Californian woodpecker. Like others of its kind, this bird is an insect-eater. Yet in view of the approach of winter, it prepares a store of food of a wholly different character, and arranges this with as much care as an epicure might devote to the storage of his wine in a cellar. In the summer, the woodpecker lives on ants. For the winter it stores up acorns. To hold each acorn it hollows a small hole·in a tree, into which the acorn is exactly fitted, and is ready to be split by the strong beak of the climbing woodpecker, though too tightly held to be stolen either by squirrels or other birds. A relation of this woodpecker inhabits the driest parts of Mexico, where, during the droughts, it must die of starvation, unless it made a store. To prevent this it selects the hollow stem of a species of aloe, the bore of which is just large enough to hold a nut. The woodpecker drills holes at intervals in the stem, and fills it from bottom to top with the nuts, the separate holes being apparently made for convenience of access to the column of nuts within. The intelligence which not only constructs a special storehouse, but teaches the woodpecker to lay by only the nuts which will keep, and not the insects which would decay, is perhaps the highest form of bird-reasoning which has yet been observed. The common ant of Italy— *inopæ metuens formica senectæ* of the Romans—if not so strangely ingenious as the gardener ants of the tropics, which prepare a particular soil on which to grow within their nests the fungus on which alone they feed, exhibits what is probably the most complex form of instinctive industry shown by any European animal. It stores up oats and various kinds of grain, making hundreds of little rooms as granaries, of about the size of a watch. But grain lying in the ground naturally germinates. How the ants prevent this is not known. Probably by ventilation, as bees ventilate their hives by artificial draught. All that is certain is, that if the ants are removed the grain sprouts. When the ants wish to use the store, they allow the grains to germinate, until the chemical change takes place in the material which makes its fermenting juice food suitable for their digestion. They then arrest the process of change by destroying the sprout, and use the stock of glutinous sugar and starch so left as their main food in winter.   M. Houssay might have drawn his parallel between human and animal industries still closer, if he had referred to the curious partnership which modern observation has made possible between men and bees.   By giving the bees a foundation of wax stamped with the shape of the cells, the beekeeper saves the hive the time and trouble spent in this non-productive labour ; and the purpose of the artificial aid so given is at once comprehended and turned to use by the otherwise stereotyped intelligence of the bee.

If we are ever to discover the origin and nature of instinct, it must be by the multiplication of facts and observations such as M. Houssay has endeavoured to co-ordinate.   At present it cannot be maintained that the last word has been said as to the origin of those astonishing creative acts by which the bee and his kind rival the mathematician and mechanician, or of the means by which the carrier-pigeon, and even four-footed domestic animals, find their way to their home across tracts of country absolutely new to their experience.   The wonderful facts as to animal journeys across the sealess and almost riverless continent of Australia, increase the difficulty of finding a suitable explanation of instinct, which must necessarily cover this wholly unexplained power of local divination. So far as a recognised theory of the origin of instinct may be said to exist, there is very little to be added to the form in which it is presented in M. Houssay's treatise. He considers that by a careful comparison and classification of observed facts, it is possible to find in animals all the intermediate stages between a deliberate, reflective action, and an act that has become instinctive, and so inveterate to the species that it has reacted on its body, and produced new and special organs. 'If an individual is led to reproduce the same series of actions, it contracts a *habit*; the repetition may be so frequent that the animal comes to accomplish it without knowing it; the brain no longer intervenes; the spinal cord or chain of nerves alone govern this order of acts, to which has been given the name of *reflex actions*. This tendency to reflex action may be transmitted by heredity to the descendants, and then becomes an *instinct*.' In the case of the bee, assuming this hypothesis to be the true one, the determination of the hexagonal form for its cells, which is just that which calculation shows to demand the least quantity of wax for the storage of the greatest quanity of honey, must originally have been due to trial and reflection. No one can doubt that there is a mind somewhere behind the astonishing finish and adaptation of bee-architecture and the social life of the hive. But of the process of development there exists no trace. We can only guess that it may have been so from the analogy of other cases of the formation of an instinct which have come within reach of human experience. But there are numbers of bees which make round honey cells, like pitchers, and which, though presumably equally intelligent with the hive bee, show no tendency to make their work more perfect mechanically. In the case of the moss-carding bee, the community may be supposed to be even more intelligent than the honey bees; for the latter always seek a ready-made home, while the moss-carder builds one for itself. If instinct is to be regarded, not as a rudiment of intelligence, but the result of a series of reasoned acts, which by frequent repetition became habitual, then reflex, and finally instinctive, the part played by time in its production becomes of the first importance. It does not matter whether the lives of the creatures which at present perform acts by instinct are long or short, if we grant the power of hereditary transmission demanded by the theory. The results of yearly experiments by successive generations of bees or wasps, most of which die at the end of twelve months, may survive in the consciousness of the race equally with the longer experiences of man in his generations. Looking at present facts — that in the case of the queen wasp, for instance the sole survivor does transmit to her offspring the whole permanent instinct of architecture and social polity of her race—the power of heredity cannot be denied, because the facts do not admit of any other explanation, except on the hypothesis of the existence of some additional sense which, owing to the limitation of our own we could by no possible means comprehend. The growth of instinct, if the theory of its development given above is correct, should be a process of abnormal length, and it would almost follow that the antiquity of species could be estimated from the degree of perfection in which instinct is exhibited. The difference of structure and diversity of needs in different animals, in some so simple and in others so complex, need not waken this conclusion, if we only compare those in which the order of daily life is somewhat similar. The life history of the hive bee would seem to demand a far longer period for its complex instinct to become stereotyped than the life history of the solitary species ; and man, with his few forms of instinctive action and reliance on individual intelligence, would be assigned a place among the latest developments of nature. Our knowledge of the facts of instinct is as yet too ill-assorted for the construction of more than a working hypothesis as to its origin; and until the question of the inheritance of acquired characteristics is more completely answered than it is at present, the whole structure hangs on a doubtful link. But there is one point on which the theory of instinct which M. Houssay reproduces is eminently satisfactory, though he does not claim it as an argument for its value. It accounts for the uniformity and subordination of individuals in the life of the social animals and social insects, which is almost inexplicable on any other hypothesis. That thousands of beings so intelligent as the bee can live together and exercise an intelligence which is used solely for the good of the community, and never for the personal advantage or aggrandisement of an individual, transcends reason, as we understand it. Yet it is just possible to conceive a human community in which the system of caste might become so stereotyped as to eliminate the initial difference between man and man in each class, and produce uniform types of workers, soldiers and the like. But in such a case, what is instinct but a degradation of intelligence, producing perhaps a higher level of work but a lower type of mind?

'SWEATING' BEES

THE pamphlets and newspapers which deal with the minor forms of live-stock farming are generally amusing reading, even to an outsider. But the columns of *Poultry* and other fanciers' journals, whether devoted to fur or feather in domestication, are more practical than scientific. They belong, as Aristotle would say, to the sphere of art which treats of production and avoids philosophy. An apparent exception occurs in the case of modern books on apiculture and the *British Beekeepers' Journal*. The nature of the subject is attractive ; but it is not to this that the difference is traced. The modern beekeeper is not specially interested in the bee as an architect and engineer, nor, except for ends of his own, does he 'go out' on the moral excellence of the bee, 'the model of patience, industry and thrift.' It is not till after a careful course of apicultural study that the 'root-thought,' the text of the whole matter, becomes clear to the curious reader. All these books and pamphlets and articles are written with a single object. That object is 'sweating' bees. All the nice little pictures of new hives and 'feeders' and 'smokers' and artificial comb foundation, are so many tips from old hands to the sweaters of future generations of the most industrious insects in the world. The moral aspect of this enterprise is, it must be owned, rather perplexing. It is open to those who advocate 'sweating' bees, to urge that, if it is good for the bee to be busy, it is perhaps better for him to be busier. In any case it was a great thought; and it forms the common bond of union which unites and animates the powerful society known as the British Beekeepers' Association. The humorous side of this latest effort to expand the limits of animal service to man, has apparently escaped the notice of the members of the Apicultural Association; but it is sufficiently obvious to the general reader, and more to anyone who watches the working of the new contrivances which have been so kindly introduced to the notice of the bees. Ingenious as these contrivances are, their success is due in the main to the absorbing desire for work which possesses the bees themselves. It is the artful diversion of this praiseworthy energy into new and remunerative channels which is the beekeepers' object; and in contemplating the difference of purpose which animates the industrious insect and his thoughtful owner respectively, the joy of 'observing' bees and beekeepers mainly consists. Practical people, who desire to get more work out of the bee than heretofore, do not deny that he is naturally industrious. Mr S. Simmins, the author of *A Modern Bee-Farm*, notes that 'bees are never idle except from sheer force of circumstances; when it is cold in winter they simply cluster in one compact mass; but with each returning spell of milder weather this living ball expands, and many of the insects travel to the most distant sealed combs of honey, and commencing on the *outer surface* of each *outside* comb, the whole of the honey there stored is carried to those cells in close contact with the cluster.' The bee code of industry will not even permit it to begin work at the easiest end. If this mental attitude were constant, it would baffle the aims of the modern bee-owner who seeks to provide his insects with the means to do more work in less time. They might refuse to use the labour-saving apparatus provided, on the ground that hard work was their *summum bonum*. But the bees are not so perverse. On the contrary, they welcome any contrivance which will enable them to do the maximum of work, and then, disdaining the temptation of shorter hours, use it for the maximum of time, day by day. The 'personnel' of the hive being thus disposed, the object of the practical bee owner is first to obtain the largest number of workers before the honey-bearing flowers blossom, and then to set them to work in the factory on improved principles. This is the point at which most bee-keeping manuals begin, after references to the mental solace derived from the pursuit, and encouraging tables of profits made by the sale of honey. Large 'stocks,' or single communities, are produced by the best queen bees. At what age the queen is 'best' is a point not agreed on by the authorities. Mr Simmins holds that none should be kept after the second summer. Queen bees are a special product, provided as an article of separate purchase, and are often 'mailed' from America in cages, though we learn that 'recently, through the short-sightedness or the prejudice of the postal authorities, many foreign queens have been returned to the senders.' The travelling-cages of queen-bees are among the minor appliances of the new bee-machinery. They are made in three compartments, one of which is ventilated for a saloon in hot weather, one less airy in case of cooler temperature, while a third contains the food-supply. The 'sweating' process begins with the queen, who is encouraged to lay 'early and often.' British queen bees are admitted to do their duty in this respect. But foreign labour is introduced into the hives in competition with native industry, either by crossing with Cyprian, Carniolan, or Syrian queens, or by importing the foreigners in a swarm. Carniolans are pronounced by Mr Simmins to be '*the* bees for beginners.' They have all the energy of the most industrious mountain races, have learnt the necessity of making honey when the sun shines, and are in all respects model creatures, with a capacity for working to order beyond the usual limits even of bee energy. Some idea of the amount of labour exacted from a colony propagated by an ideal queen bee, may be gathered from the area of flowering plants sown to keep them busy. Seventy-five acres of ground, planted with white clover, borage, or sanfoin, will occupy one hundred hives profitably for the three months of June, July and August. This the bees are expected to work in addition to the flowers which grow naturally in a rural district. To prevent loitering, the crops are planted near the hives. The return of honey due from the bees is calculated as accurately as was the return due from farm stock under the ancient manor system. Clover and sanfoin should produce 10 lb. of honey per acre each fine day ; and as they flower twice, and remain in full blossom for a week at a time, the seventy-five acres, if properly worked by the bees, are expected to yield more than 10,000 lb. of honey.

The triumph of the 'sweater's' art is in inducing the bees to fetch this enormous quantity of honey, without neglecting the arrangements for storing it in the hives. The honey, being liquid, must be bottled, and the bees will only put in comb of the exact size and texture which instinct has taught them. Comb-making is also much lighter and safer work than honey-gathering, with its dangers from storms, wasps, and birds. Young bees are generally told-off for the purpose, while their elders go a-field. But conscience will not allow a bee to stay at home if he is not wanted to work. The beekeeper therefore makes it his business to provide ready-made foundations for the cells, stamped in real wax, and of the natural size. He also removes the combs full of honey, spins them round in a tin churn, and replaces them in the hive empty—a hint which the bees take as an invitation to refill them. The ancient task-master said, 'Ye are idle, ye shall have no straw.' The modern bee-master says, 'Ye are industrious, here is the straw ready chopped.' The bees seem delighted to make the most of the opportunities so thoughtfully provided for them. By using the mechanically stamped 'foundations' for their cells, they make a more perfect and symmetrical comb than is often constructed without help. The bottoms being regular, no 'crooked comb' is ever built upon it. The size stamped is also uniformly that of worker-cells ; thus there is no room for drone-cells, producing bees which cannot be 'sweated' or made profitable in any way. The visible results of the system are a vastly increased store of honey—nearly 1000 lb. were recently made by the bees of fifteen hives — and so far no sign of 'overstrain' among the bees. When the system has had another twenty years of trial, it may possibly show certain strains developing a tendency to forget how to construct comb-foundation, just as some breeds of fowls are forgetting how to hatch their eggs. We cannot suggest an improvement in the architecture of the cells, because they are mechanically perfect in economy of material and space. But the readiness with which the honey bee has accepted and incorporated in its comb the materials supplied by man suggests the possibility of further experiments to determine how far its mechanical instinct is capable of modification.

THE RE-DOMESTICATION OF THE AFRICAN ELEPHANT

GERMANY, which feels the want of a reliable beast of burden in her East African territory even more than England, seems to have resolved on the re-domestication of the African elephant. Some time ago a German officer commenced a series of visits to the Indian 'keddahs,' and after mastering so far as possible the Indian methods and system of catching and training wild elephants, has hired a staff of experienced Indian catchers and trainers, and is to establish a Government 'Elephant Stud' in German East Africa. Mr Carl Hagenbeck, proprietor of the Thierpark at Hamburg, has recently contributed an interesting article on this subject to the *Hamburger Nachrichten*. Mr Hagenbeck's name is a household word in Germany and the United States, and his name became familiar in England last summer, when he exhibited his Somalis and their animals at the Crystal Palace ; but it is perhaps worth noting that

he has for many years been at the head of the wild
beast trade, both in Europe and America, and that
he is not only the owner of the largest menageries
in the world, with trading-camps on the outskirts of
civilisation in three continents, but a very practical
and successful man of business. Mr Hagenbeck's
paper took the form of a plea for the preservation
of the African elephant. But with him preservation
is merely the necessary preliminary to their re-
domestication, for the probable success in which he
gives reasons which should be very encouraging to
those now pledged to the undertaking. Mr Hagenbeck
writes with authority on the subject. Out of two
hundred African elephants brought to Europe in
recent years he has imported one hundred and seventy,
and many of these have remained in his Zoological
Gardens at Hamburg and in America. With the
histories of the rest since they passed into other
hands he is perfectly familiar. He was recently able
to tell the present writer the exact number of African
Elephants, and the owner of each in the different
countries of Europe; and he has a natural insight
into the ways and means of animal domestication.
He gives it as his opinion that the general belief
that 'African elephants are not so strong as are
wilder and less easily tamed, and possess less endurance
than the Indian species, is wrong.' He maintains,

on the contrary, that they are stronger, and at least as tractable, and as useful as beasts of burden or to be ridden, as Indian elephants ; and he claims to have convinced the Berlin Geographical Society that this view was correct, as early as 1878, when he had a number of African elephants in that city.

It will be quite sufficient for practical purposes, if a part only of these anticipations are realised. If the African elephant can be trained and made an obedient slave, it will be a factor of enormous importance in a district where the tsetse-fly stops all animal carriage, and where for generations human— that is, slave — transport has been the sole means of conveying goods from the interior to the coast. The African elephant may well answer this purpose without becoming such a marvel of intelligence and docility as his Indian relative. Moreover, he is not only as strong, but far stronger in mere physique than the Indian, the males being, on an average, two feet, and the females one foot, higher than the Asiatic species. Whether they have quite the same massive dray-horse build may be doubted ; but for most purposes they would probably be even more serviceable as beasts of burden, and the question of general constitution would hardly arise in the case of animals used in their own country, as these would be in the German Colonies. The experience of English

owners of African elephants can scarcely be set against
the opinion of Mr Hagenbeck, because the purposes
for which the African species is needed in Europe
are not those of the beast of burden. The European
'elephant herd' is, generally speaking, the property
of the large circus owners; and these prefer the Indian
elephant, which they allege to be more docile, and
more reliable for their purposes, than the African
species. The trainers say that the latter have bad
memories, and that this makes them uncertain per-
formers in the ring. They will learn a few tricks
without difficulty; but when called upon to perform
in public, they sometimes seem to forget their accomplishments, and either stand still or bolt to their
stables. It has been recently pointed out that this
lack of memory, or perhaps of brain-power, in the
African, when compared with the Indian species, may
possibly be accounted for by the descent of the former
from the mastodon, an earlier extinct type than the
mammoth. The teeth of the African elephant corre-
spond with those of the mastodon, while in the Indian
elephant they are analogous to those of the more
recent mammoth. When kept in England the African
seems to have less respect for 'humans' than the
Asiatic, and is less trusted by its keepers, who seem
to look upon it as unsafe. But this is only a
comparative estimate of a creature judged by the

side of one which has long held the first place among domesticated beasts of burden. Dr Sclater, who has summarised the general experience of the Zoological Society for nearly twenty years, gave it as his opinion that they are quite as intelligent as the Indian species, though perhaps not equally docile. He suggested that a 'keddah' of Indian elephants and their attendants should be transported to the East African Coast. General Gordon, whose practical wisdom was seldom at fault, had the same idea; and with such encouragement the German enterprise has every reason to hope for success. The modern estimate of the relative intelligence and usefulness of the two species of elephant may be compared with what seems the only record of their employment by hostile armies in the same battle, at a time when they played an important part in the highly trained forces of the successors of Alexander. At the battle of Raphia, between Antiochus and Ptolemy Philopator, the former employed Indian, and the latter 'Libyan' elephants. 'Of the elephants,' writes Polybius, 'forty were placed on the left wing where Ptolemy fought in person; thirty-three protected the left wing. Antiochus put sixty of these beasts before his right wing, where he himself proposed to encounter Ptolemy.' The battle began with an elephant charge, and the men mounted on each engaged hand to hand. 'But a far finer sight it was to see the warlike beasts themselves engage with the utmost fury, and charging each other. For the manner of an elephant-fight is as follows : They lock their tusks, and standing where they are, they push until one gets the better of the other, and pushes the other's trunk somewhat on one side. The moment its flank is exposed, the other buries its tusks in it, and wounds it as a bull uses its horns. But many of Ptolemy's beasts declined the combat. For a mischance occurred to which Lybian (African) elephants are liable, in that they cannot endure the smell or the sight of the Indian, but frightened, in my opinion, by their size and strength, take to flight.'

The African elephants stampeded and broke the ranks behind. Polybius is wrong as to the relative size of the elephants, for, as we have said, the African is the larger. But it seems clear that, when tried by actual experiment, the African race was inferior in docility. Yet judged on their merits, the African elephants must have answered the purpose of their owners well enough. Hannibal was able to bring thirty-two through Spain and across the Alps into Italy, and those of Hasdrubal numbered ten at the battle of the Metaurus. These were a failure in the battle ; but as Indian elephants seem, according to Mr Rudyard Kipling, usually to decline going into action at all under modern conditions, this can hardly be ground for assuming that the Punic elephants would not have been useful and obedient if employed as beasts of burden. Pyrrhus landed no less than fifty elephants in Southern Italy, and there seems little doubt that these were all African beasts. As the Indian elephant line ends at the eastern border of the Punjab, it is not conceivable that they could have been imported directly overland. They were lent to him by Ptolemy Ceraunus, King of Macedon, and though he (Ptolemy) *may* have obtained them from Antiochus, who probably imported them from the Persian Gulf, it is much more probable that they came from his half-brother, Ptolemy Philadelphus, the reigning King of Egypt. Pyrrhus's elephants must have been very 'handy' beasts, for he seems to have taken them across to Sicily from Italy, and also to have used them in the Peloponnesus to attack Laconia. The wonder is, not that the Libyans tamed their elephants, but that they ever lost the art of doing so. Possibly the decay of Egyptian power in the interior may have discouraged their use on the Upper Nile. But it is in the more western regions, in the 'Hinterland' of the Mediterranean coast, that their use seems to have been most general and their training best understood. Libya did not cease to be civilised because Carthage was destroyed. But the elephants seem at last to have been used solely for the purposes of war ; and when they were found wanting as military machines it is possible that their usefulness for other purposes was forgotten, or that other animals, easier to rear, though less highly specialised for use in tropical jungles, had taken their place. Then the African elephant became merely an object of the chase to the negro and Arab ivory-hunter.

ANIMALS IN SICKNESS

THE circumstances which attend the illness and death of wild animals are perhaps less well known than any other part of their history. Yet when we consider that animal life, though in some cases of great duration, is naturally brief, and liable to an infinite number of accidents without remedy and sudden dangers unforeseen, the subject of the last days of the nobler sort of beasts has a certain pathetic interest. No doubt, all animals, from the healthy and natural lives they lead, have strange powers of self cure in case of accident. Those whose profession it is to prepare the skeletons of wild beasts, large and small, for museums and collections, speak with surprise of the number of injuries and fractures which the bones exhibit, but which have set themselves in a rough but effective fashion. But the 'chapter of accidents' in animal life spares none, from the stags which die with horns locked together on the mountain side, to the locusts which impale themselves upon the barbed wire of the Transvaal farms, or the cicalas which rend their wings upon the thorns of the mimosa. Death by violence seems to be the rule in the lower forms of animal life, except in the case of sudden plagues or changes of season. To the largest quadrupeds, human fancy has conceded the boon of a painless death; but the remote, untrodden jungle where the elephants go to die lies still among the undiscovered countries.

The saddest side of these millions of unrecorded deaths, from the human and humane points of view, is that the creatures, for the most part, suffer unaided and die alone. There is, however, good reason to believe that this is not always the case, and that there are many instances of animal sympathy, and some of animal aid for animal suffering. On the other hand, it must be admitted that there is often a strong and apparently natural impulse among animals, as among savage men, to hasten the death of a sick comrade, which, in some cases, take the form of deliberate and premeditated murder of the sufferer.

If ever human sentiment at the sight of fellow creature's suffering be analysed, the two emotions

of pity and disgust are constantly at war. Pity is
generally prior, but, except in the highest natures,
it weakens with time. 'Pity,' says Cobbett, 'is not
a lasting emotion,' and instead of pity passing into
love, it often turns to disgust, and disgust to dislike, after a long contemplation of disease and
deformity. The ruder the state of society, the
harsher becomes the law, for we may assume that
the dislike of the weak and sickly by the healthy
and vigorous, is an indirect and unpleasing form
of the working of natural selection. Maternal affection must, of course, be exempted from this general
tendency. So long as any young creatures are
dependent upon their parents, the tendency of the
old is to give most to the young who need most.
The devotion of the bird or animal varies with the
helplessness of the offspring.

But we must look further and consider the
relations of the non-related, the conduct of the
society to the individual, and of the different
species to each other. In doing so, we find something parallel to our own development, for
domestication, the animal equivalent to civilisation, does produce a tendency towards the emotions
of pity and benevolence. But in animal communities, there seems to exist little sense of pity when
the weakness of a member inconveniences or en-

dangers the safety of the whole. Bulls and wild stallions fight for the herd, but that is the price of their own supremacy. The wounded and sick are usually driven away, and perhaps killed.

The wild cows of Chillingham Park hide their calves from the rest, and, as in the days of the Psalmist, the calving hind 'discovereth the thick bushes,' and does not venture to show its young till it can keep up with the herd. Shakespeare, in 'As You like It,' does no injustice to the general indifference of deer to their injured comrades ; and the stag, 'left and abandoned by his velvet friends,' which excited the pity of Jaques, suffered the general fate of wounded deer. But there are exceptions to the rule. The scene of the wounded stag, attended by the hinds, which Sir Edwin Landseer painted in his beautiful picture, called 'Highland Nurses,' was, we believe, actually witnessed by the painter or his host. But the *Storch Gericht* condemns without mercy those that cannot join in the Southern migration ; ducks and canaries peck sick and ailing birds to death, and pigs are born bullies, the smallest of the litter— the 'petment,' as it is called in East Anglia— being invariably bitten, and deprived of its food. Carnivorous animals rarely injure a sick or wounded member of their tribe, though wolves, when pressed by hunger, devour the weakest, and jackals will at once assemble and tear to pieces a wounded member of the pack. But I lately heard a curious instance of the instinct to destroy the injured among the larger cats. Some rough ground in Oudh was being driven by beaters, when a cheetah appeared before one of the guns and was badly wounded. Another cheetah appeared immediately after, and came up to the first, which it seemed to urge to follow it. The wounded cheetah was unable to move, and the second, on discovering this, sprang on it, caught it by the throat, and killed it, and was shot as it bounded away after this deliberate murder. Monkeys, with some notable exceptions, are some degrees worse than savage men in their treatment of the sick. On the new Jumna Canal at Delhi, monkeys swarm in the trees upon the banks, and treat their sick comrades in true monkey-fashion. The colony by the canal being overcrowded and, as a consequence, unhealthy, did, and probably does still, suffer from various unpleasant diseases. When one monkey is so obviously unwell as to offend the feelings of the rest, a few of the larger monkeys watch it, and taking a favourable opportunity, knock it into the canal. If it is not drowned at once, the sick monkey is pitched in again after it regains the trees, and either drowned, or forced to keep aloof from the flock.   At the Zoological Gardens, the monkeys torment a sick one without mercy; and unless it is at once removed from the cage, it has little chance of recovery.   The small monkeys bite and pinch it; the larger ones swing it round by its tail; and when quite exhausted, or dead, as many monkeys as can find room *sit* on its body.   Frank Buckland's monkeys, so far as we remember, exhibited considerable affection towards one another when ill.   But that may have been due to the civilising influences of his society.   Generally speaking, monkeys mope and seek solitude when sick.   But 'Sally,' the chimpanzee at the Zoo, during her last illness behaved exactly as a human being might in similar circumstances.   While the large gibbon in the next cage, which died just afterwards, retired to the furthest corner, and refused all assistance, 'Sally' came to the bars in front, where she could most easily receive her medicine and food, and took her balsam of aniseed for bronchitis, as her keepers dictated.   Only when very ill did she retire to her kennel, and even then would reach out her hand to the 'doctor.'   But there is not much faith in 'physicking' at the Zoo.   Prevention is better than cure — though one bear generally takes castor-oil, which it likes, when suffering from a bad throat; and a very fine bird, the African hornbill, would allow medicine to be given to it by its keeper. A lady-visitor was good enough to leave a prescription to cure the savage Indian wild dogs of mange. But as she left no directions as to whether the remedy was for internal or external application, the dogs were allowed to cure themselves by taking 'sulphur baths' in straw sprinkled with the remedy.

Domestication modifies, and often changes, the instinct of wild animals to persecute, or at least neglect, the sick or injured, perhaps because the lessened strain of the struggle for existence leaves room for sentiment to grow. Both dogs and cats often aid their kind when sick, and strange alliances spring up between pets of different species. Perhaps the best-known instance is that of the raven which Dickens saw at Hungerford, which used to carry bones to a broken-legged retriever; and the quickness with which dogs learn that their master is ill, and show sympathy, is well established. The following anecdote of aid given by one animal to another has not, we think, been published. An elephant-train was on its way from Lucknow to Seetapore, and one elephant, becoming lame, knelt down and refused to go on. The elephant next in the column stopped of its own accord, and when driven on, turned back; and began, without instructions, to remove some part of the load. Instances of aid rendered by birds to others in distress may also be found, showing that the instinct of sympathy exists, and takes form in action, when the causes of the suffering are such that the fellow-bird can understand, and see its way to remedy. The writer was informed that some years age, at a hawking party on Salisbury Plain, a falcon was flown at a carrion-crow, which it struck after a long flight, and the two birds came down like a parachute to the ground. The party galloped up, and were about to dismount to take up the falcon, when the mate of the crow suddenly descended from a great height, with such velocity that the wings made a whizzing sound like that of a falling stone, and dashed on to the falcon. The force of the blow struck the hawk from its quarry, which was uninjured by the grapple in the air ; and both crows flew off unhurt into a copse near. In this case the crow clearly understood the cause of the danger, and the possibility of a rescue when the falcon was on the ground and least able to act on the offensive. But the courage and devotion which prompted it to overcome the natural dread which the falcon inspires, and the added terror of a party of mounted men in pursuit, place the crow's claim to admiration on a very high level. A pair of terns have been seen to aid a wounded companion on the water.   In this case they lifted it from the surface and tried to assist it to fly.   The terns, like the carrion-crow, not only showed sympathy, but were able to translate it into action.   Other birds, either less intelligent or less indifferent to the danger which the presence of a human spectator suggests, exhibit the same concern for wounded mates or companions by flying round them or alighting near the sufferer.   St John mentions a case of a sheldrake which would not leave its wounded mate ; and peewits will sometimes return and hover over wounded birds, especially early in the year, before the full-grown young have learnt the extreme caution which marks their behaviour later in the season.   But perhaps the most remarkable instance of 'aid to the weak' recorded of birds was shown by a brood of young swallows.   These had left the nest, and were sitting in a row along the gutter, while the old birds fed them alternately as they flew past.   One of the young ones, weaker and more backward than the rest of the brood, was unable to raise itself sufficiently to attract the notice of the parent birds as they flew past, and two of the other young were seen to close in on either side, and by shuffling underneath its body to raise it until it was on a level with the others, and able to receive its share of food.   With such instances ·to the contrary, it cannot be maintained that the animal instinct is uniformly selfish towards the sick and weak. The emotion of sympathy exists, though circumstances are usually too strong for its development.

ANIMAL 'MATERIA MEDICA.'

THE legend that the young Æsculapius cured a man by the use of a herb which he had seen a sick goat search for and eat upon the slopes of Pelion, is evidence of the antiquity of the belief that animals are acquainted with the use of medicinal plants. The belief did not lose in force in later days; and in the 'bestiaries' and medical works of the Middle Ages, the medical knowledge possessed by animals was almost as much exaggerated as were the healing virtues of various parts of the animals themselves. But enough is now known of the nature of animal *materia medica* to excite interest and curiosity without the aid of fable. There is abundant evidence that very many species know and constantly make use of simple remedies for definite disorders, and at the same time observe rules of health to which only the highest civilisation or the sanction of religious prescription compels man to conform. It has been noted that the general condition of animal health, especially in the case of the herbivorous creatures, corresponds not inexactly with that of such tribes as the Somalis, men feeding almost solely on grain, milk, dates, and water, living constantly in the open air, moderate in all things, and cleanly, because their religion enjoins constant ablutions. Like them, wild animals have no induced diseases; the greater number do not eat to excess; they take regular exercise in seeking their food, and drink only at fixed hours. Many of them secure change of climate, one of the greatest factors in health, by migration. This is not confined to birds and beasts, for the salmon enters the soft water partly to get rid of sea-parasites, and returns to the sea to recruit after spawning. With change of climate, change of diet, and perfectly healthy habits, their list of disorders is short, though they readily fall victims to contagious disease, just as recently numbers of the Hamran Arabs of the Soudan, as healthy livers and good Mussulmans as the Somalis themselves, friends and fellow-hunters with Sir Samuel Baker, perished of contagious fever on the banks of the Nile tributaries.

The medical precautions of animals are thus mainly directed to the preservation of the health, which is partly obtained by the conscious search for a change of food and locality. Cleanliness is their next object of solicitude, and in this the various forms of animal toilet play an important part. It is almost more necessary that the *outside* of an animal, whether skin or scales, should be free from disease, than that the interior functions should be in perfect order. Nature seems to cure the latter, but not the former. On the contrary, animals when wild constantly die a lingering death from injury to the skin, whether caused, as usually happens in tropical countries, by wounds aggravated by insects, or by cutaneous disease. Hence the pains which they take in making their toilet, and in the use and selection of 'cosmetics.' Nearly every tropical animal, including the tiger, bathes either in water or in mud. Perhaps the best-known mud-bathers are the wild boar, the water buffalo, and the elephant. The latter has an immense advantage over all other animals, in the use of its trunk for dressing wounds. It is at once a syringe, a powdering-puff, and a hand. Water, mud, and dust are the main 'applications' used, though it sometimes covers a sun-scorched back with grass or leaves. 'Wounded elephants,' writes Sir Samuel Baker, 'have a marvellous power of recovery when in their wild state, although they have no gifts of surgical knowledge, their simple system being confined to plastering their wounds with mud, or blowing dust upon the surface. Dust and mud comprise the entire pharmacopœia of the elephant, and this is applied upon the most trivial, as well as upon the most serious, occasions. . . . I have seen them when in a tank plaster up a bullet wound with mud taken from the bottom '

In Europe the pig is credited with the discovery of the use of the mud bath, and of the healing virtue of the waters of Bath itself, unless the story of the cleansing of Prince Bladud by the use of the water which cured the skins of his swine is a baseless fable. There is indirect evidence of the success of the different forms of treatment used by animals to keep their skins in health, in the disaster which sometimes overtakes those which neglect them. In the last few years great numbers of foxes, from South Berkshire to the Badminton country, have died of virulent mange. The disease was said to have been introduced by some foreign foxes which were turned down near Aldershot. The earths became tainted, and the infected foxes seemed quite unable to shake off the. disease, or to discover any natural remedy to cure it. Birds, such as rooks and ducks, which live in companies, soon stamp out sporadic disease by killing the sufferers ; but in great epidemics, such as the grouse disease or the plague which destroyed the reindeer of Northern Russia, birds and animals alike seem helpless, and die passively. An exception must be made in the case of those grouse on the moors near the sea. These birds, in many cases, moved down to the coast and ate the salt crystals left among the rocks.

The maintenance of a good digestion holds the next place to a healthy skin in the animal practice of medicine. To this end they do seek and use what might be termed 'drugs,' or substances which are their equivalent. As each creature is its own doctor and has to judge of its symptoms by the light of Nature, the uniformity of 'practice' in their use of medicines is not a little curious. Salt is the remedy most generally used by all the larger herbivorous animals. Both in America and India certain places are resorted to by animals, often coming from a great distance, to eat the salt-impregnated earth, or to lick saline exudations from the rocks. In North America this habit is so well known that hunters wait at the 'salt-licks' to shoot the deer which come to them at night. A tea-planter in Assam was recently watching at night under a salt-yielding hill-side with the same object when he was himself attacked. An elephant with a young one came on to the bank above, and smelling an enemy below, picked up large stones and threw them over, thinking, as a native gun-bearer remarked, that a tiger was hidden below. Red deer will also go down to the shore and eat the seaweed and even devour the bones and horns of dead deer for the sake of the salt and lime in them, while all cattle and sheep will eagerly eat rock-salt when placed in low, wet pastures. Many birds, especially pigeons, are salt-eaters, though the carnivorous birds, like the carnivorous animals, do not seem to need it. Pheasants, which, like turkeys, have a delicate digestion, especially when young, require hot and pungent food in addition to their usual fare. It has been noticed that when wild they scratch up and eat the roots of the wild arum, which are so hot that they will blister the tongue, and in the Caucasus they eat the colchicum root. Pheasant-breeders have taken the hint from this, and mix hot spices with their pheasant-meal, just as turkey-rearers give their poults peppercorns. It has been noticed also that birds, and some animals, require drugs far stronger and in larger quantities than are needed to produce an effect on men.*

The carnivorous animals avoid salt, and take an emetic instead. This at least seems to be the object with which dogs eat the harsh and sword-like blades of 'spear-grass.' But they also eat other grass merely as medicine. Cats also eat grass, and not always as an emetic. There is a wide-leaved kind which grows in some gardens, though not in

---

* The brent geese, which feed mainly on a sea grass, roll this into little balls or pads and push it into shot holes when they have been wounded.

others, which is known as 'cat-grass.' Cats will come to eat it from a distance, and some will take it from the hand if it is plucked and brought to them. This medicinal use of grass seems common to most of the larger cats. At the Zoo, when the grass is cut in the spring, a few handfuls are generally given to the lions and leopards, which eat it just as a dog does.

A third panacea for indigestion among birds, and used also by the larger lizards, is the swallowing of stones of all sizes, from a pound-weight in the case of the crocodile to the tiny grit and gravel in the gizzards of birds. This can only be done for purely medical reasons, for not even a crocodile would swallow stones, as famishing negroes do earth, 'to deceive the stomach.' Breeders of prize poultry have recently been engaged in one of those controversies, which rage with such unbridled warmth among the 'fancy,' as to whether 'grit' is necessary for the well-being of fowls, and if so, what grit, and whether it should be patent grit or common mortar and gravel. Judging from the habits of fowls and pigeons other than those bred for show, there can be no doubt that they naturally eat gravel and grit as medicine, the pigeons taking it more freely at the time when the eggs are about to be laid. It has been noticed also that dogs, when always fed from platters, and not given food upon the ground, will eat ashes, apparently to supply the want of this natural digestive. This knowledge of remedies available for animal use is as difficult to explain as the instinct by which they avoid poisonous plants, for even domestic cattle refrain from eating the leaves of the yew tree if they are kept in districts where the tree is commonly found.

THE LENGTH OF ANIMAL LIFE AT THE ZOO

THE great age attained by the polar bears in captivity at the Zoo—twenty-three years in the case of that which died at the end of 1894, and thirty-four in that of its predecessor, lost in 1880—is a creditable result of the experience in animal maintenance acquired since the foundation of the Zoological Society's menagerie in 1831. It suggests the question whether the records of the Society could throw any light on the unknown but interesting problem of the real duration of wild animal life. By the necessities of the case this is still unknown in the case of the larger animals when free. Conclusions formed from the results of their life in the Zoological Gardens must be modified by their unfavourable site in Regent's Park. As long ago as 1848 Sir Richard Owen, commenting on the death of a male aurochs from inflammation of the lungs, described this disease as the 'fatal enemy to exotic animals which have been exposed to the

An Aged Bison. *From a photograph by Gambier Bolton, F.Z.S.*

cold fogs incident to the undrained clay by which they are surrounded in Regent's Park—a pregnant but happily remediable source of ill-health even to its human inhabitants.' The park was drained in 1851, with marked results in improving the health of the animals at the Zoo. Experience also was not thrown away. Fifty years ago, when lion-keeping was in its experimental stage, the records of the Society showed that lions, leopards, tigers and pumas lived, on an average, for two years only in the Gardens, which gave a rate of mortality of about one per month. They were then confined in small stuffy cages, artificially heated throughout the year. They were transferred to cages, now occupied by the bears, in which no artificial heat was supplied at all, with greatly improved results. The fine new lion house, in which they have warm winter quarters, with an open summer garden attached, answers admirably, and the records of mortality seem to give some clue to the natural length of life of species. Lions, for instance, live on an average for fifteen years, tigers for eleven, and leopards for eight years. 'Duke,' the old lion recently dead, was—we speak from memory—eighteen years old. The oldest living lioness was brought to the menagerie in 1877. With a curious coincidence of name, the Patagonian sea lion is sixteen years old, and though it shows

M

signs of age is by no means failing. In the 'felidæ' size seems an index to longevity, the lions living longest, and the tiger cats seldom reaching more than the fifth or sixth year after their arrival.

When once established in the Zoo, many of the bears survive to a considerable age, though none have as yet attained the years of the Arctic species. Even Malayan bears, natives of a hot climate, have been known to live and thrive into their 'twenties.' The old 'honey bear,' which died last spring, had been over twenty years in the Gardens. The oldest of the family, now confined in the terrace, is a brown bear, which came into residence in 1878. The age of deer in the Scotch forests is probably as well determined as that of any wild animal. Yet though it is agreed that after twelve or thirteen years the horns of the stag deteriorate in size, the normal limit of life is not certain. The Wapiti deer at the Zoo are usually in splendid condition. A hind born in 1880 has not only borne a number of calves, but last year suckled a pair—one belonging to another hind. The mother of this animal lived twenty-two years in the Gardens, and its father, a splendid stag, twenty-four years. In the case of the deer and antelope size also seems to bear a relation to length of life. The oldest of the latter tribe in the Gardens is an addax antelope, rather larger than a fallow deer, which was brought to the menagerie in 1876. The Zoo elephants, though of the larger size, are quite young as elephant life goes—not yet grown up, though one stands 10 feet high at the shoulder. The Indian elephant, which died in the spring of 1896, was just twenty years old. Elephants in England seldom live more than fifty years. In the Government keddahs of India the average is eighty years, though individuals have lived beyond a hundred. The eagle, which, with the crow, shares the tradition of being the longest lived of all birds, suffers like all the raptorial birds from confinement. The oldest hawk in the Zoo is a Brazilian Caracara, presented by Lord Lilford in 1876. To judge by the analogy of the known limit of life in dogs, the foxes attain their full age at the Zoo; many of these live for ten, and some for twelve years. Monkeys, in spite of all the disadvantages of climate, are kept far longer than is generally supposed. The northern Chinese Tcheli monkey, which has an outdoor cage, is eleven years old; and one Indian hill monkey which, oddly enough, was subject to fits and required to be revived with cold water like a human being in a faint, lived to the age of eighteen. Such facts are interesting as data, but the accumulation of instances increases the difficulty of forming any clear view as to the causes or conditions of animal longevity.

Parrots live longer than eagles ; three years ago one died at the Zoo which came there before the Crimean War. A fruit-eating bat which died in 1880, and spent its life in the monkey house, was eighteen years old. The doyen of the Zoo at present is an Indian rhinoceros who is thirty-seven years old, and the next oldest inhabitant is, if we are not mistaken, an ugly water-lizard from North America, with rudimentary legs and blind-looking eyes, which has been in the collection for four-and-twenty years.

THE LIMIT OF SIZE IN MODERN ANIMALS

THE largest pair of horses shown at the Cart-Horse Parade on Whitmonday 1894, were two bays owned by the Thames Bank Distillery. These gigantic animals stood eighteen hands, and probably weighed at least a ton each, and were capable of drawing a weight of over four tons, in addition to their driver, Compared with the average size of the nearest approach to the wild horse existing, the tarpan of the Khirgiz Steppes—for the animal which Prejvalski claimed to have discovered in the highlands of Gobi is too like a wild ass to be accepted as the primitive ancestor of the horse until more evidence is forthcoming than is at present available from such remote and inaccessible regions—these mammoth horses show an increase of about one-third in height, and three-quarters in bulk and weight, as the result of human effort directed mainly to the increase of size in just proportion in a particular animal. The natural inference from this fact is a doubt whether the limit of size, which Nature seems to have set to the growth of particular species, is really as fixed and arbitrary as might appear. The general weight of what is called 'palæontological' evidence shows that many of the modern forms had corresponding species of gigantic size, while others, which are only recently extinct, or survive in small numbers, were larger than the present forms. Take, for example, the gigantic tortoises, one of the last members of whose respected family died at Colombo at the age of at least one hundred, and whose epitaph was written by Dr Gunther in the *Times*. Dr Gunther has always had a true naturalist's sympathy for these last survivors of a race whose unwieldy bulk suggested to the fancy of Eastern cosmogenists the picture of the tortoise bearing the world upon its back. When they have completed their allotted century or so of blameless life, they become their own monuments in a chelonian Valhalla at South Kensington, and dedicate themselves in little votive tablets to the musing reflections of mushroom humanity. There are exhibited the remains of the great tortoise of Aldabra, a small uninhabited island in the Indian Ocean, north-west of Madagascar. It was quite young, its known age being only eighty years, and it was still growing at the time of its death; but it weighed 870 lb., and its legs were like those of a small rhinoceros. Compared with this, the tortoises from the Galapagos Islands in the Pacific, whose strange and solitary existence is so curiously described by Darwin, are mere dwarfs, the largest having only weighed 200 lbs. ; but the contrast in size between these surviving giants and the dwarf scale of the many forms which seem destined to survive and flourish, down to the tiny ' tortoisettes ' no bigger than a watch, would, even if these creatures stood alone as examples of the dwindling tendency of species, be enough to suggest that the limit of animal dimensions had long ago passed its acme and entered on its decline. The evidence of the gigantic forms which fill the long galleries of the Museum, seems to point to the same conclusion. Those for whose monstrous bones existing life affords no parallel except to the instructed mind of the biologist, merely present themselves as objects of wonder, without suggesting a comparison. But the skull of the elephant found in the Sewalik hills of India, with tusks 12 ft. long, like the limbs of a tree, and the horns of the Irish deer, which stood 2 ft. higher at the shoulder than the largest wapiti of the Rocky Mountains — remains of creatures identical in character with those which now frequent the regions they once inhabited — seem visible evidence of a steady and universal decline of which instances might be multiplied without number.

The theory that great size was in itself a bar to the well-being of the giant species, is an easy, if not a wholly satisfactory, means of accounting for the degeneration, for the failure of food can hardly have been such, in the Indian forests for instance, as to account for the dwindling of forms like the 'Elephas ganesa' into the smaller but still enormous bulk of the herds which still survive and multiply in the jungles of Hindostan.

But if the limit of the food supply is the key to the apparent limitation of size, in the case of most animals which are widely distributed, there seems no reason why the loss should not be made good, in the case of domesticated animals at least, by a process of generous feeding continued for generations, until, if it suited the needs of human society, we produced oxen far larger than the Bos primigenus, rabbits as large as sheep, dogs as tall as a polar bear, and a breed of horses between twenty and thirty hands high, which would, of course, be too large for riding, except with a howdah or a camel-saddle, but would draw loads of from four to five tons.

The argument of a natural limit set to size, derived from the circumstances of wild animals, must not be pushed too far. In the case of many domesticated animals the contrary has been proved by experience. Its application to the case of those which are wild and free is only partial ; and its working is often accompanied by variations which leave it quite open to doubt whether even now the power of wild animals to increase greatly in size under favourable conditions is altogether lost. The great difference in bulk between the small hill tiger and the 'cattle eaters' of richer districts is well known. Stags in an English park, such as Windsor, probably average one-third more in weight for age than those of the Scotch mountains, and the leopard varies from a creature almost as large as a jaguar to a creature scarcely bigger than a jungle-cat. A very complete example of the nature of the limits set to the size of animals when wild, or in conditions exactly similar to those of the wild life, is seen in the case of the New Forest ponies. The whole of this vast tract of country not subject to inclosure has been the feeding-ground of the ponies of the foresters for a period of time which must have begun far earlier than the date of the removal of the deer ; and even in the reign of Henry III., the King himself seems to have 'run them' in the forest, as he made a grant from his herd to the monks of Beaulieu. In any case, the forest ponies are now wild, living in herds dominated at particular seasons of the year by a master stallion just as in the prairies of America, and so attached to particular localities that, in whatever part of the forest a captured pony is released, it usually finds its way back to that in which it was bred. Various attempts to improve these ponies have been made, which have met with marked success in all respects but one, that, namely, of size. The influence of the thoroughbred sires which have been let run in the forest, is still seen in their fine shape, high Arablike quarters, elegant heads, and extraordinary endurance. But the experiment of getting direct crosses from larger animals always fails, if the object be to run them in the forest, for the simple reason that an animal above a certain size cannot find sufficient food to maintain it. By browsing all day, and the greater part of the night, little 'foresters' of twelve or thirteen hands high can just 'make both ends meet,' though after the winter they are extremely thin and ragged. But anything above that size requires artificial support, and its progeny naturally deteriorates. On the other hand, the size does not tend to fall *below* the standard at which Nature sets the limit, the natural appetite and wants of these hardy creatures prompting them to do the best for themselves from day to day with a constancy hardly to be understood by beings whose minds are not concentrated by necessity on the absorbing effort to satisfy the hourly cravings of hunger. It is doubtful whether there is an average difference of half a hand in the height of the four or five score of ponies admitted to the annual show held at Lyndhurst by the Association for the Improvement of New Forest Ponies. Though many of these are dragged in, rough and unkempt as a mop, and shaggy as a poodle, unbroken, and almost unhaltered previously, and bred by promiscuous intercourse in the wildest parts of the forest, Nature levels up as it levels down, and the two forces tend to produce a uniformity in size which may be due to outside, rather than to inside, forces. The case of the horse is the more interesting, because its ancestral types were, unlike those of most modern creatures, smaller than the existing species. Its earliest known ancestor was no larger than a fox. These were succeeded by others of the size of sheep, and in Pliocene times by creatures the size of donkeys. Modern breeding, it must be remembered, has not been directed solely to increase in size. Yet the average of the thoroughbred has gained three inches since the introduction of the Arabian horse. Size is restricted by convenience and economic considerations; and the tendency at present is rather to diminish than increase the bulk of the most useful

kinds ; but it is not long since a horse of admirable
form, inneteen and a quarter hands high, was exhibited in London, and with the ancient history
of its kind before us, there seems no reason to
doubt that we could, if we chose, produce a
gigantic breed, which at least could hold his
own in size with the monstrous stags that once
inhabited the Irish hills.

DANGEROUS ANIMALS OF EUROPE

THE author of *Happy Thoughts*, on comparing the information received in a country visit as to the habits of domestic animals, concluded that they were nearly all dangerous, and those that were not were 'very uncertain.' The same charge cannot be brought against most of the wild animals of Europe, and against none of those of our own island, except the wild cat, and the rats, which recently bore out Mr Burnand's theory by trying to eat three children at Paisley.* But the causes of the survival of some, and the disappearance of others, of the larger carnivora of Europe, are not clearly known. The best authority for the ancient haunts of the European lions is the gossiping traveller Pausanias. This natural history note is embedded in a long catalogue of the trophies and records of athletic victories at the Olympian games, which he saw in the great temple on the plains of Elis. There stood a monument to

* See the chapter headed Recent Rat Lore in the present volume.

Polydamas. 'He was the strongest man of our days,' says Pausanias; 'stronger than any man except those who have always been considered as gods and heroes. Among other feats, he imitated Hercules by killing a lion, unarmed. The mountain region of Thrace,' he adds, 'south of the river Nestus, which flows through the territory of the Abderites, produces both other large wild animals, and also lions. So many are bred there that in ancient days they attacked the camels of Xerxes' army (when marching to attack Greece) and killed numbers of them. These lions especially frequent the district below Mount Olympus, one side of which is in Thrace and the other in Macedonia; and it was on this very mountain that Polydamas killed a large and very fierce lion.' Though the lion has disappeared, the other three carnivorous creatures most frequently mentioned by classical writers, the bear, the wolf, and the lynx, are still inhabitants of Europe, and are found from the Arctic circle to the shores of Southern Spain. Of these the lynx seems to be about to disappear from the Swiss forests, but is still common in Spain, Portugal, the Carpathians, and the Swedish woods. It can hardly be classed as dangerous, except that, like the cat, its habit is to sit perfectly still if discovered, and if wounded to spring straight at the aggressor's head. The European bears differ much in size.   Some can scarcely be considered as dangerous in any sense.   Few of the Pyrenean bears which reach England are formidable.   They are neither large, nor have they good coats, but are dwarfed and dusty-coloured, inferior in every way to the splendid brown bears of Nothern Russia.   In Switzerland they occasionally reach a large size ; some have been killed which weighed as much as 420 lbs.   But the Swiss bears, even when less rare than they are now, were always more formidable to sheep than to the shepherds. The European wolf is also in the main a destroyer of livestock and game, and has not aroused that intense hatred which its attacks on children seem to have caused in primitive England and Wales.*

The only bird besides the albatross which may be accurately included in the list of animals dangerous to human life, is still an inhabitant of Europe.   This is the lammergeier, or bearded vulture, a few pairs of which still nest in the high Alps.   The French name 'gypaète,' or 'vulture eagle,' best describes the bird, which has the appetite and almost the dimensions of a condor, and more than the strength of any eagle.   The wings sometimes measure

---

* A melancholy contradiction to this view appeared in the papers at the opening of the present year. A husband and wife had engaged to walk across Europe, pushing a wheelbarrow. In Hungary they were attacked by wolves, and though the wife shot one which had seized her husband, the others bit her so severely that she died in a few hours.

10 ft. from tip to tip, and the beak, which is from $4\frac{1}{2}$ to $5\frac{1}{2}$ in. long, is modelled for seizing and *biting*, like that of the cormorant. Its powers of swallowing and of digestion are as remarkable as its physical strength. The stomach of one was found to contain the large iliac bone of a cow, the thigh of a chamois, a chamois's ribs half digested, a quantity of small bones, fur, and the claws of a blackcock. Instances of attacks made on man by these birds when engaged in defending their nests are numerous ; and, considering the size of the lammergeier, and the advantage of position from which it delivers its onset on the human biped, crawling up or down the face of a precipice, it would be strange if such experiences did not occur. In the canton of Glaris a turpentine gatherer climbed to an eyrie, and took two young lammergeiers, which he tied by the legs and slung over his back, while he climbed down the precipice. . There he was attacked by the old birds, who, though they did not succeed in throwing him from the rocks, followed him for four miles to the village of Schwanden. Joseph Scherrer, a hunter, shot a male lammergeier, and was climbing to the nest when the female flew up, and settled on his back, driving her claws in deep, and trying with furious backward beats of the wings, to drag him from the face of the rock. The man's gun was

loaded, but he dared not let go his hold on the rock to fire it. His attitude was for a time that of a reversed Prometheus, the vulture tearing his back, instead of making a meal of its victim's liver. In this predicament the hunter contrived to shift the position of his gun, so that the muzzle almost touched the breast of the lammergeier, and cocked and fired it with his foot. But in these cases the vulture was not the first aggressor. Unfortunately, the cases in which it has carried away young infants are not rare, and are well authenticated. A number of these are mentioned by Tschudi, the naturalist of the Alps. In the canton of Uri a woman was living in 1854 who had been carried off by a lammergeier when a baby; at Hundwyl, in the canton of Appenzell, a child was carried off in sight of its parents. On the Silberalp a vulture attacked a little boy who was watching sheep seated on a rock, and had time to knock him over the edge of the cliff before the shepherds could drive the bird away. At Murren, above the valley of Lauterbrunnen, a vulture carried an infant to an inaccessible rock opposite the village and devoured it. Portions of the baby's red frock lay there for some time. Another child of two years' old, but very small and feeble, was lost when out with her sister. The remains of the body were afterwards found on a rock, separated from that where the child was last seen by a precipice ; a vulture must have taken it there, either dead or living. But the most striking instance of the child-devouring tendencey of these birds occurred in the Bernese Oberland. A child of three years' old, called Anne Zurbuchen, was taken up to the high alp at haymaking time, and left asleep while the father fetched a load of hay. He returned to find the child gone. At the same time another peasant, called Henri Michel, was coming up the mountain by a rough path when he heard a child cry. At the same time he saw a lammergeier rise and sail away. Running up to the place he found the little girl, unhurt except for wounds in the arm and left hand where the bird had clutched her. She had lost her socks, shoes, and cap while being trans-ported by the bird, the distance traversed being about three hundred and fifty yards. The facts were all entered in the parish archives of the village of Habkeren ; and the girl, who lived to be an old woman, was always known as 'Geier-Anni.'

The mountain vultures have decreased in numbers, partly because it is the ambition of the Swiss hunters to shoot them, partly because a reward was for many years offered for their destruction. But the retreat of some of the quadruped carnivora, such as the lynx

and wolf, and the total disappearance of the lions
from Eastern Europe, are less easily explained.
Game in abundance is the first condition for the
existence of a creature like the lion. It is clear from
Pausanias's account that large game was very plentiful in Thrace and Macedon ; there are still deer
and wild boars ; and though forests which sheltered
the lion in Argos have perished, there are still thick
woods on the Macedonian ranges. Natural causes
are not enough to account for the disappearance of
the lion. It was probably due to organised hunts
for his destruction. The ancient myths, in which
the names of killers of noted pests are honoured,
shows that the lion was an object of dread in ancient
Hellas, and Hercules gained credit for ridding the
country of the Nemean lion, just as Theseus gained
credit for killing off brigands and making the roads
safe. The process as it took place in England is
known to history. Royal wolf-hunts, in which the
King takes the lead, tributes of wolves' heads, and a
fixed reward for killing them, destroyed the wolf, and
possibly the bear in Britain. Organisations for the
destruction of wolves are part of the existing social
order in every European country where they survive
except Turkey and Greece. In Brittany the office
of *Grand Louvetier* is something more than a picturesque survival, and in most cantons of Switzerland

and near the Jura Mountains, there are societies for the destruction of wolves.

In the Vaudois Jura the societies have regular meetings, officers and laws. Part of the society serve as beaters, while others carry guns ; it is an honour to belong to them, and as no one is eligible as a member until he has assisted at three successful hunts, children in arms are sometimes carried a short distance in the beat in order to qualify as members when grown up. The bear is hunted in this cantonal fashion in Russia ; and only the vastness of the forests and mountain ranges of Northern and Central Europe enable him to escape the extermination which overtook the lion. As things are, they do escape, and both bears and wolves maintain their numbers without decrease beyond a certain point. It was noted that after the disarmament of the Poles by the Russians, after their first rebellion, the number of wolves much increased, and human beings were attacked by them even in summer. Wolves are daring travellers, and will journey hundreds of miles in search of food. Consequently, their numbers in Switzerland, the Italian Alps, the Ardennes, and the minor forests of France are replenished every severe winter by immigrants from the east, whose place is again taken by Russian wolves moving westwards.

THE MYSTERY OF MIGRATION

THE 'sense of locality' awakens more interest when shown by the bird than by the bee, because the former has a mind of an order more human, and more cognisable by our senses. Yet the mystery of migration remains a mystery still; and this year's arrival of the tens of thousands of spring migrants from Asia, Africa and the Mediterranean has not found us much better informed as to the means which guided them on their way. When the movements of birds on migration were first noted and set down, the results were unexpected and bewildering. Movement, not rest, seemed the general law of their being. The greater number of species were found to pass their lives in travel, though the motive and the routes chosen for their journeys were less accountable as the facts were multiplied. The simple and easy conclusion of the older naturalists as to migration, from the days of Virgil to those of Gilbert White, was that their own particular country was the natural home of all the birds which we call ' spring migrants,' such as the swallow and the nightingale ; and that when winter came, bringing cold and hunger, these deserted their home and sought a temporary shelter in warmer climates, whence they hurried back to their *dulces nidos*, like ships' crews impatient to revisit a frozen port which was nevertheless their home. This accounted for the departure of the birds in autumn and their return in spring. The visits of northern birds in winter were only a result of the same causes, working in more northern lands. It was a theory as simple as Homer's notion of the ocean stream circling in endless flow round the rim of the inhabited world. When the naturalists grew dissatisfied, and demanded more data, and began to sit in lighthouses through the winter nights to note the migrants coming and going, and sift reports from those whose duty makes them watchers by the shore, the apparent simplicity of birds' travel could no longer be admitted. There seemed neither limit nor law in the incessant and perplexing streams of bird movement. The problem of the real ocean currents, compared with the ancient belief in the constant ocean stream, was simple in comparison with the crossing and recrossing, the apparent contradiction and want of purpose in the journeys of the birds.

The first task undertaken was to note and separate these lines of flight, and to determine whence and whither the birds were going. We now know whence the birds ·come to us for the summer, and the roads by which they come. Africa sends perhaps the greatest number. Some of these start for England from Algiers and the Mediterranean coast. Others have wintered in the Nile Valley, and descending to its mouth—for the Sahara desert is almost as dreaded by the birds as the Atlantic Ocean—skirt the shore towards the Straits of Gibraltar. Some fly across to the Balearic Islands, and thence through Catalonia, and down the Garonne Valley to the Biscayan Coast. Others pass by Sardinia and Corsica to the valley of the Rhone. But the main body cross at the Straits of Gibraltar, follow the east coast of Spain, pass up the valley of the Ebro, cross the Pyrenees near Pampeluna, and then follow the Bay of Biscay till they reach Cape Finisterre, and fly across the channel to the Lizard or the Start. France contains the three other main roads of the spring migrants. The most southerly stream passes up the Rhone Valley to Lyons, crosses to the Loire Valley at Orleans, and passes thence *via* Cape La Hogue to the Start Point. The stream from Turkey and Greece passes up the Italian coast, through the Swiss passes, into central France, down the Seine Valley, and across to Selsey Bill. The most northerly route is that of the birds that are coming from the Danube Valley. These pass through Zurich on to Rheims, and reach the channel coast near Boulogne and Calais, whence they cross the channel at the Straits of Dover. In these journeys, the land-routes are preferred, and the straits are as a rule chosen for sea passage ; but some birds fly straight across the Mediterranean at its widest part, from Algeria to Marseilles ; while birds making for Ireland, though mainly crossing *via* England and that part of the Irish Channel which lies opposite Milford Haven, often cross directly from Brest to Cape Clear.

Next to the success and persistence of the birds in making good their point across unknown continent and seas, the most striking features of the migration is the enormous number of the birds which sometimes journey together. The ' *locus classicus* ' on this subject is the late Mr Seebohm's description of a ' migration night ' on Heligoland, where he had been in 1870 to visit Dr Gätke, the results of whose observations have recently been published and translated. This is Mr Seebohm's account of the scene by the lighthouse.

He was awakened at ten o'clock to find that the whole population was moving towards the lighthouse, nets in hand, to capture the birds which strayed from the main body :—

'The whole zone of light within range of the mirrors was alive with birds coming and going. Nothing else was visible in the darkness of the night but the lantern of the lighthouse vignetted in a drifting sea of birds. From the darkness in the east, clouds of birds were continually emerging in an uninterrupted stream ; a few swerved from their course, fluttered for a moment as if dazed by the light, and then vanished with the rest in the western gloom. Occasionally one wheeled round the lighthouse and then passed on, and occasionally one fluttered against the glass like a moth against a lamp, tried to perch on the wire-netting, and was caught by the lighthouse man. I should be afraid to hazard a guess as to the hundreds of thousands that must have passed in a couple of hours ; but the stray birds which the lighthouse man succeeded in securing amounted to nearly three hundred. The scene from the balcony of the lighthouse was equally interesting ; in every direction the birds were flying like a swarm of bees !'

It remained for naturalists to find a probable reason for the northern migration of birds, and to explain the means by which, given the desire to

do so, they find their way across seas and lands,
unknown to many of their number, to a goal
which, in the case of young birds of the year re-
treating to their winter homes, must be unknown,
and which, in the case of their first return to the
land in which they were bred, can at best be but
an imperfect memory.   One hypothesis supposes a
reason for the northern migration of birds in the
desire of species to return to districts from which
they were formerly driven by the advance of ice in
the glacial age.   Mr C. Dixon, in a recently
published book on the Migration of British Birds,
suggests another.   He notes that all migration has
for its object to increase the breeding area of a
species, and that the tendency of all birds is to
move in the direction of the Poles, which tendency
he calls the 'Law of Dispersal.'   Thus, in our
hemisphere, there is no known migration route
which goes south in summer or north in winter.
Hence, our migratory birds winter in the countries
in which their ancestors escaped extermination in
the glacial epoch, and go north to extend their
breeding area at a time when the individuals need
more space and food than at any other time, in
obedience to instinct used strictly in Paley's sense
of a 'propensity prior to experience and independent
of instruction,' for Mr Dixon can hardly mean that

the 'constant endeavour to regain and re-people the area once occupied during pre-glacial times' is a conscious effort on the part of birds, though his language almost suggests it. This he calls the 'impulse to migration,' though why he should not call it the 'instinct of migration,' is not very clear. The 'propensity' in all the young birds must be prior to actual experience, and independent of instruction in many cases, such as that of the young cuckoo, in which the parent bird leaves the young to find their way back to Central Africa from Kew Gardens or Richmond Park.

Mr Dixon seems in difficulties between the theory that the 'impulse' to migrate is a transmitted instinct due to descent from ancestors who once lived in the northern regions, and a 'corollary' from his Law of Dispersal, that birds never retreat before adverse conditions, but, 'if overtaken, perish, so far as the species is exposed to them.' If the members of a species, say, of the swallow tribe, which were exposed to the glacial period, died, and did not migrate, and only those were left which were secure in 'refuge areas' (parts which the ice did not reach) survived, these lattter could have had no recollections of their old home to suggest migration to their descendants. This 'law' that species all tend to migrate northwards in spring to regions from which they are supposed once to have been driven by the advancing ice, is not new either in idea or form. But whether 'impulse' or 'instinct' sends them northward, Mr Dixon attempts no explanation of the exceptional power which enables them to achieve their journey. He even suggests that they need none. 'Once a bird begins its migration,' he writes, 'all instinct as a guiding medium ceases; memory and knowledge of locality, in fact, experience, assist it to perform that long journey.' Until this conclusion is supported by more evidence it may safely be neglected. Whatever the 'impulse' which sends them out, it cannot yet be shown that it is not instinct that shows them the way. It is not instruction, for no parent bird could leave with its young in England a way-bill for the Nile Valley, though the young birds may possibly find their way here in the wake of the old ones. It is not example, for though many species travel in flock, with old and young together, such as the swallows, others force their young to migrate separately, and Temminch states that the flocks of old and young *always* travel separately. Other birds force the young to migrate while they remain on their breeding ground, or, as in the case of the cuckoo, leave England a month before the young. The 'follow-my-leader' instinct accounts for much of the marvel in the case of some species on certain routes of migration, where the flocks of species as different as chaffinches and cranes, pass on in such quick succession that the flocks are always in sight, while the lateral width of the travelling multitude feels the way, like a fleet extended over a great width of sea. But this does not account for the safe passage of isolated species to lonely spots, such as the crossing of the Wheatears from Cape Finisterre to the South of Ireland. The assumption that migration is due to a mere automatic impulse guided by experience, does not take into account the conscious end proposed by many birds as the object of their journey. The sentimental motive which induces many birds to seek the old nesting place, is one of the strongest factors in migration. Without some such eager desire, those birds which have once faced the dangers of one journey might refuse to persevere in a second, or to call to their aid those astonishing faculties which direct their path. To conclude that, because a domestic species of homing-pigeon performs its flights better after experience, the Australian cuckoo, which traverses a thousand miles of open ocean to nest in New Zealand, or that the midnight flights of birds so tiny as the golden-crested wrens across the North Sea are guided by experience alone, is too hasty and imperfect a

generalisation. The birds are guided by some
faculty not yet understood, and our daily-growing
acquaintance with the facts of migration does not
in the least diminish the difficulty of its discovery.*

* Slatin Pasha's history of his captivity among the Dervishes contains a
notable instance of the identification of a migrating crane. He was summoned
before the Mahdi and his cadis, and asked to account for some writing inside a
brass case attached to a ring. The paper contained a note written minutely in
four languages, stating that this crane was hatched on a certain estate in South
Russia, and asking anyone into whose hands it fell to communicate with the
writer, whose name and address were given. The Mahdi then said that the case
had been found fastened to a crane which was shot at Dongola in December. The
date of the letter it bore was September.

MR SEEBOHM'S DISCOVERY

THE death of Mr Henry Seebohm removes from the list of English ornithologists the most original figure since the days of Macgillivray. He came of an old Quaker family, was born at Bradford, and from childhood was an enthusiastic observer and collector. He became a large steel manufacturer at Sheffield, and while carrying on his business visited Russia, Siberia, Greece, Asia Minor, Norway, Denmark, Heligoland, Germany, Austria, the Engadine, Holland, and France, to see for himself the English migratory birds in their foreign homes. He held that this kind of original observation was the work in which English naturalists excel those of the Continent ; but he wrote much and well, and the result was the best History of British Birds and their Eggs ever written, a connected theory of the geographical distribution of English birds, and accounts of his visits to the valleys of the Petchora and the Yenisei,* which rank among the best de-

* *Siberia in Europe*, and *Siberia in Asia.*

scriptive natural history ever written. It was when visiting the 'frozen rim' of the north of Europe and Asia that he discovered the *motive* which takes certain birds to the Arctic regions to rear their young.

The author wrote under all kinds of difficulties, at Russian post-stations while the horses were being changed, in peasants' and fishermen's cottages, on wrecked ships, and often after eighteen or twenty hours of outdoor work ; but the reader feels always in the open forest, by the banks of the great rivers, or on the mysterious 'tundra' between the forests and the frozen sea. His expedition to the Petchora was suggested by two lines of thought. There were half-a-dozen of by no means rare birds, constant winter visitors to Britain, which vanished every spring as completely as if they had flown to another planet. Their breeding place might be either an unknown land, or more probably some region which was not undiscovered, but was never visited by educated Europeans. The birds were the grey plover, the curlew sandpiper, the sanderling, the little stint, the knot, and 'Bewick's swan,' a small wild species found on our coasts in winter. Secondly, but in reference to this first quest, Mr Seebohm, on two visits to Norway and Archangel, had noted the great difference between the birds found on the

White Sea and those of Norway. He concluded, therefore, that if he went some ten degress further to the east, he might find, not only the breeding grounds of new species, but the unknown summer home of those which vanish for a season. The desired position coincided geographically with the valley of the Petchora river, which flows from the Ural Mountains northwards, and falls into the Artic Ocean opposite Novaya Zembla. There was a delightful uncertainty as to the results of the contemplated expedition. The only existing records of previous visits to the river were exactly the same as those used by Milton to compile his pamphlet on 'Moscovia,' the latest being an account of old voyages in 1614 and 1615 to Ust Zylma, on the lower Petchora, to trade in beaver-skins, for which the river was then famous. But the promise held out by the map was sufficient. The thousand miles of the Petchora's stream, though lying inside the boundary of Europe, cut the two characteristic tracts of the North Siberian region which runs without a break from above Archangel to Behring Sea. On the upper river was the great Siberian forest, while on the lower, on either bank, beyond the limit of trees, was the 'tundra,' which fringes the whole length of the northern coast. On the maps the tundra has a bad name. It is called the 'region of treeless swamp.' It is uninhabited, and for eight months out of the twelve it is covered with snow. Yet this Mr Seebohm found to be the unknown land which drains the Old World of half its bird population, at the time when the temperate and tropical zones are in their most enchanting mood. For love of 'the region of treeless swamp' the birds gladly turn their backs on the English spring, and fly across Europe to sojourn in what Mr Seebohm terms 'an ornithological Cathay.' He not only discovered the fact, but the still stranger reason which accounts for it ; but his story should be followed without anticipating its conclusion. At the beginning of April, he reached the town of Ust Zylma, three hundred miles from the mouth of the Petchora. The river was fifteen times as broad as the Thames at Hammersmith Bridge, the surface was frozen as far as the eye could reach, up stream and down stream, and the frozen forest was as 'bare of life as the Desert of the Sahara.' Except one or two ravens, there was not a bird to be seen.

Suddenly summer came, and with it—almost on the same day—the birds arrived also. The ice on the Petchora split and disappeared, the banks steamed in the sun ; geese, swans, ducks, gulls, redstarts, wagtails, pipist, chiff-chaffs, willow-wrens, dotterels, snipes and hawks pursuing them, arrived in forty-eight hours after the first warmth ; the cockoo sang all day long ; and the Siberian forest became a paradise of beauty peopled with birds, and stocked with last year's fruits, preserved by seven month's frost and snow. But among all the migrating myriads, not one of the species whose nest he sought passed over the upper Petchora. Mr Seebohm and Mr Harvie Brown, who had accompanied him, then descended the river, and encamped on the tundra. The tundra was, in fact, a moor, with here and there a large flat bog and abundant lakes. It was covered with moss, lichens, heath-like plants, dwarf birch, and millions of acres of cloudberries and cranberries. As far as the eye could reach, this region stretched east and west, intersected by low ridges of tussocks, like the rind of a melon. Here they found the nests of three of the six species whose eggs were unknown. The eggs of the grey plover were found in the first day's 'birdnesting' on the tundra, and the birds were identified. These plovers, which feed in the Thames marshes in autumn, thus fly to the most northern corner of Europe to rear their young. Lower down the river the eggs of Bewick's swan were also found by a fisherman, and later, the eggs of the stint, on the tundra itself. The knot and sanderling were not found breeding on the tundra ; they go further north to Grinnell Land — the furthest limit of human as well as of bird migration.

In summing up his observations, Mr Seebohm declared that the number of birds which go to the Arctic regions to breed is 'vast beyond conception.' They go, not by thousands, but by millions, to rear their young on the tundra. Of the cause which attracts them he was equally certain. It is because nowhere in the world does Nature provide, at the same time and in the same place, 'such a lavish prodigality of food.' That the barren swamp of the tundra should yield a food supply so great as to tempt birds to make journeys of thousands of miles to rear their young in a land of plenty, only to be found beyond the Arctic circle, seems incredible. Mr Seebohm explained the apparent paradox. The vegetation largely consists of cranberry, cloudberry, and crowberry bushes. Forced by the perpetual sunshine of the Arctic summer, these bear enormous crops of fruit. But the crop is not ripe until the middle and end of the Arctic summer, and if the fruit-eating birds had to wait until it was ripe they would starve, for, as has been already noted, they arrive on the very day of the melting of the snow. But each year the snow descends on this immense crop of ripe fruit before the birds have time to gather it. It is then preserved beneath the snow, perfectly fresh and pure, and the melting of the snow discloses the bushes with the unconsumed last year's crop hanging on them, or lying ready to be eaten, on the ground. The frozen meal stretches across the breadth of Asia. It never decays, and is accessible the moment the snow melts. Ages have taught the birds that they have only to fly to the Arctic circle to find such a store of ' crystallised fruits ' as will last them till the bushes are once more forced into bearing by the perpetual sunlight. The same heats which free the fruits bring into being the most prolific insect life in the world, the mosquito swarms on the tundra. No European can live there without a veil after the snow melts ; the gun-barrels are black with them, and the cloud often obscures the sight. Thus the insect-eating birds have only to open their mouths to fill them with mosquitoes, and the presence of swarms of tender little warblers, chiff-chaffs, pipits, and wagtails in this Arctic region is accounted for. Having found by his visit to the Petchora where the birds went to and why they went, Mr Seebohm made his next expedition to the valley of Yenisei, in Asiatic Siberia. This adventure was hardly so fruitful in results as the first. It included 'two shipwrecks, which were not part of the original programme,' and he wintered too far north to encounter the main stream of migrating birds. But he was able to define the geographical limits of many European, Central Asian, and Chinese species, and recorded, among other observations in his second book, *Siberia in Asia*, that Siberia 'is a second Canada in reserve, waiting for a European overflow.'

The interesting point about the birds' migration to lands of promise is that they do not 'wait.' They have a colonial agency quite independent of time, and working with an accuracy which no 'labour bureau' can equal.

THE PROBLEM OF PERMANENT
ARCTIC LIFE

Mr SEEBOHM's discovery of the unlimited 'iced' food
supply waiting ripe and ready for the melting of
the snow, explains the attraction of the North Polar
region to migrant birds. But it does not explain
why other creatures ever consent to stop there through
the Polar winter. The persistence of animal life in
the region of Arctic cold appears only less unaccountable than its presence in the ocean abyss. The
existence of deep-sea creatures in perpetual darkness,
and under a weight of waters four miles deep, was
incredible, because inconceivable. The existence of
life in Arctic darkness and Arctic cold is unaccountable,
because it seems to be of necessity intolerable. Grant-
ing that highly-organised creatures can exist there,
it is passing strange that they should consent to do
so, or make a voluntary habitation in that hell of
cold and darkness which Norse fancy imagined as
a place of torment more appalling than the lake

of liquid fire. One would have thought Arctic life must cease, because, even if possible, it was not worth living ; that there would be a voluntary exodus of beasts, as of birds, before the winter setting of the sun ; and the slower-moving mammals would go, to return no more.

Yet in the deep seas the inconceivable has been found to exist ; highly organised creatures live and are reproduced where no light penetrates, where no plants grow, in eternal cold, and in a pressure twenty times greater than that which drives a railway train ; and in the Arctic circle mammalian animals, birds and plants endure a five months' night, and a temperature far lower than that of the deep seas. The lowest temperature of the ocean abyss was found to be 29° Fahr. below freezing point. That of the 'Polar' night falls from 70° to 90°. The cold endured by the Arctic animals is almost as astonishing as the pressure borne by the creatures of the deep sea ; yet in neither is there any notable change in structure to meet these conditions. The Arctic mammals do not differ greatly from those of kindred species found elsewhere. Why, then, do they stay where they are ? And how do they continue to endure the plague of darkness and the desperate cold ?

The problem is explained in part by Mr A. Trevor-Battye, in a suggestive and well-written paper, read before the British Association in 1895, on 'Life and its Conditions in Arctic Lands.' Mr Battye's observations were mainly made in the island of Kolguev, off the Petchora river, and, compared with the records of explorers who have lived through the Artic night, they explain much of what has hitherto appeared unaccountable.

In the first place, he attaches due importance to the beneficent effect on life of the nightless Arctic summer. At Kolguev, which lies at no great distance north of the Arctic line, the year falls equally into six months of perpetual sunlight and six of unbroken night. The never-setting sun of the first forces the powers of life at high pressure—'life beating strongly under perpetual sunlight ; life, and the propagation of life, by birds as clamorously, by flowers as brightly, as in the lands of the south.' Of the flowers, 'buttercups, dandelions, forget-me-not, hawkweed, cuckoo-flower, sedum, and saxifrage are found in blossom, and no English meadow can outvie these Arctic pastures in masses of purple and blue and gold.' But these are the halcyon days of the Polar region. When the winter and darkness settle down on the land, the birds, ducks, geese, knots, sanderlings, and plovers fly south, except the raven, the ptarmigan, and two species of gull. But with these remain all the mammals, not only the whales and seals, but the land creatures, all of whom might, if they chose, migrate—reindeer, musk-sheep, polar-bears, blue foxes, and lemmings prefer to stay, and abide for six months in this circumpolar 'city of dreadful night.' The nature of this polar night, of the cold it brings and its effect on animals, may be gathered from Colonel Feilden's notes made during the winter passed by H.M.S. 'Alert' on Grinnell Land in 1875-76, at a point nearer the actual Pole than has been reached before or since. The sun sank on October 12th, and did not reappear till March 2d—a night of only twenty-nine days less than its calculated disappearance at the actual Pole. Yet it is certain that this protracted night was never dark in the sense that it is dark inside the galleries of a coal-pit. The Arctic animals, unlike the deep-sea creatures, need to develop no light-organs to illuminate their path, though they live only in 'darkness visible.' 'On November 30th,' writes Colonel Feilden, 'with a perfectly clear sky, from a distance of half-a-mile in a southerly direction, the ship was visible from eleven A.M to one P.M. At noon, just topping the eastern hills, was a faintly-tinted, pearly-green sky, through which stars of the first magnitude had a difficulty in shining. On January 24th, the twilight at noon had increased sufficiently to enable us to distinguish a comrade at a distance of one hundred and twenty yards.

By the beginning of February, a month before the reappearance of the sun, we were able to take walks of considerable extent, and by the middle of that month we were carrying our guns in pursuit of game.' In addition, moonlight and starlight were brilliant, and enabled them to cross the country almost throughout the winter. This account somewhat dispels the thickness of that Cimmerian darkness in which tradition wraps the Polar night. But at best it is bad enough. Men, even Arctic voyagers, feel its gloom intolerable, though cheered by artificial light. Strange to say, the animals do not, so far as we can tell. Their eyes are not modified by the prevailing darkness, either in the direction of greater power, or by degeneration, through which the shallow water forms which have invaded the deep seas have become blind. At the same time, Mr Battye has noted, and satisfied himself by repeated experiments, that the faculty of sight is inferior in the Arctic fox and Arctic hare to that of the common fox and common hare of Britain. The 'nervous depression' with which darkness affects men is quite absent in the case of animals in the Arctic nights. Their vital activity is unaffected by the absence of sunlight which, though protracted for so great a time, seems no more irksome than it does to those animals which have by choice become nocturnal in their habits in temperate lands.

Their indifference to cold is still more astonishing. The Arctic animals do not even hibernate. The polar-bear does not imitate the winter sleep of the black and brown bears, but is a rover through the winter, and is hunted and killed by moonlight ;* and Mr Battye found on Kolguev the traps and half-frozen baits of seal fat which had been set for blue-foxes in the previous winter. The Samoyeds also urged him to stay through the winter, saying that there would be plenty of hunting. More strange still is the experience of Colonel Feilden-when wintering with the 'Alert.' When the temperature was at 80° below freezing point (Fahrenheit), the lemmings were seen peering from their burrows in the snow, and he had 'ample proof that animals were moving all the time' in this stupefying cold.

Man in this case was also able to withstand the extreme of low temperature, drawing his food from artificial stores, and clad in the skins of the Arctic animals which have developed a special cold-resisting covering. But how are the Arctic animals fed while the cold prevails? The carnivorous creatures live on the weaker animals. But the reindeer, musk-sheep and lemmings must procure vegetable food even at such times. The life of plants must be preserved, in

---

* The female bears, when pregnant, do hibernate, and produce their young beneath their snow burrows.

spite of conditions which seem to make it impossible. The explanation is that the absence of the sunlight, which is absolutely necessary for the nutrition of plants elsewhere, does not prevent their growth in the night of the Arctic winter. The lemmings which were seen by Colonel Feilden were found to have been feeding on a saxifrage common in the district, which, though exposed throughout the winter to a temperature of 70° below zero, and often to greater intensity of cold, showed a small green bud at the extremity of each stalk, proving that it was growing in spite of the darkness.

The immunity from destruction possessed by Arctic plants and animals exposed to such conditions is thus established. But the struggle for existence must, even so, be most severe and exhausting—so severe that the impulse to migrate to a less rigorous climate seems suggested by nature. Yet the mammals do not migrate, and the birds return faithfully every summer. The usual explanation of the presence of the Arctic mammals is the assumption that they are the remains of a previous migration northwards. This is rejected by Mr Battye as a movement from favourable to unfavourable conditions, and so contrary to probability and the facts of experience. The objection is not conclusive. It is certain that the creatures which inhabit the deep left light, warmth, and food, and invaded the realms of cold and darkness, where their eyes lost the power of sight, while retaining the outward form which they possessed for use in the sunlight. But Mr Battye has an alternative theory to take the place of that which sees in the existence of the Arctic mammal the relics of a northern migration. He considers 'that the Arctic plants and animals are there because they were born there;' certain plants existed in the northern region before they descended into temperate Europe; and there is 'no reason to suppose that contemporary animal life could not have begun there also, when we remember that these regions had then cooled down from a temperature sufficiently tropical to have supported the corals of the Silurian era which formed the reefs now shown to have existed in those regions.' Such a theory explains the northern migration of birds by supposing that they are returning to their old home; and the musk-sheep, reindeer and polar-bear remain there and refuse to leave for the same reason.

But it does not explain why the beasts, like the birds, do not leave the country in the winter, and settle in more southern latitudes, whence no temptation would induce them to return.

THE CONDITIONS OF ANIMAL DOMESTICATION

MR BARTLETT recently stated an opinion that only four species of wild animal were at present on the border line of domestication. These are the elephant, the gayal (the wild ox of Assam), the ferret, and the yak. Mr Shaler, Dean of the Laurence Scientific School at Harvard, has also published a series of papers on 'Domesticated Animals,' most of which appeared in *Harper's Magazine*. He deals rather with the uses of domestic animals in the relation to man, than with the conditions which determine the domestication of some species, and the neglect of others, but two phrases which occur repeatedly in these chapters indicate the direction in which a part of these conditions must be sought. The first is 'temperament' and the second, 'previous communal association' or social intercourse when wild. Those animals which live by preference in association—

not 'society,' as we understand the word, but in company with one another—rather than in anti-social seclusion, only do so because they participate in that general stock of animal good-temper which is the rule, not the exception, in the animal world. If the aim of domestication were to make one solitary species the companion of man, the consideration of temperament might be neglected. The North American Indians, for example, only tamed a single species, the dog, which, judging from the analogy of the wolf-like dogs of the Hare Indians, was probably derived from the domestication of the fox or wolf. Even had its disposition not been modified by time and training, there was no reason to suppose that the wolf-like dog, though as hostile in temperament to all other animals as the dingo of Australia, might not have remained a solitary but successful instance of domestication by a race who themselves were at war with every other form of living animal. But among all progressive races the domestication of animals means not the maintenance of a single species in semi-commensalism with man, like that of the Red Indian and his dog, but the enforced association of many species in daily intercourse. It is a condition of the successful existence of any species in domestication that it shall be equable in temperament towards other species, and benevolent rather than not in its attitude towards man. For a complete and subtle analysis and estimate of the likenesses and differences of temperament in domestic animals, we must turn to those chapters of Buffon in which, after satisfying his imagination by the poetic description of the sensations of man awakening to find himself equipped with every faculty in a world in which he was destined to be supreme, he reviews the different species of domestic animals, and accounts for the uses severally found for them, not so much by difference of structure as by constant variations of temperament which have modified their treatment by man, and permanently affected their development. While all domestication presupposes an equable, and in some degree sympathetic, temperament in the species when wild, such slight differences of disposition as the restlessness and vivacity of the goats, as contrasted with the more staid and tranquil character of the sheep, have relegated the first to wild and uninclosed regions of mountain, and to the care of races who are poor and comparatively unenterprising, and so retarded over the greater part of the globe the development of the goat ; while its relation, the sheep, whose wool is at best not so valuable as that of the Angora and Kashmir goats, has been improved, refined, and developed, until it marks the most successful example of domestication in temperate climates. The ungenial, sullen temper of the wild ass, repeated in the domestic breeds, is a more marked instance of the effect of the personal factor in rendering domestication a practical failure. The measure in which slight differences of temperament affect the progress and development of birds under domestication, is seen in a marked degree in the case of the peacock, which would be far more commonly kept and reared were it not quarrelsome and dangerous to other poultry, and of the guinea-fowl, which though fairly friendly with the other members of the poultry-yard, never quite loses its fear of man, and is therefore less favoured by him in return. There is no reason why the game-birds should not have been domesticated equally with the fowl and the pigeon, except that the greater number of pheasants in Asia, and the bustards and florikins in Africa, seem, even when artificially reared for several generations, incapable of acquiescing in the familiar presence and good offices of man. In cases where obvious similarity of form and habit exist between species which have been domesticated and others which have remained wild, or have been imperfectly trained, 'incompatibility of temperament' more often than not supplies the reason for their remaining outside the ranks of the reclaimed. The causes of these inbred differences are unexplained, but the facts are

not denied. In the ox tribe there are three species apparently well suited for domestication, the yak, the gayal, and the African buffalo, whose very partial entrance into, or absence from, the ranks of domesticated animals is clearly due to some mental defect discovered by experience. The two former are found both wild and tame, the yak being commonly used as a beast of burden in the Central Asian plateau, while the gayal, a very large wild ox of the Assam forests, is commonly reclaimed from among the wild herds, and breeds well in this state. But the bull yak always tends to become dangerous as it reaches maturity; and the gayals, even those crossed with domestic cattle, have a bias to revert to savagery, and 'go Fantee' like a West African negro. The African buffalo is so morose and savage by nature, that it would be impossible to make the first experiment of domestication by catching and taming the wild specimens, and by this distinguishing feature of ingrained evil temper it has secured a 'splendid isolation' which must end in the destruction of the species. It is not clear that the exclusion of the two allied forms of bison, the American 'buffalo' and the European aurochs from the list of domesticated *bovidæ*, is due to temper, though those kept in confinement are usually dangerous animals. The law of the survival of the fittest runs not only among wild, but among domesticated species, and appears in the competition of the latter with the former. Had the white man's cattle not been available to compete with the red man's bison, the whites might have domesticated the bison, instead of killing him off to make room for the more useful domestic species. Had the wild ancestors of our cattle not proved more useful when tamed than those of the still wild aurochs, the latter might be fattening for Christmas beef, while the former survived only in the forests of Esthonia.

Two obvious instances of animals whose instinct, when wild, is certainly not benevolent to other species, occur. The dog, when wild, whether as wolf or 'hunting dog,' is the inveterate foe of all those kinds with which he has to live in domestication, and the cat is by nature hostile to the whole class of domesticated birds. These anti-domestic instincts have never yet been completely lost by either, but are held in check—in the case of the dog, by intelligence and quick sympathy with the desires of man ; in the case of the cat, mainly by intelligence also, and the fear of punishment. The sheep-killing instinct is never wholly eradicated from the canine brain. It breaks out among all breeds of dog, and is often indulged with curious cunning and consciousness of criminal intent. Few domestic cats, when young, can resist the temptation to kill a cage-bird, and though they can be taught to respect particular individuals, no pigeon or canary is safe from the 'strange cat'—in other words, all other cats but those living on the same premises.* That none of the larger cats except the puma have been even partly domesticated is not surprising. They are the representatives, beyond all others, of the non-communal instinct in animals, living alone or in temporary association limited to the family, and, with the exception of the cheetah, are too dangerous to admit of the encouragement of any initial effort to train them to the service of man. Physical causes only affect domestication in a minor degree. That animals should reproduce their species is an essential condition to their continuance as domesticated species ; and Mr Bartlett considers that the elephant is only 'on the border-line' because it will not, as a rule, breed in captivity. Its length of life counterbalances this disadvantage. But other species tend to become rather more than less prolific when accustomed to their new conditions. Among water-fowl the widgeon is the only example of a bird which as a rule refuses to pair, and this may in part be due to arrested migration. The turkey of our farm-yards was originally

* A friend asks, ' Are there no mice in Persia ? because Persian cats always seem to kill birds and neglect mice altogether.'

brought from Cuba, but mates freely with the continental American species. When the latter is introduced to English plantations, it tends to degenerate in size, and is a less free layer;* but this is probably due to inbreeding, with a view to preserve the wild form. The eland breeds when domesticated as readily as cattle, and the failure to acclimatise this and other African antelopes is due, not to natural, but to economic objections; it is a gross feeder and fattens slowly, and so fails to hold its own in competition with modern breeds of cattle.

But though we seem to have reached the limit of profitable domestication, we have no evidence except that of our present experience. The same objection might have been raised with equal force thirty years ago. But the recent reclamation of the ostrich, which may before long be improved in size and in plumage like the fowl, and the impending education of the African elephant, are instances to the contrary. Meantime, man is, in the case of most animals, the sole arbiter as to whether they shall survive or be presently destroyed. In view of the enormous service to man of each single species which is domesticated, he would be improvident to allow one of those which are still wild to disappear;

* This has been observed at Whitestaunton Manor in Somersetshire, the property of C. Elton, Esq., Q.C., where the American turkeys have been kept for many years.

and it is some such underlying notion which is dictating measures in almost every civilised and semi-civilised State for their future protection and preservation.

SANCTUARIES FOR WILD BIRDS

Referring to an account of the wild fowl on Holkham Lake, published in the *Spectator* of January 18th, 1896, Mr Francis Darwin wrote from Arthington in Yorkshire :—'At Walton, in the late Mr Waterton's time, I often, in an evening, used to watch the birds congregating for their flight to their evening feeding grounds, on the Humber and Lincolnshire coast ; and I have wished, and almost hoped, to see the time when large areas of sea and country, such as the Wash and parts of the Lincolnshire coast, with the Cromarty Firth, in Scotland, should be made sanctuaries for wild birds, in which they, as the deer in the forest sanctuaries now do, could feel themselves at rest from the sportsman, and where those who like to watch the birds in their usual natural state could see them.'

This suggestion of creating a 'reserve' on a given area of sea and adjacent coast, deserves attention. The nearest approach to such a sanctuary is

WILD FOWL ON LANGMERE, NORFOLK. *From a drawing by Lancelot Speed*

that inside the Chesil Beach, where both sides of the lagoon are the property of Lord Ilchester. There, in and below the swannery, immense numbers of fowl congregate and are left in peace during the greater part of the winter, and though not so complete a 'sanctuary' as the Holkham mere, where Lord Leicester has for many years refused to allow a shot to be fired, it is a concrete instance of the success attained by protecting a given area of sea water. Great inlets, like the Wash and the Northern Firths, are less well suited for such 'reserves' than inland lakes or land-locked harbours, partly because the fowl cannot obtain shelter from rough weather on such extensive tracts of sea, and also because, even in calm weather, their habits and appearance could scarcely be observed when the flocks are scattered over many thousands of acres. An ideal place for such a sanctuary would be the land-locked gulfs of Poole Harbour, where not only the diving and surface ducks, grebes, coots, cormorants, and occasional wild swans, would assemble in thousands in the winter months if a truce could be proclaimed, but also the flocks of still less accessible shore fowl, curlews, plover, redshanks, knots, and the like, might be observed on the shores as the ducks may now be observed on the inland lakes. Even these waders, the shyest of all shy fowl, learn to recognise a 'sanctuary,' and in one such reserve, suited for these birds, the writer has seen several species, such as the redshanks, snipe, and grey plover, usually unapproachable elsewhere, sleeping or resting within thirty yards of the furze bush behind which he was concealed. Those who have seen the shore fowl on the eastern coasts, the knots, stints, plover, and curlew, rising literally in thousands, and drifting like dark clouds across the sands, but unapproachable either by the naturalist or the sportsman, will realise the interest and novelty of seeing them at close quarters.

A large area, whether of land or water, is a desirable but not a necessary condition for the establishment of a sanctuary. Confidence in the friendliness of human beings, and not the absence of mankind, is what wild fowl rely upon in selecting a home for the hours of daylight. The wholly wild ducks exhibit none of that natural preference for total seclusion which is instinctive even in coop-reared pheasants. The brain power of the duck is very considerable—greater probably than that of any other bird (except the goose) commonly domesticated. There is no reason to doubt that they gauge accurately the limits of danger and safety when passing from the open country to protected waters, and by a process of reasoning as quick as that of human beings, they adapt their behaviour to the treatment which their intelligence warns them to expect. At Monymusk, in Aberdeenshire, the home of Sir Francis Grant, numbers of wild ducks used to take sanctuary on a pond adjoining the stables. The place was described by a writer as 'a large duck-pond adjoining the stable square; the ducks are not tame wild ducks, but *bonâ-fide* wild ducks, wild wherever else they go, but tame the moment they settle on the pond. They swim up to be fed within a few feet of anyone, evincing no fear. Outside the precincts of their pond they are as wild as the wildest duck can possibly be.' Sir Francis Grant, in answer to a question addressed to him by Sir R. Payne-Gallwey, wrote of this wonderful 'duckery'—'Every word in the account is perfectly true; a gentleman is staying with me to-day who never saw the ducks in the stable square before. He saw about one hundred and fifty, and the coachman called them and fed them with oats. Last Sunday I fed them, and they came within the length of my walking-stick.'

The park at Walton Hall, which Charles Waterton inclosed and protected, only covered two hundred and sixty acres; the lake was large in proportion to the size of the park, containing twenty-four acres of water. But the modest limits of this park afforded complete and permanent sanctuary to most of the larger species of English birds, with the exception of a few which do not care for woodland or inland districts, and to many, including a colony of cormorants, which are only occasional visitors to other inland waters. The gathering of fowl was retarded for some time because he shot the widgeon, not believing that these birds, which he knew were only winter visitors, would be likely to remember the hospitality offered, and to requite it by a second visit. When he discovered his mistake, and the use of the gun was interdicted, the widgeon not only came in numbers, but remained both by night and day, feeding on the grass of the park like geese. On one occasion he counted sixteen hundred and forty wild duck on his lake, besides a flock of Canada geese, which came from a distance and enrolled themselves as part of its regular population. Though occasionally fired at when 'out of bounds,' they seldom lost any of their number. Wild fowl, unlike game, gain almost complete immunity from this source of danger by confining their journeys to the hours of dusk and dawn, and their preservers have little to fear from human prowlers round the fold. Waterton's worst enemy was a fox, which climbed his 9 ft. wall by the aid of a pole left leaning against it. Rats and rabbits were the only other creatures banished from the park, and the latter only on account of their undue increase. The taste for maintaining near country houses some form of protected area, in which birds and animals may multiply unmolested, is already partly established. The gun is now banished from most country gardens, and here the wood-pigeon, magpie, and other large birds have accepted a year-long sanctuary and show themselves without fear, where formerly they only ventured to appear in the nesting season. The increase so obtained in the numbers of wild birds and animals has struck others who desire to preserve these on the largest scale, mainly with the very opposite view of securing great numbers at certain times for the purposes of sport. In this case a 'single and mighty Nimrod' often creates a semi-sanctuary which offers the opportunities to the naturalist which our correspondent desires. The system has been extended from the deer forests of Scotland to the preserves of Norfolk. At Sandringham the Prince of Wales has created a 'partridge sanctuary,' set with protecting plantations and sown with agreeable seed plants. At Merton, in Norfolk, the number and variety of the fowl on the two meres owned by Lord Walsingham is a remarkable result of partial sanctuary; the list of birds either seen or shot in one day at the end of the season

includes snipe, wood cock, teal, herons, gadwall, poch-
ards, golden-eyes, swans, coots, moorhens, tufted duck,
pintail, widgeon, shovellers, water-rails, gulls, kingfishers,
and a sand-grouse. But it is in the economy of the
'decoys' that the nearest approach to the establishment of sanctuaries on a large scale is now seen.

Sir Thomas Browne was right when he attributed
the abundance of wild fowl in Norfolk to the 'very
many decoys, especially between Norwich and the
sea.' 'It may seem strange,' writes Mr Stevenson,
the author of *The Birds of Norfolk*, 'to speak of
the decoy, perhaps the most deadly engine ever invented for the purpose of luring wild fowl to their
destruction, as being favourable to their abundance;
but it is strictly in accordance with fact. The great
attraction of the decoy pond is its absolute seclusion;
here, the fowl which return in the morning from
their nocturnal feeding grounds find perfect rest, and
pass their time peacefully, in happy unconsciousness
of the destruction which may be going on within
a few yards of them.' Decoys are being revived
both in Norfolk and Suffolk. The main require-
ment for success is proximity to the coast, and
absolute quiet, with, if possible, a thick plantation
round the pool. The conditions which attract fowl
to the decoy, would serve equally to establish a
sanctuary in any of the home counties, or near any

part of the coast. Even the neighbourhood of salt water is not indispensable; there is one decoy working in the central Midlands. But the sites for the future establishment of sanctuaries for wild animals as well as for wild birds are to be found in the national forests. At the beginning of the next reign the terms on which these are held by the State will once more be arranged with the Crown. The 'sporting rights' should be secured, and their administration placed in the hands of practical naturalists. In Woolmer Forest there is a pool and marsh, in which the wild fowl are now shot annually by the officers of the Royal Engineers at Aldershot (the forest being leased to the War Office), which seems designed by Nature as the site of the first national experiment in this direction.

THE INVISIBLE FOOD OF FISH

RECENT experiments on the food of the oyster show that the oatmeal commonly given to fatten them causes them to lose weight and die, and that flour, often used for the same purpose, soon poisons them, though, on the other hand, the typhoid bacillus is destroyed by passing through the oyster's alimentary canal.

The latter discovery will be good news to the owners of oyster beds. But the study of bacteriology is a new one. What strikes the average reader as more curious is the lateness of the discovery that the food commonly used in shops to fatten oysters disagrees with and kills them. Yet it is only one of the results of what, until recently, was a very general ignorance of the main food supply, not only of shell-fish like the oyster, but of all the swarming vertebrate fishes of the sea, except such as are entirely carnivorous and live by preying upon other fish. The food of river fishes was better known ; but what was, until recently, thought to be their principal food now appears to play only a limited part in their maintenance, and the common fisherman's view, that river fishes work hard for their living and subsist mainly on worms and grubs, with a change to may-fly in the season and occasional feasts of ground-bait and paste, is almost as far removed from fact as the showman's description of the elephant's diet as consisting mainly of cakes and hay.

But the case of the river fish did not settle the obvious problem suggested by the question of the food supply in the sea. The sea, except in the shallow-water fringe along the shore, is devoid of vegetables. It contains in general no growth of weeds and plants to harbour swarms of possible food creatures with their eggs and larvæ, and where such vegetable growths do occur, as in floating weeds of the Sargasso Sea, a race of fish and crustaceans at once appears, limited to that locality, and obviously fed from that source alone. Neither does the sea, except in certain areas, greatly abound in vertebrate fish. You may catch large fish at any point on the voyage in the narrow seas, from Gibraltar down the Mediterranean to Aden. But the open seas are not full of the fry of fish which might form a good supply for others, and in the Atlantic, except on the Newfoundland banks, there are no fish found near the surface at all. A bucket of Atlantic water is to the eye simply a vessel of transparent brine, unfouled with weed, void of fish, and, in most cases, not visibly infested with any form of floating marine organisms. Yet at any moment shoals of fish numbering millions of individuals may elect to enter this apparently foodless waste; the herring shoals disappear from the coast at intervals into the deep Atlantic, and return in good condition, oily and exuberant, and the whales find sufficient food to make them the 'fattest' creatures in creation.

Many of the whales are carnivorous; some, including the 'right' whale, have long been known to live on small sea crustaceans, which were supposed to be found in exceptional numbers in the Arctic Seas. But the case of the typical 'shoal' fish, such as pilchards and herrings, offered special difficulties. When caught near land they were often found to have been living on sand-eels, roe, and small fish and crabs. But in the greater number of cases the contents of their stomachs were quite unrecognisable, and the immense size of the shoals increased the difficulty of believing that on the migration they could live on fish or on vegetable food. For fish moving in a serried shoal extending for a square mile, and perhaps 30 ft. deep, it would be impossible to find room to chase and capture smaller fish, even supposing these could be found in sufficient numbers to form food for the numberless herrings. The rapidity and order of their movements make it equally unlikely that they should stop to chew and browse on vegetables, even when arrived in the shallow seas where seaweeds grow. It was just possible that previous to spawning the fish could for a time abstain from food. But it was equally certain that after spawning their numbers were the same, and that they must require food, and that in large quantities, in an area no greater than that occupied by the herring or pilchard shoal, so long as the fish remained in that formation. The explanation is that the microscopic creatures which are in parts of the Atlantic massed so thickly in the water as to discolour the surface, and give abundant food for the whale, are present, not so thickly, but in numbers comparable to the motes in the air, in all parts of the sea. For the purposes of the herring and the pilchard, and countless other vertebrate fish shell fish, and zoophytes, the upper waters of the sea are in fact a nutritive soup, teeming with food exactly suited to their needs. These microscopic creatures are the basis of all the larger life of the ocean, and in a great degree of the growth and increase of fresh water fishes. Some of these tiny creatures are water-fleas, others like carapaced shrimps, others occupy shells like miniature bivalves, others are forms of the one-eyed microscopic monster of the ponds, the *Cyclops*. All are of prodigious fecundity, and proof against astonishing changes of temperature, and the eggs and young, the microscopic offspring of the water-midgets, pervade every drop of the surface ocean, the rivers, and the ponds. In fresh water the common water-fleas often discolour a pool; they produce three broods a month, with forty or fifty eggs in a brood; other species swarm on the leaves of every water growth, and adhere to every filament of the *fuci* and *confervæ*. The *Cyclops* will, it is calculated, beget four hundred and forty-two thousand young in the course of a year; and the *Cetochilus*, or 'whale-food,' is said, even in the Firth of Forth, to form almost exclusively the food of the herrings and the sea-living salmon and salmon-trout. Their existence is one of the greatest economic triumphs of nature. They are the creatures which dispose of the refuse of the world in the sea, and keep it sweet. Dead vegetable and animal matter feed these *entomostraca*, and they are converted without further machinery into the food-fishes of the world, or at one remove, when these are eaten as food by other fish, such as the tunny, the cod and the mackerel, which follow the herring-shoals. Nothing short of assimilation in the digestive organs of fish seems to kill these *entomostraca*. They swarm in the distilled brine of the salterns on the Solent. Their eggs are proof against frost, and survive being baked by the sun. They even come to life without being fertilised. Yet they undergo infinite changes of form, and their cast shells are piled like billows of dust on parts of the Cornwall coast. Detached and self-supporting, they wander over the whole ocean, swimming mainly upon the surface. At times they descend to the deeps, and this, it is surmised, causes the temporary disappearance of shoal fish, which necessarily follow them. Their countless numbers are also recruited by the microscopic larvæ of fixed shells. The barnacle, for instance, begins life in this form, taking its place in the ingredients of the 'sea-soup' as a one-eyed swimming crustacean, then growing a pair of eyes, and finally settling down as a fixture in proper barnacle style.

In rivers they are almost the sole food of all young fish, and probably the main resource of the older fish when other supplies fail. In the first days of spring, the creatures in every stage, eggs, larvæ and perfect, though microscopic *entomostraca*, swarm in the water, on the mud, and on the foliage of the water-plants. At such times even trout feed mainly on them. In the Hertfordshire streams the trout are then said to be 'tailing.' They push their heads down into the weed, and raise their tails, which wave about in the weeds, or even above the surface of the water. They are eating the weed bare of the clinging film of microscopic larvæ, of water-fleas, *Cyclops*, and other fresh water *entomostraca*. The trout is the most easily fed of all fish, being greedy, omnivorous, and not afraid of artificial food, such as bread or paste. But the kind of food with which it is supplied makes a vast difference in its growth. Experiments made on trout showed that when fed upon worms only they grew slowly; others fed on minnows did better, but a single fish fed upon insects weighed twice as much at the end of the experiment as a pair of those reared upon worms and minnows respectively. For feeding all young trout the microscopic food is now admitted to be best of all. Mr Armistead, in a recent lecture on 'Fish Culture' at the rooms of the Royal Institution, dwelt on the necessity for making separate pools, full of weeds and plants, in which the millions of *entomostraca* might increase, and serve as food for the young trout below. Carp were formerly believed to be vegetable feeders, and the carp ponds of Germany used to be drained and planted with rye as carp food. So it was, but only as being itself food for the microscopic millions. The carp chews the water-weed, sucks off the insects, and then spits it out again. It may be doubted whether there are any of our common food-fishes, except the grey mullet, which are vegetable feeders ; and by a curious reversal of the rule obtaining among birds, the fish-eating, or '*entomostraca*-eating,' fishes excel in flavour the vegetable feeders. The red mullet, which lives mainly on 'sea-soup,' is among the dainties of the table, while the grey mullet is almost worthless.

This unseen but omnipresent source of food, nourishing either directly or at second-hand almost every creature of sea and river, from the tiny jelly-fish to the 'right' whale, explains the truth of the old saying, that an acre of sea is worth four acres of land. In the words of a recent writer :—'No other source of food can compare in economic value with this. Even the smallest pools and ditches swarm with the *entomostraca*, and wherever life can find a lodging in the water they are found in countless numbers ready to become the food of the higher animals, and able, by their surprising rapidity of re-production, to maintain their numbers. Without them the life of the fresh water fishes would become impossible, and lacking their innumerable swarms, the schools of herrings and other sea-fish would hardly be able to exist.'

THE ANIMAL VIEW OF CAPTIVITY

An evening paper recently raised the question whether the menagerie in Regent's Park did not contribute as much to the unhappiness of its animal captives as to the pleasure of their visitors? If that were so, the enjoyment of the latter would inevitably be diminished, though the sufferings of most of our native birds and beasts in severe weather, such as that which in the beginning of 1895 drove the wild deer of the Highlands to the farmyards, and actually caused hundreds to die of cold and famine in Ross-shire, must suggest the reflection that the comforts of captivity afford some compensation for the loss of freedom. There is good reason to believe that the surmise to which we have referred, though not unnatural, is wrong, and that, though some creatures do suffer in confinement, the balance leans rather towards an increase than a loss in the sum of animal well-being.

What makes the happiness of wild animals?

The question is not very easily answered. The abstract idea of liberty certainly does not enter into it in the case of the greater number; they cannot, like the man who has consciously sought a life in the wilds in order to enjoy the sense of freedom from social restrictions, say, 'I am free, and my own master, and therefore I possess one element of happiness.' What the happiness of wild creatures consists in can perhaps be best judged by their daily habits. Within certain limits they are free to choose their life, and presumably they choose that which pleases them best. In nearly every case this is one of pure routine. It consists in the daily repetition of a very limited series of actions, the greater number of which seem to give them satisfaction rather than pleasure, but make up in the aggregate the sum of animal happiness. Unlike the domesticated dog, which welcomes any break in the monotony of life, they never, except in the courting season, seem to seek change, or adventure, or excitement. It may be doubted whether, if the food supply were plentiful and constant, animals or birds would ever care to move beyond the circle in which they can find enough for their daily wants. The probable whereabouts of deer at any time in the twenty-four hours, and their occupation, whether feeding, sleeping, or resting, are known with the

utmost certainty to those whose business it is to
watch the forest, and could be predicted for any
month in the year; and though the Scotch deer
move considerable distances, owing to the bad
weather and want of food on the mountains, a fat
Exmoor stag remains in the same haunt, and goes
through the comfortable round of eating, sleeping,
and occasionally bathing, as regularly as its tame
relations in Richmond Park. Change, excitement,
or even the desire to visit another part of the
forest does not seem to come within their notion
of what constitutes happiness in the wild life.
Comfort seems to be its aim, though this secured
by natural means, bestows what in the case of
human beings it often withdraws, the condition of
perfect health. The adventurous life, if it is found
anywhere among wild creatures, belongs to the
carnivorous animals. Yet most of these only wander
just so far as is necessary to find their prey, and
then prefer to kill some creature that will provide a meal for more than one day. They are
naturally indolent, and active only from necessity.
Even the peregrine falcon, the fastest and boldest
of English birds, lives 'in a groove' when it can.
Those in the Culver cliffs not only remain there
during the whole year, but at no time during the
day are they absent for more than an hour from

the cliff face. Though they could cross the Channel after breakfast and return by mid-day without fatigue, did they choose to do so, they are as much attached to a small area as the birds which haunt our gardens. Another clue to the passive character of animal happiness is that given by the behaviour of those creatures which have voluntarily established what is called by naturalists 'commensalism' with man, living only where he lives, and feeding on what, in a sense, 'falls from his table.' Sparrows, starlings, and the half-wild pigeons of London are in the transition state between the freedom of the fields and the confinement of the Zoo, where, by the way, these birds are perhaps tamer and more confident than in any other place. Their life, in its hours and habits, is almost identical with that of the bird inmates of the cages. They eat when they eat, bathe when they bathe, and on cold nights will come and sit in the aviaries of the larger birds which admit their passage through the bars. In no case do they seem anxious for more 'liberty.' It may be doubted if a Zoo sparrow has ever visited Hyde Park, or whether, if the caged birds were given their liberty, they would leave the Gardens. This has in some instances been proved. Some years ago the snow broke in the wire roof of a cage of wild wood-pigeons. These birds remained in the Gardens, and nested next spring in the adjacent trees. For the wildest creatures the state of nature has its evils, which disappear in captivity. Every class, except the strongest, has its 'natural enemy' for ever seeking to kill it, of whose existence it is painfully aware, and which keeps it constantly in nervous dread. For most, a change of weather or of season causes a dearth of food ; and for all the inevitable time of injury and sickness, though not foreseen or dreaded, comes at last, without the chance of aid or recovery. An example of the advantages of life at the Zoo, even to the largest animals, when attacked by illness curable by human treatment, but likely to cause lingering death in freedom, occurred only recently in the Gardens. An Indian rhinoceros developed a large and painful abscess under its eye. This was suspected to be caused by a bad tooth ; but as it ate the twigs of a birch-broom which was cut up and given to it, it was decided to treat the case as one requiring the surgeon, and not the dentist. The creature allowed the abscess to be lanced, and later to be syringed daily with a large garden squirt, and the treatment was successful.

The absence of self-consciousness in animals distinguishes their case from that of human beings in confinement. They feel none of the exasperation of the prisoner who knows that another will could, did it choose, release him. They feel none of the corroding sense of injustice. On the other hand, many creatures, if kept in solitary confinement, suffer from dejection and often die. But that is not a form of captivity known at the Zoo. Though the birds and animals at the Zoo do not always attain that exuberant health, which to many wild creatures is the chief delight of life, it is worth mentioning that even these only enjoy this ecstasy of physical vigour at certain seasons in the year, when food is abundant, temperature agreeable, and the season of moulting or rearing the young is passed. On the other hand, wild animals when confined can enjoy the comforts of semi-domestication with less risk than wild men can endure the comforts of semi-civilisation. Wild cattle, antelopes, zebras, cats, large and small, elephants, the hippopotamus and rhinoceros, and semi-Arctic, as well as semi-tropical birds, live in perfect health and condition in houses artificially warmed ; and in the case of the ruminant animals on food artificially prepared. The wild cattle, elephants and antelopes, are in condition equalling or exceeding that in which they are found in their native jungles or plains, a curious contrast to the fate of the tamed Fuegian Indians. These men, whom Darwin describes as ' savages of the lowest grade,' were, according to a writer in *Scribner's*

Magazine subsequently civilised by the missionaries into a general conformity with European habits. But the Indians, 'who had thrived when naked and living on whale blubber, did not thrive as clothed farm labourers living on bread. The woollens of the whites were less efficient as clothing than whale oil. Fatherless children, who had been strong and sturdy when naked in the storms of sleet, died when well dressed and living in a warm orphanage. Every child taken into it died. Pneumonia and consumption became plagues.' These complaints were once the scourge of the Zoo, until the Park was drained, mainly as the result of a report by Sir Richard Owen. Now they are almost unknown, except occasionally among the larger apes and delicate monkeys.

Even want of space is not a serious drawback to the happiness of most animals at the Zoo. The lions and tigers feel the confinement of their inner cages, and often strike impatiently the doors which separate them in winter from their summer palaces, and the wild cattle would enjoy life far more if a roomy paddock could be added to their pens. No hawks or eagles can be happy in cages, because exercise in flight is essential to their health. Parrots, on the other hand, dislike exercise, and consequently live to the greatest age of any creatures in the Gardens.

Bears seem to share this dislike for unnecessary movement, and 'My Lords the Elephants' and all the
camels, with true Oriental indolence, would prefer to
stand still all day doing nothing, if they were not compelled to earn their living by carrying visitors. All
the reptiles lead the life of lotus-eaters, and so far as
their brief day lasts, the tropical butterflies in their
cages seem equally happy with those which flit among
the flowers which fringe the Garden walks.

HOUSEHOLD PESTS

Antipathy, and not fear, is, according to Dr Johnson, the basis of that horror to which most persons are willing to admit themselves subject in touching, or even seeing, the 'noisome beasts' which in various forms combine to form the intruding army which invades the houses of civilised man. One of his acquaintances, to whom we are introduced in the pages of the *Rambler*, was free to confess that he could not see a rat, even when dead, without palpitating; and another threw his reputation for courage at the feet of his mistress, unless she could condone the fact that 'among all the animals upon which Nature has impressed deformity and horror, there was none that he durst not encounter rather than a beetle.'

Those who share the feelings of repulsion so magnificently expressed by the great master of Ciceronian English, will not notice without a qualm the accounts of the recent surprising increase in the numbers and ferocity of these plagues great and small, from rats 'as big as rabbits' to clothes moths and cockroaches innumerable.

Since the hot summer of 1893, Fleet Street itself has been invaded by armies of starving and thirsty rats, which are said to leave the dry sewers, and take up their summer quarters within easy reach of the river; Dublin has suffered from a plague of rats unknown in the memory of man; and in the interval which must elapse before the complete emancipation of Ireland from the upas tree of English rule, the Lord Mayor has so far sacrificed patriotism to expediency as to employ an English rat-catcher for their extirpation, and rewarded his success with a gratuity in addition to his stipulated wages. It is high time that the services of this gentleman were secured by his suffering countrymen in London; for one of the most audacious rat outrages yet chronicled was recently reported from a western suburb. A baby, left in a perambulator by the child in charge of it, was attacked by rats issuing from a sewer at Acton, and badly bitten before it could be rescued from these vicious and unexpected enemies. It is high time that we set our house in order, otherwise our neighbours beyond the Channel may be tempted to see in the sufferings of our middle-class a requital for that last indignity offered to the captive Napoleon at St Helena, so touchingly described in the *Mémorial*, when an 'irruption de rats, énormes, hardis, et très méchants' was suffered to deprive the Emperor and his devoted followers in exile of their *déjeuner à la fourchette*.

'As for rat-catchers,' says St John, 'find me an honest one, and I will forfeit my reputation.' So far as the writer's experience goes, want of skill, rather than of honesty, is the chief failing of the profession ; though on the sole occasion in which he knew one of the craft to be employed to poison rats in a dwelling-house, a demand for the surrender of the key of the 'silver hutch'—East Anglian for the plate-chest — in addition to those of all other rooms and receptacles possessing a lock in which poison might be laid, excited some not unnatural misgivings. He poisoned all the rats, which died under the floors of every room on the ground-floor, and gave employment for weeks to his friend the village joiner in ripping up and replacing planks ; and an intermittent crop of dead mice, which by preference chose the hearthstones as a suitable covering for their bodies, gave to the same rooms the aspect of a small pavior's yard at intervals for some months after. On the other hand, the rats, when allowed to resume their old quarters, made an immoderate use of victory. Food, linen, paper and carpets were devoured ; and screams from the larder from time to time announced the success of the great practical joke, so long familiar to successful rats, of leaping swiftly from a pie-dish when it was wanted for the servants' supper. Though the best that the house afforded was at their disposal, they were dainty and capricious in their appetites, taking infinite pains to secure what their fancy suggested might prove new and interesting, either as diet or furniture for their nests ; and the writer, after lying awake for hours listening to the operations of the enemy on a steep flight of stairs and in a wardrobe in the passage above, discovered in the last a couple of hard dumplings, made for the dog's breakfast, which had been carried up the stairs, and hoisted over a panel two feet high into this ancient piece of furniture. Deliverance came at last, not by human aid, but in the shape of the stable cat, which thereby won for itself a seat on the hearthrug, and a local reputation which rivalled that of its reputed ancestor owned by Sir Richard Whittington.

The sole virtue of rats in a house is that they drive out the mice. The long‑tailed and short‑tailed field-mice are chiefly gardeners' pests, eating the mushrooms, store-peas and bulbs, as well as the sown peas. They never touch any but *good* bulbs, and the knowing gardener feels a melancholy satisfaction when the mice pay marked attention to the stock he has selected. Those whose industry has led them to spend a vacation reading 'in College,' realise the full burden of the house mice when all those on the staircase 'trek' to the solitary student's room, and make merry on his stores. They, like the rats, have their own sense of humour. A landed proprietor of our acquaintance had invented a peculiar form of rent-audit for a set of 'small holdings.' He chalked a rough diagram of the 'plots' on a cupboard shelf, duly labelled with the names of the tenants, and deposited on each the sums paid in on Lady Day. The little piles of gold or silver were a visible witness to the punctual payment of his tenants; and among them was one new and crisp £5 note. The mice explored the cupboard also, and abstracted the note, leaving behind one or two small fragments which had been bitten off as samples.

The odious 'black beetle,' which is, properly speaking, not a beetle at all, is, like a number of other insect pests, not indigenous to England, though it is now a 'resident alien.' The only use which we ever heard found for black beetles, was to feed the first birds of paradise brought to England by ship from the Malay Archipelago. No four-footed creature that we know will eat them except the hedgehog, and cats, which are said to be poisoned by them. This is hardly strange, for everything which they touch is contaminated by their repulsive odour. Even hedgehogs are a failure, though tradition makes them thrive on cockroaches. An early ambition of the present writer's was to live in a house stocked with black beetles, in order to keep a hedgehog. At last this came about. The new house swarmed with the insects; and we had the luck to find a hedgehog in a cow-shed, and brought it home. It would not uncurl in the kitchen, so we put it in a dark cupboard, where there were enough of the creatures to 'feed right a great hog,' as the cook, who was disappointed in the animal's size, remarked disparagingly. But the hedgehog *never* uncurled. We looked at him night and day, and found beetles running over him, and speculating when they would begin to eat *him*. At last we carried him to the lawn, where he did move, and walked into the tennis-net, and had to be cut out, to the great destruction of the meshes. Black beetle killing is a limited but respectable calling in London; and a leading member of the craft sends his card round at intervals to owners of the larger mansions in London, to intimate that in his opinion the time has come when his services ought to be required in the houses which he has attended during many changes of ownership or occupation. One habit of the beetle, if the observers are correct, itself tends to their destruction. The eggs are carried under the body of the female, and not dropped at hap‑hazard. So that if the creatures are once exterminated, their quarters can only be repeopled by immigrants. On the other hand, it is asserted that the cockroach 'gums' its eggs in cases to the walls. Which of the statements is true, the writer has not yet been able to discover. It will be new to many readers that the mosquito is now firmly established in London. It is to be found in certain large hotels which are the resort of visitors coming from the Continent, and the supply seems to be maintained by constant importations from abroad. Visitors who are familiar with the noise and bite of the mosquito assert that it is the true pest in its worst form, and there is no reason for doubting their experiences. A ludicrous mistake in identity on this point recently occurred at a large colliery in the North of England. The men in a distant part of the mine complained that the work‑ings were full of 'mosquitos,' and refused to enter the gallery. As it takes something worse than a mosquito to frighten a collier, the manager went down to explore, and discovered, much to his amazement, that the workings were full of huge, hornet-like, yellow – banded flies, whose larvæ were hatching out from the wooden props which supported the roof in the warm atmosphere of the pit. The buzz and rustle of wings was indeed formidable, and the bite of the supposed 'mosquitos' would, by analogy, be something very terrible indeed.

RECENT RAT LORE

A JUROR in a coroner's inquest held recently in the East End complained that his attendance on the jury had cost him a sovereign. He explained that he was a rat-catcher in the Docks, and that a ship in which he had been employed to kill rats had sailed that morning, before he was able to return and call for his money. He explained that, unlike the coroner, he was paid by the job, and that unless that official would give him one, he should be out of pocket to the extent he named. The coroner, who apparently resented the rat-catcher's references to the practice and emoluments of their respective professions, only offered him sympathy, and not much of that, to which the rat-catcher sarcastically replied, 'Sympathy without help is like pudding without fat,' and left the court, declaring that next time he should refuse to serve unless paid.

The amount of the rat-catcher's earnings incidentally threw a light on the number of rats which

may be found on an outward-bound ship, even in
in these days of steel bulkheads and tinned provisions.
At twopence per head, the usual price paid for rats
killed, we gather that on this ship one hundred and
twenty were killed; enough to make the ship's company uncomfortable for the whole voyage, and to
damage any perishable cargo. The responsibility
would in this case lie with the shipowners. It is
not long since an insurance company refused to pay
damages claimed for a cargo of grain spoilt by water,
which had run in from pipes gnawed by rats, alleging
the negligence of the owners in not having them
destroyed—a contention in which they were partly
supported by the court.

The summer of 1895 saw a greater plague of rats
in large towns than has been known for many years.
The most striking instance of their numbers and
boldness was shown in the case in which they
attacked a family of children in Paisley, during
the great heat in the middle of September. The
accounts which appeared in the papers at the time
were somewhat exaggerated, but the following notes,
communicated to the writer by the senior house-
surgeon of the Paisley Infirmary, do not diminish the
interest of the story :—'The family, named Weaver,
lived in an old house, between which and a stable
next door there was free communication. Near the

house there was also a brewery. About 6·30 on the morning of September 18th, Mrs Weaver, hearing screams, got up, and found that her children—Patrick, nine years old ; John, four years old ; and Michael, two years old—were being attacked by a swarm of rats. The mother had some difficulty in driving off the rats, which were large brown ones. Patrick was bitten on the arms, fingers and nose ; John on both hands, the right being badly bitten ; and Michael on the cheek. The wounds were scratches and bites, the marks of teeth being in some places quite distinct, but none of the children were so badly hurt as to be detained in the infirmary. Except that in one case there was inflammation and swelling round the wounds, none of the children suffered any ill results.'

There is not the least doubt that the rats intended to eat these children, and would have gnawed and mangled them to death just as they do fowls and rabbits, and if help had not been at hand to drive them off when the pain made the children scream, they would probably have succeeded in killing the baby. The most curious fact of the story is that they deferred their attack until after sunrise, and that they were not afraid of the elder boy. As all three children probably occupied one bed, the rats may have failed to distinguish the difference in size between the boy of nine and the baby. In other respects the enterprise was conducted in the usual rat fashion when a raid is made on living animals, those attacked being bitten on all the exposed parts, and treated rather as food ready to be eaten than live creatures which need artistic killing. Ferrets, which have more than once attacked sleeping children, act on the principle which all true carnivora practise, and endeavour to attack a vital part by biting the veins in the neck. The exploit of the Paisley rats coincides in time with a great increase in the number and boldness of Thames-side rats, which was noted after the long drought and heat of September in the same year. Good houses near the river, which had formerly been exempt from the pests, were found to be full of the vermin when their owners returned from their autumn holiday.

Fresh holes were gnawed in doors and floors, and it was said that parties of rats were seen at night hopping down the water-side streets and disappearing through the gratings and down the areas. The 'water-famine' in part accounted for this. The drains and large sewers in the higher parts of North London were so dry that the rats moved down towards the river, where the level of the sewers is lower, and food and water more abundant. A great fire which raged among the warehouses on the Surrey side of the river in the middle of August, sent fresh recruits to the army of rats on the Middlesex shore. The bridges were crowded with sightseers, watching the line of wharves burning, when the river was seen to be covered with rats swimming across, from the direction of the burning buildings. The number was estimated at many thousands, and one of the crew of a river fire-engine, which was moored off the burning wharves, states that the greater number of the rats entered the water almost at the same time, apparently struck by some common and simultaneous conviction that safety could only be found on the opposite side of the Thames. The rural rat, partly because it is in the main a clean-living, 'outdoor' beast, does not inspire the repugnance which every one feels for the urban or 'sewer' rat. Its cleverness, its courage, and the audacity and cunning with which it maintains its position in the midst of dangers which would daunt any other wild creature, gain for it a measure of that admiration which is part of the tribute paid to depraved greatness. In its character as an outdoor wild animal, it has recently received compliments from such an accurate observer as Mr A. Trevor-Battye, while as a beast of the chase it is the subject of an admirable monograph—*Studies in Rat-catching*,* by Mr H. C. Barkley. Mr Barkley's book might, for minute detail and devotion to the

* Longmans & Co.

sport, have a place in the 'Badminton Series.' He describes and accounts for 'good' days and 'bad' with dogs and ferrets in the hedgerows, with a seriousness which would do credit to 'Brocklesby.'

The reason for this business-like treatment is to be found in the age of the writer when he engaged in these pursuits. As a boy, he had trained his dogs and ferrets so well, that his services were in request as a competent and paid rat-catcher; and the total of the day's earnings, at twopence per rat, is duly entered after the description of each day's sport. Old ladies living in large country houses used to send for him to devise means for ridding them of demon rats who baffled the regular practitioners, and the discoveries made in these visits are as curious as anything yet published in the history of household pests. In one case, a house was apparently perfectly free from rats, yet every night a rat came to the fowl-house, and carried off hen's eggs, or young ducks and chickens. Hedges, ditches, sheds, out-houses, and stables were examined with the aid of a trained dog, yet not a trace of a rat could be discovered. The dog was even made to run over the roofs of the buildings, in case the rats were lurking under the tiles. One afternoon, Mr Barkley requested that a dog, which was tied up in a kennel in a backyard, might be removed, as its barking disturbed his dogs when at work. As soon as the house dog was removed, one of Mr Barkley's terriers 'pointed' a rat, apparently under the kennel. No hole was visible, but the dog then entered the kennel, and 'pointed' a hole made through the floor. The predatory rat was found beneath, and as there was only one hole, it was evident that it must have passed and repassed the dog when asleep every night. In another house the dogs 'pointed' a sofa in a bed-room—a rat had eaten a hole through the sacking near one of the legs, and made a nest among the springs; a ferret was put in; 'there was a rush and a scuffle, the sofa seemed alive; then three or four small rats bolted out; another squeak and rush, and out came the mother, and then, as the ferret did not come out, I ripped open the sacking, and found it eating a tender young rat.' Church mice are common in the Eastern Counties, which were the scene of Mr Barkley's experiences; they are alleged to live on the samples of wheat and barley which the farmers pull out of their pockets at vestry meetings, and drop on the floor and desk. But Mr Barkley discovered, and in due course caught, a church-rat. He was amusing during the sermon, sitting on a bench opposite, a score of village school-children, when he was suddenly struck by the curious resemblance of expression—not in one, but in the whole row—

to that of his own dogs when they found a rat. He was reproaching himself with dreaming when he noticed that all the eyes were turned in one direction, and there he saw the cause—a rat, just peeping out of a hole in the brick floor, and apparently listening to the sermon. It was duly caught next day. Mr A. Trevor-Battye has watched the rats transporting eggs on level ground. They rolled them in front of them with their chests ; but the means by which they carry them unbroken up and down stairs, is not yet known. On the only occasion on which Mr Battye saw them try to do this, they broke the egg.

A BOOM IN ANIMAL LIFE

In the *Field* of February 22d 1896, the following
letter appeared from Sir R. Payne - Gallwey :—
'Sir, — I send you a cutting from the *Eastern
Morning News* of Feb. 10 which accurately describes
the extraordinary invasion of rats that has recently
invested 'Reed's Island,' in the estuary of the
Humber. This island consists, or rather *did* consist,
of 600 acres of very rich and valuable land (grass
and clover), formerly reclaimed from the sea. Four
or five years ago between 2000 and 3000 sheep and
cattle might be seen grazing on its then extremely
verdant surface. Now there exists scarce sufficient
pasture to feed one rabbit, and the entire island is
as brown and rough as a ploughed field from the
excavated earth thrown out of their burrows by the,
I may safely write, millions of rats. The island is
throughout as flat as a billiard-table, and is surrounded by earthen banks about 10 ft. in height

to keep out the sea. These banks were, last month, cut through in several places, and the apertures made were fitted with sluices to retain the tide on the island, which was then completely flooded. It was hoped, through this drastic measure, the rats would be drowned. The animals are, however, at present, masters of the situation, as though a few thousands, a trifle only of their numbers, have doubtless succumbed, the great majority have taken refuge in the broad banks, which, for their entire length of several miles, are so riddled with holes that they are like sieves. As the animals are the common water rat, I fear that the idea of drowning them is akin to trying to drown a fish. Starvation may eventually have some effect if their burrows and the ample store of roots to be seen laid up therein are covered with water ; but, rather than starve, the rats are sure to escape by swimming to the mainland, as many have done already, and we shall be no nearer an extirpation than now.

'Perhaps some of your readers can suggest an effective system of destruction. From more than one personal inspection, I consider that ferrets, trapping, smoking out, and terriers would be mere child's play, and make no impression on the myriads that are now on the island.

'As the burrows and underground runs are only

a few inches below the soil, perhaps deep ploughing or a heavy roller would have a good result.

'RALPH PAYNE-GALLWEY.'

The account referred to runs as follows :—

'The Humber Conservancy Commissioners have not yet solved the difficult problem of how to rid Reed's Island of the plague of rats that now infest it, nor are they—the most ready means, the flooding of the island having failed—likely to do so in a hurry. What a few year ago was a splendid pasture land, and sustained thousands of sheep in its rich verdure, is now the home of myriads of rats. It is burrowed from end to end, and so densely populated is this habitat of the rodent that it is said that it is almost impossible to put your foot down without standing upon a rat hole. It is only about a year ago that the rats got the upper hand, and the commissioners have of late been very much exercised as to the eviction of their unwelcome tenants. It was decided to cut openings in the banks which surround the island, and thus let in the Humber waters at spring tide, with a view to drowning master rat and his numerous family. The openings having been made at considerable expense, the water was let in a week ago last night, but not with the result anticipated. As the water advanced the rats fled from their holes in tens and hundreds of thousands, and made for the banks which remained high and dry. The screeching and snarling of the rats as they fought for foothold beggared description. Many were, doubtless, drowned by the inundation, but, being for the most part expert swimmers, the impression made in the numbers of the great army was practically nil. Adjudging rightly that a day's sport might be had shooting the vermin, a party of gentlemen went down on Saturday in the commissioner's launch, among them being Sir Ralph Payne-Gallwey, Col. Burstall, Mr Legard, Col. W. H. Wellsted, Mr M. Samuelson, Mr E. T. Sharp, Mr H. Saxelbye, Mr E. D. Davis, Capt. Hume (the Humber conservator), and others. Hundreds of rats succumbed to the firing of these gentlemen, and it was manifest that extraordinary measures will have to be taken to rid the island of the pest. The inundation seems to have done little good, and to shoot them down would be an impossibility. Poisoning has been thought of, but that is deemed of no value, since the Reed's Island rat appears to live on the roots of grass and herbs under which he burrows. Already considerable excitement prevails in North Lincolnshire, on account of the invasion of these rats. Nightly they swim across in swarms, notwithstanding that the channel between the island and the Lincolnshire coast is at least 500 yards wide.   Their 'footings' have been observed on the foreshore, and their location in fields hard by is certain.   The farmers are, however, almost helpless to check them, since they shun the stack-yards and granaries.   In fact, the rat of Reed's Island appears to be a rodent of an altogether different kind to the common rat with which we are familiar. He has a tail and hindquarters like the latter, but his head and ears are more like those of a cavy, while he has a soft furry skin of a rich tawny hue. It is said that in some places this kind of rat is bred in captivity for the sake of their rich skins, which are a marketable commodity.   Who knows, then, but what the rat plague of Reed's Island will not turn out the ill wind that will blow the com-missioners good?   A rat farm with such furry-skinned inhabitants might prove a little gold mine to them if it were only exploited.'

The rats of Reed's Island were, as the *Eastern Morning News* surmised, not grey rats, but water rats, or water voles, and one probable cause of their extraordinary increase was that this island, and another near it, had recently been overgrown with a dense crop of some succulent weed supposed to have been imported from a distance.

For the next season or two the 'boom' will probably continue. But the best evidence that this plague of water voles will be combated by a host of natural enemies suddenly rising round them, and, ultimately reduced to natural limits, is contained in the history of the vole plague in Scotland. This is contained in a *Blue Book*, giving the 'Report of the Committee, appointed by the Board of Agriculture, to inquire into the plague of field voles in Scotland.'

This Report is in many ways one of the best works on natural history which has appeared during the last few years. It gives at length, and in admirable arrangement, the first-hand observations of men who spend their lives on the moors of the Scottish Border — shepherds, foresters, gamekeepers, farmers and naturalists, often in language as quaint as that of Dandie Dinmont. The whole question of the natural or unnatural increase and decrease of wild animals in a wide district has been the subject of the most careful inquiry and evidence. The numbers, lives and habits of such creatures as weasels, voles, sparrow-hawks, kestrels, stoates, short-eared and other owls, rooks, ravens, rats, rabbits, moles, pheasants, grouse, merlins, hobbys, herons, gulls, foxes, crows, buzzards, falcons, badgers, and even snakes and adders, have been deposed to by men whose solitary and serious lives on the upland sheep farms afford them few other distractions than those which may be obtained from watching the ways of the wild creatures, which, except their masters' flocks, are the only inhabitants of the moorlands. Excellent bird portraits, by Mr George Lodge, so well known for his illustrations of scenes in the hawking field, serve to emphasise the distinction between the useful kestrel and the destructive sparrow-hawk, and introduce the reader to the short-eared owl, which has now settled in numbers in the vole-infested region; and if the mind wearies of the woes of the Scottish dalesmen, the description of the visit of the enterprising chairman, Sir Herbert Maxwell, and of the secretary, Mr Harting, to the vole-infested plains of Thessaly, presents a picture of the impact of the restless West on the brooding East which cannot fail to raise a smile. The chairman of 'your Committee' landing, eager to see the results of the introduction of the 'mouse-typhus bacillus' among the voles, was met by a steamer chartered by Turkish landowners to bring holy water from Mecca to sprinkle the infected district! According to the evidence of Mr David Glendinning, a shepherd, the short-eared owls and weasels increased in numbers almost proportionate to those of the voles. Speaking of the latter, he says, 'I followed a weasel which was hunting voles up one of the sheep-drains. I followed it up, and it was killing its sixth. A week past, on Sunday morning, I came down a drain for 250 yards or so. A weasel had been before me, and there were twenty-two dead voles in the bottom. I kept a specimen last night to show you the way a weasel destroys a vole. The blood is entirely drawn from below the left ear. There is not a bit of the vole marked otherwise, except by the teeth-marks on the head.' Another shepherd had counted fourteen nests of short-eared owls on his ground, and stated that a small wood behind the farm of Howparley presented a remarkable appearance, his ground being thickly covered with the 'castings' of owls, composed of the fur and bones of voles. The Committee state that 'it would be difficult to condemn too severely the foolish and cruel action of those who allow or encourage the destruction of this useful and beautiful family of birds,' and note that many landowners have issued orders for their preservation. Next to the owl, and hardly second in merit, as a check upon voles and mice, comes the kestrel. Yet its death-warrant is a standing order in most preserves, and the Committee feel so strongly on the subject, that the following portions of a keeper's evidence are embodied in their Report :—

' Why did you kill the kestrel ? Well, it was an enemy of the game, of course, and that is why I killed it. How long have you been a gamekeeper ? Six or seven years. How often have you seen a kestrel take game ? Many a time. What kind of game ? Young pheasants. Had you many young pheasants at West Buccleuch ? No. Then why did you kill the kestrel ? Because they will kill young grouse. Did you ever see them take young grouse ? No. Did anybody of your acquaintance ever see them take young grouse ? No ; but I have heard of their taking young grouse. Would you believe a man if he said that he saw a kestrel taking young grouse ? Yes, if he said it I would. Any man ? Yes, if he was not drunk.'

Against this may be set the evidence of the head-keeper at Drumlanrig, where kestrels, as well as owls, are preserved by order of the Duke of Buccleuch that in his experience of over thirty years he thought that he could only remember twice seeing a kestrel take a young pheasant. Buzzards, which on the occasion of a former plague of voles, assembled in numbers almost as great as those of the short-eared

HAWK KILLING A WILD DUCK.
From a Japanese woodcut.

owls, are nearly extinct ; but these large hawks, with the smaller sea-gulls, owls, and kestrels, are scheduled as deserving complete preservation, being harmless to sheep, crops and game.

Ravens, hoodie-crows, great black-backed gulls, and foxes have always had an evil reputation among shepherds. Weakly lambs dropped among the hills suffer wherever any of their species are found. But strange to say, the rook is now an object of suspicion, not only to game preservers, but to farmers on the Border. It was matter of general complaint in the evidence, that the rook has changed its habits, concurrently with the appearance of the voles, and become almost as disreputable a bird as the hoodie-crow. ' It is not madness,' said Mr Bumble, accounting for the audacity of Oliver Twist, ' it's *meat.*' ' So,' within the last ten years—that is since their dish of voles became habitual—the rooks in the district ' have developed marked carnivorous habits ; taking eggs, young birds, young poultry, hares and rabbits, and so forth, to an extent which they never did before.' Consequently, though the rook is by far the most deadly enemy to the voles, digging out their nests and eating their young by thousands, when they visit the hills, the forays on game and poultry in the low ground have led to their wholesale destruction. Perhaps the most remarkable evi-

dence as to this change of habit in the rook, is to
be seen in the physical alteration which accompanies
it. 'Along with this increase of carrion-crow-like
habits, there has been a great increase of rooks with
feathered faces.' These birds are quite unlike the
ordinary rook, which has a bare white patch at the
base of the bill. Many specimens were exhibited
before the Committee, and in an engraving by Mr
Lodge, which appears in the Report, the face of the
'carnivorous' rook can hardly be distinguished from
that of the crow. Whether the destruction of the
voles does not more than counterbalance the damage
done by demoralised rooks, is for the farmers and
landowners of the district to decide. But now
that a competent and impartial tribunal has pronounced for the complete protection of the owl, the
kestrel, and the buzzard, and the smaller sea-gulls, it
is not too much to hope that a clause may be added
to the Wild Birds' Protection Act which may preserve them, not only in certain months, or in particular districts, but at all times and in all counties
of the Kingdom.

THE MODERN ART OF BIRDSNESTING

THE winter publishing season of 1895-6 produced two books of special interest to outdoor naturalists.* These are Mr Kearton's photographs of the nests and young of birds, and Mrs Blackburn's drawings of the birds of Moidart. Among the latter are some of the best and most original portraits of the young of birds ever painted. Mr Kearton's work is, perhaps, more new in form. He has taken his camera to the hedgerow, the mountain, and the loch-side, and photographed the nests *in situ*. An examination of these beautiful pictures explains in part why it is that 'birdsnesting' is so attractive an art. They recall a hundred forgotten details of the minor beauty of the country, and enable us to estimate in some degree how much positive beauty, as well as charm of association, go to make up the pleasure of a day's birdsnesting.

* (1.) *British Birds' Nests*. With Original Illustrations. By R. and C. Kearton. London : Cassell and Co.—(2.) *Birds of Moidart*. By Mrs Blackburn. Edinburgh : D. Douglas.

The greater number of these photographs of nests 'compose' naturally into a picture. Some seem almost too perfect; yet no one who has found such nests himself will fail to realise their truth. Take, for example, a coot's nest, on the top of a single tussock, with the delicate, upright flowers, stems of the grass, rising straight above it; while the lower leaves fall off like bending sheaves of corn. The difference of nest position and surroundings is shown in the two examples of the moorhen's nest. One, in early spring, set among the bare alder stumps, the other—a common example—in a bed of upright water flags. The broad-bladed leaves rise vertically all round it, but some have been crushed down to form the nest, and others bent horizontally across to screen it from view above.* The wonderful beauty of hawthorn foliage is best shown in the pictures of the blackbirds, greenfinches, and hedge-sparrows; of the leaves of the oak, in that of the turtle-dove. The bullfinch's nest is embowered in hawthorn and wild-rose leaves. The reed-bunting's nest gives the wealth of growth in the damp ditches crowded with rank grass, nettle, and lovely stems

---

* Mr Kearton informs the writer that this particular nest was so well concealed from the view of anyone looking at it from above, that half-a-dozen country boys, who were wading about in the marsh looking for nests, failed to discover it.

of meadow-sweet. Tree tops—seen from a point of view which brings them level with the eye—are to most a reminiscence of boyish days of climbing. To photograph the larger nests—crow's, heron's, magpie's, and sparrow-hawk's—Mr Kearton climbed the neighbouring trees, lashed his camera to the boughs, and so presents us with a true 'bird's-eye view' of the site. Some of these pictures are as decorative as the Japanese studies of trees, notably one of a magpie's nest in a straggling pine. Then down to earth again, and we see the kingfisher's hole beneath the bank, taken from the middle of the River Mole, the artist being knee-deep in water. All the pretty rusticity of thatchroofs, straw-built sheds, old orchard trees, the homes of starlings, missel-thrushes, and tits, are here,—things only studied closely by the prying birdsnester.

The great incident of a day's birdsnesting in the woodland and hedgerow districts is the discovery of a cuckoo's egg. Pure luck, and nothing else, in most cases leads to this success, and, as in other enterprises, this present of Fortune is perhaps unduly valued. But it lends as much excitement as the chance woodcock does to a day's covert-shooting. On Whit-Monday 1895, the writer, according to custom, spent the morning in seeking nests, and the only egg found was a cuckoo's. The fact was unusual in itself; but the circumstances were such as to suggest a doubt whether the cuckoo is as clever as is supposed. The place was a perfect site for the smaller common birds to build. A spring broke out in a sloping meadow, filling a deep pool, while the high banks were surrounded with pollard willows, tall elms, and low ivy-covered stumps and bushes. But the long frost of last January had killed off nearly all the indigenous birds, except a few thrushes, whose nests had been robbed by the village boys. In the ivy growing on a pollard with a thorn bush round its trunk, was a hedge-sparrow's nest, so ragged and dilapidated that it was obviously deserted, though the moss of which it was built was still green enough to suggest that it might be a nest of the year. The lining was out of place, and filled the inner cup with untidy rubbish. No birdsnester, certainly no sensible bird, would have given a second look at it, viewed in the light of a 'going concern.' The writer felt in the untidy lining to ascertain if the young had been hatched out, in which case some fragments of shell might have been left at the bottom. Instead, deep among the dishevelled lining, was an egg. It was a fresh cuckoo's egg, just laid. It could never have been hatched, and it was clearly a case, perhaps one of many, in which cuckoo tactics lead to failure. This was not the only curiosity in the nest. It was, partly lined with fragments of newspaper wadded into the fabric. Some of these when taken out proved to be part of the financial column of a daily paper, which, when pieced together, were found to be from the list of South-African Gold-Mining shares, including some of the popular favourites, such as 'City and Suburban,' 'Croesus,' 'Crown Reef,' 'Durban Roodsport,' 'Ferreira,' and 'Geldenhuis.' Those who seek omens from birds may perhaps find a field for conjecture in this 'selection' by a hedge-sparrow, near the White Horse Hill. Mr Kearton's picture of a wagtail's nest containing a cuckoo egg shows the former set in a bower of ivy leaves, growing on a garden wall. It is a beautiful study, both from the grace with which the leaves fall, and the contrast of the nest with the dark background. Turning from this to Mrs Blackburn's drawings, we find a most interesting first-hand confirmation of an account of the behaviour of the very young cuckoo, given by Sir William Jenner in a letter to John Hunter in 1788. Jenner wrote that the 'little animal, with the assistance of its rump and wings, contrived to get the bird (a young hedge-sparrow) on its back, and making a lodgment for it by elevating its elbows, clambered back with it up the side of the nest till it reached the top, where, resting for a moment, it threw off its load with a jerk, and quite disengaged

it from the nest. . . . . . it remained in this situation a short time, feeling about with the extremity of
its wing, as if to be convinced that the business was
properly executed, and then dropped back into the
nest again.' This was a *newly-hatched* cuckoo; and
even Waterton rejected the story as incredible. Mrs
Blackburn saw the same operation, and not only
describes it, but has drawn the scene with wonderful
skill. The almost blind, naked cuckoo, with its head
so big and neck so weak that the former drops forward as if it were dead, is standing almost on tiptoe
backing a half-fledged young pipit out of the nest.
'The most singular thing,' she writes, 'was the way
in which the blind little monster made for the open
side of the nest, the only part where it could throw
its burden down the bank. I think all the spectators
were struck with horror and awe at the apparent
inadequacy of the creature's intelligence to its acts.'

Both Mr Kearton and Mrs Blackburn have
pictures of eagles' nests. Of the two, the latter is
the more interesting. The pencil has beaten the
camera. But Mr Kearton's photograph was taken
under great difficulties. It shows a pair of downy
eaglets, lying flat on a 'messy' nest of small twigs
and rubbish, with a half-plucked mountain hare beside
them. Mrs Blackburn was able to draw her eaglet
from a rock close by; and she has added what is

necessarily an impressionist picture, but one of great interest and obvious truth, of the attack made by the old birds on a pair of collie dogs which accompanied a shepherd to the top of the cliff, not many feet above the eyrie. The eagles look heavy and 'lumpy,' just as they do in some of the old Greek sculptures of eagles carrying prey, striking awkwardly, with the feet brought under and forward, like a game-cock spurring. The snarling, snapping dogs are also admirably drawn. Nesting sea birds and wild ducks have always been favourite subjects with photographers, from their tameness and stillness when sitting. But no more interesting scene has ever been represented than that of the gannets' nests on a ledge on Ailsa Craig, photographed in the clear light at four o'clock in the morning of an early summer day. The adventure had its dangers, and the story of the picture is typical of the difficulties, as well as of the success, of this new form of birdsnesting. 'In getting down to the edge of the cliff,' writes Mr R. Kearton, 'my brother placed too much dependence upon the stability of a large slab of rock, which commenced to slither down the terribly steep hillside at a great pace directly it received his additional weight. He narrowly managed to save himself and the camera, with which he was encumbered at the time, from being shot over the lip

T

of the precipice into the sea below.' Then the screw fastening the camera to the tripod fell out, and it had to be fixed by some strong wing-feathers picked up on the crag; and 'while the artist held the camera to the tripod, the writer, from a more secure footing, held the artist by the coat-tails on to the Craig.' The picture is notable in its way, showing the steplike cliff, the single sitting bird, and the infinite distance of silvery sea. The pictures of the red-throated diver's nest, by a Scotch lakeside, of the razor-bill's and other sea birds' eggs on flower-adorned shelves of rock, are admirable; and of its kind we have never seen anything so charming as the newly-hatched goslings of the grey-leg geese among the deep heather. But these are matched by Mrs Blackburn's drawings of the young black guillemots—perhaps the best picture of young birds of any kind which has yet been published. For living objects, even birds, the pen and the brush are still first. But for such 'cameos' from natural history as the nests of birds in their natural setting, Dr Bowdler Sharpe's judgment on Mr Kearton's photographs will not be questioned. They 'mark a new era' in the illustration of natural history.

HOMES FOR WILD BIRDS

Though Aldrovandus declared that storks would only build their nests in free Republics, there is little doubt that modern birds are less particular; and if anyone wishes to increase the number and variety of birds near a house, the one thing needful is to provide them with suitable nesting-places. Nearly all our garden birds migrate more or less during the winter, and there is not the least doubt that when travelling, they, like ourselves, often say : 'What a capital place for a house!' If the tempting spot is met with in springtime, they instantly establish themselves there, and will remain, either as permanent tenants, or, if they are migrants, until the autumn sends them once more across the sea. A good example of this occurred during the year 1894. The severe cold forced all the bullfinches to move southwards, and for months the handsome red-breasted cocks and their darker mates thronged the hedgerows in the Vale of the White Horse.

The meadow-land in the Vale abounds in the tall, dense thorn fences in which these birds like to build, and in the spring so many of these immigrant bull-finches were tempted to stay, that four times the usual number of nests were found near one village, with the bird - population of which the writer has long had an intimate acquaintance. In one garden in the Vale, more than thirty kinds of birds build annually, mainly because some pains are taken to secure them a variety of nesting-places. Dead limbs are not sawn from the apple trees in the orchard, and in them the nuthatches chisel out their homes. Nettles are left to grow under the rooks' trees, and the whitethroats like these almost as well as the wild-rose bushes for their delicate nests. Branches that have been pruned from an overhanging elder are left upon the ground near the paths for the blackcaps to nest in when the wild hemlock has grown up through them, and the heavy masses of ivy left cling-ing round elm, birch and fir, give shelter to wrens and greenfinches, blackbirds and wood pigeons, and later, to the turtle-doves. But many of those who wish to entice the birds to build would hardly care to obtain this result by the simple but effective plan of letting things alone. A little ingenuity will secure the same objects, without incurring the reproach of ' untidiness.' Artificial nesting - places can easily be

made, and these 'eligible building sites' need no advertisements to secure tenants for the ground land-lord. Charles Waterton was perhaps the most successful founder of bird colonies ever known, and made Walton Hall a real paradise for his favourite tenants. He had a special tower, so built that no rat could gain access to it, for the starlings; and many pairs of owls, both brown and white, took possession of the holes which he excavated for them in the elm trees. Whenever he saw one of the large bracket fungi growing from the stem of a tree, the first sign that the centre of the trunk has begun to decay, he used with mallet and chisel to cut a circular opening, and scoop out a cavity in the half-rotten wood within. This made a dry and warm nesting-place which no owl could resist, and a pair used nearly always to occupy it before a year had passed. No bird was ever killed in the park, and hawks and owls nested in the same trees with stock-doves and woodpigeons. No doubt the hawks sometimes killed their neighbours; but hawks, as St John rightly observed, seldom interfere with birds nesting close to their own eyrie, though ruthlessly destroying the same species at a little distance. But all ground vermin, especially rats, were exterminated by Waterton, who built a high wall round his park to keep them out, paying for it by the wine he did *not* drink.

Though modern acquaintance with the nesting of the storks obliges us to forego the old belief in their special love for lands of freedom, there can be no question that in the greatest of all Republics, the United States, the desire to protect birds and to attract to the home and garden, has taken the form of a national sentiment. In the New England States, besides the strict laws passed for the preservation of the birds themselves, and against the robbing of their nests, special homes are provided where they may bring up their young in safety. These retreats are known as 'bird houses,' and nearly every human dwelling, whether mansion or cottage, possesses one of them. Some are built in the most elaborate and fantastic styles of architecture, while others are no more than a cigar box with a hole in the end. But usually a great deal of rather misplaced ingenuity is expended on the bird-houses, and the New Englanders delight to have opposite their windows a model of a church or a large hotel, with doors, windows and floors, painted white or some bright colour, and stuck upon a pole where all men may behold it. Sometimes a whole village decides to put up a bird house as a public edifice, in which case the size, paint and architecture are very grand indeed. But these houses, which would answer to all the varieties named in the children's game of fortune, 'Church, castle, cottage, out-house, barn,' are in high favour with such birds as build naturally in nooks and corners of farm buildings or holes in walls and trees. Their most frequent tenants in the New England States are the bluebird, the house-wren, the purple martin and the sparrow, a 'resident alien' imported from England. 'The first to arrive from the South,' writes an American friend 'is the bluebird, which in the States is looked upon much as the robin red-breast is in England, on account of its beauty, its tameness and its song. The male arrives before his mate; generally about the middle of February. If the weather turns cold, he disappears again, but by the end of March both birds are generally established in the room in the bird house which they occupied the year before. Soon after the nest is finished, another visitor arrives from the South. This is the house-wren, a larger bird than its English name-sake. The wrens often try to drive out the blue-birds, and take every opportunity of their absence to pop into the hole, and steal or throw away the sticks and moss collected by the previous tenant. But both are often driven out by the sparrows. who maintain their post against all comers. The last visitor is the purple martin, which is such a universal favourite that even the wild Indians hang up a gourd or a calabash under the roof of their huts for the bird to nest in. This martin is larger than a swift, with plumage of a lovely deep purple, and is a bold and unflinching assailant of hawks, or even of the eagle itself, if it comes near the nest.'

In England, as in America, most birds that build in holes can be easily attracted by anything like a box with a hole in the side. Woodpeckers, nuthatches and wrynecks nearly always prefer to hollow out a hole for themselves ; and a few dead branches, or even dead trees left in the garden, will nearly always attract one or the other. The wrynecks always like a dead willow better than any other tree. If there is a pond, waterhens are sure to know of it, for they are great travellers, especially at night ; and a pair are almost certain to take possession of it, if there are one or two bushes on the bank with boughs just touching the water, so that they may form a basis for the floating nest. But the birds most wanted in a garden are all those warblers which come to us during the spring and summer. They are the most useful, for they are exclusively insect-eaters, and the most charming, for, except the chiff-chaff, they all sing sweetly. They can be won over with ease, for they come to us on purpose to nest ; and every cock-bird that arrives selects some pleasant spot, where his mate, when he has won her by outsinging his rivals, can build her nest. The redstart, the most beautiful of them all, will nest in the boxes ; the blackcap and garden-warbler, the best songsters after the nightingale, are very fond of bramble bushes, and a few long runners planted in the corner of a shrubbery will soon find a tenant. The nightingales are harder to entice, for they insist on thicker covert, if possible in the neighbourhood of oak trees, with the dead leaves of which the nest is always finished ; but they may be invited by keeping a piece of coppice or clump of shrubs cut low, and so forcing them to grow close and bushy. It is by no means necessary that the spot shall be a retired one, for small birds during the nesting season are almost indifferent to men. The writer knew of a nightingale which nested in a window box, and has found many nests within a few feet of a path. Only one precaution need be observed —the birds must not be frequently disturbed, nor the eggs handled. Rooks are probably more often the object of direct request for the 'honour of their company' than any other bird ; but the writer cannot recall a single instance in which such invitations have been successful. Probably a few sham nests put in suitable trees might attract the young birds driven from neighbouring rookeries ; but they are more exacting and particular than any other species as to their choice of a residence. For the following story the writer could give both place and date if necessary.   A farmer drove away his neighbour's rooks from a rookery by placing carrion in one or two of the nests.   Six years later their enemy's farm was sold and occupied by a new owner, and in the next spring the birds came to the house and built a large rookery close to it.   Some rooks taken out lately to Australia met a curious fate.   They had completed their moult when shipped, but on arriving in the splendid aviary built for them, were affected by the hot weather, and moulted again.   The exhausting effect of the double moult seems to have gradually killed off the whole colony.

But few birds besides the rook can resist one or other of the attractions which we have described, and some such provision is now needed ; for the tendency of a growing population is to banish bird-life, not in England, as in France, by killing the birds, but by destroying their nesting-places.   In the fruit-growing part of Kent, for instance, the copsewood which sheltered the warblers is giving place to currant and gooseberry plantations, and the hedges are being cut into formal lines.   Yet a family of young white-throats will do more to clear the bushes of insects than the most skilful ' garden hand ' in the county.

THE BASIS OF ANIMAL MYTH

THE awakening of interest in the emotions and intelligence of animals in the present era, is a natural reaction from the theories of Buffon and his school, that they were, so far as mind is concerned, mere automata, working out innate ideas without conscious intelligence. But Buffon's position was in its turn the result of a reaction from the 'myths' of the mediæval naturalists, who culling these stories from the works of Pliny, that great reservoir of lies about animals, used them for their own purposes, and bequeathed this *corpus* of nonsense to the travellers who, when the exploring impulse began in the sixteenth century, found themselves equipped with this singularly useless stock of 'facts' to guide them in their observations. Yet the mediæval naturalists were industrious after a fashion, and we must consider the difference of aim with which they wrote, contrasted with the modern treatment of natural history. Mr Edward Hulme, in his *Natural History Lore and Legend*,* notes that, 'In the books of travels we occasionally have the more modern and descriptive treatment; but the main bulk of the writings on animals in mediæval times had ordinarily one of two objects—the healing of the body, or the saving of the soul.' Hence the medical writers sought for the 'virtues' contained in animals, and were far less anxious to describe the form or habits of a creature than the spot at the back of its eye, where lay a stone which cured rheumatism; while the clergy, borrowing from and spoiling Æsop, sought for a moral from the creature's habits; and if the facts did not lend themselves readily to this treatment, so much the worse for the facts. Mr Hulme quotes Hippeau on St Augustine. 'L'objet important pour nous, dit Saint Agustin, à propos de l'aigle, qui, disait on, brise contre la pierre l'extrémité de son bec devenu trop long, est de considérer la signification d'un fait, et non en discuter l'authenticité.' This line of thought produced the monkish 'bestiaries,' which gave a kind of credit derived from religion to fables, which otherwise would not have been taken seriously. To this class of animal myth belong the greater number of beliefs in 'antipathies' between certain animals—in the feud between the dragon and

* Quaritch, London.

the elephant, though this may possibly be based on stories of elephants being attacked by crocodiles when drinking, and that between the polypus and the lobster. The moral carried by the assumption that moles only open their eyes when about to die was also too good to encourage inquiry into facts, though the belief is not more inaccurate than the common notion of countrymen to-day, that moles' ears are under their arm-pits. The effects of the monkish treatment of natural history reached far beyond the period in which its uses were consciously applied. It was carried on, like a spent shot, and fell into the commonplace of later commentary. As late as 1761, we find the following notes published in Cruden's *Concordance*, under the heads of 'Dragon' and 'Serpent' —'As to the dragons which are talked of, and are often mentioned in books, they are for the most part only old serpents grown with age to a prodigious size. Some are described with wings, feet, claws, crest, and heads of different figures. There is no question but there are winged serpents. . . . . . Real dragons, by Solimus' account of them, have a small mouth and cannot bite ; or, if they do, their biting is not venomous.' 'It is further said of the serpent's subtilty, that it stops up its ears that it may not hear the voice of the charmer. It is said that it applies one of its ears to the ground, and stops up the other with the end of its tail. Others say that the subtilty of the serpent consists in its agility and suppleness ; or in a secret which it has of recovering its sight by the use of fennel.'

Beside the impossible stories of the bestiaries are found another set of 'myths' mainly based on facts, and only distorted by the 'uneven mirror' to which Bacon likened certain phases of the human understanding. 'The pelican fed its young with its own blood.' Pelicans have a habit of trimming their breast feathers with their sharp, hooked beak. The plumage is of a pinkish hue, especially on the breast and when the feathers are wet. The 'moral' supplied the rest. 'Young bears suck their paws for food.' Bear-cubs do suck their paws, making an odd humming noise the while ; the Caucasian bear-cubs at the Zoo did so till they were three months old ; and though bears do not 'lick their young into shape,' which Sir Thomas Browne questioned on *à priori* grounds, the Polar bears do hibnerate when pregnant, and produce very small cubs, which they nourish under the snow, according to the evidence of Eskimo hunters. Popular ignorance on what is now the commonplace of natural history was such, even in late mediæval days, that there existed none of the ordinary checks on the misstatements of writers. It seems hardly possible that the appearance of a tiger should be unknown to any educated person in the sixteenth century. Yet in a fine illustrated natural history, published in the middle of that century, it is clear from the engravings that the artist did not know what a tiger was. He carefully read the Latin description of its appearance and habits, and was struck by a remark that it was a creature which leapt upon its victims from behind rocks. So he engraved a block representing animals of the size of large ferrets, with cats' heads, jumping through the air like a shoal of flying fish. Basilisks, cockatrices, and dragons, which were treated of at equal length with fleas, hedgehogs, and hawks, presented no difficulties to the artist. Their form and colour were as well established as that of the unicorn which supports the Royal Arms, and drawing and letterpress agreed. The danger from gigantic squids was well known and naturally exaggerated by the early voyagers. Here the illustrators were again at fault. In a very old edition of *Olaus Magnus*, the squid is represented as an enormous lobster, picking the crew out of a ship with its claws. The artist thus perverts a story which was based on truth into a myth, by substituting a species which does not grow to a gigantic size, for the octopus, which does. One of the most persistent of the explorers' myths is that of the *remora*, the gigantic sucking-fish, which stuck to the bottom of ships and prevented their progress. It was the nightmare of early voyagers, who seem to have entertained a genuine belief in its existence, though no one had ever seen a larger species than the common sucking-fish of the size of a mackerel. But there was no reason why such a creature should not exist. Voyagers encountered many kinds of whale, grampus, shark, and walrus, of a size far greater than that of the fish and seals of waters nearer home. Every day the ship's bottom grew fouler, and her speed less, and nervous tension found in a gigantic *remora* the most probable solution of the delay. The 'glutton' is another subject of Northern myth; there is no foundation for its alleged excesses in eating, or for other curious habits chronicled by mediæval naturalists; but these stories are still current among the Samoyeds, and were quoted by the voyagers just as they heard them. Milton, in his 'Moscovia,' mentions the creature by its Samoyed name, 'rossomakka.'

The early naturalists could not afford to disregard stories derived from native sources; but they gave them with too little qualification. Herodotus gave currency to animal 'myths,' some of which have been shown to be based on fact, while others seem *à priori* impossible. The story of the pygmy race in Africa, and of the pygmies fighting the cranes (Bush-men and ostriches), is always quoted to his credit. But the detailed story of the ants 'larger than dogs, but smaller than foxes,' which made ant-hills of gold dust, has yet found no rational or probable solution in the facts of natural history. Yet there is no reason to think that the ancients looked on the story of the 'golden ants' as at all more improbable than that of the pygmies. On the contrary, there is evidence that they thought the latter a very childish tale. Perhaps they were right in not rejecting the first. The Brazilian beetles recently shown at the Zoo were so exactly like gold buttons that they were daily mistaken for the 'real article,' and the keeper's attention was drawn to the fact that there were some buttons under the glass case. 'Golden beetles' are less probable than gold-hoarding ants, and in Little Thibet the gold found after storms is still called 'ant-gold,' from a belief that the insects remove the earth from above it. Modern incredulity for a time refused to believe in Bruce's discovery, of the tsetse-fly, though it was carefully described and pictured in his account of his African travels. The story of a fly 'which kills horses but cannot hurt donkeys,' was so exactly in the style of Herodotus

that it was rejected with derision.   No mediæval
naturalist would have refused the account of the
'tsetse-fly' a place in his pages, any more than he
did that of the 'oxen-born bees,' whose history and
modern extension of range to the New World have
recently been investigated by a Russian diplomatist.*
Mediæval natural history is now mainly interesting
to the student who uses it to check the progress
of ancient voyages and travel.   But from the journals
of the old discoveries, and even in those of Columbus,
it will be found that these beliefs had practical effects
on the conduct and guidance of early exploration.

* Baron C. R. Osten Sacken.

OMENS FROM BIRDS

WHILE the war between Japan and China was at its height, the Secretary-General of the Imperial Cabinet of Japan and a Member of the House of Peers presented to the Mikado a memorandum of 'an unprecedentedly auspicious omen,' which occurred just after the naval battle off the Yaloo River. The narrator further translated his memorandum into English, and forwarded it to the editor of the *Times*, so that we were able to learn at first hand what omen it was that impelled the composition of this unique document. After noting that history records many instances of sacred birds giving auspicious signs for, and assisting in, the triumph of the Imperial armies over rebels and enemies, the most remarkable being that when the Emperor Jimmu was marching against Nagasunehiko, 'a crow of dazzling brilliance perched upon the point of his bow, and the Imperial host gained a complete victory,' he adds, 'a similar mysterious incident has recently taken place. In the autumn of the present year, after a great naval engagement on the Yaloo, a hawk descended on the mast of one of his Majesty's ships. The undersigned, his Majesty's humble servant, has had the great honour to have a glance at this sacred bird at the Imperial military headquarters, where official duty requires his daily attendance. With eyes brilliant like gold, claws glittering like jewels, the bill sharp like a sword, and wings stout and strong to perfection, it has a lordly air and doughty carriage, as if ready to cause the whole feathered fraternity of China to tremble with fear.' The facts of the hawk's descent upon the ship are given, after this literary excursus, in a very businesslike fashion, much as Livy would narrate a *prodigium*, taken from the records of the augurs' college. 'It was nearly dark when the battle ceased. Just then something was observed to descend from the sky with great force, and hover over his Majesty's ship 'Takachiho,' and finally perch upon the top of her mainmast, when it was observed to be a hawk. The commander of the ship ordered one of the men to ascend and seize the hird. The latter, dropping its head, did not attempt to move, but seemed glad to be caught.' Then follows a comment exactly in the spirit of a Roman annalist. 'It was naturally welcomed as heaven's messenger, and it was decided to keep it alive with care.' There was no fresh meat in the vessel, and the ship's company, who had been fighting their vessels all the afternoon, 'were soon in a bustle to hunt for rats,' a circumstance which is properly noted as evidence of the 'inexhaustible energy of the officers and men of the Imperial Navy.' To wind up a battle with a rat-hunt is a form of exuberance which is not recorded even of British seamen. For the omen, such as it was, came not when men's nerves were over-strung with the expectation of battle, or to cheer them in the fight, but just at the moment of reaction, when even Marryat admits that the energies of a ship's company are at their lowest. The Japanese captain had the instinct of a great commander. Neither pious Æneas nor Julius Cæsar could have 'accepted the omen' at a more auspicious moment. When Rodney engaged De Grasse in the 'Ville de Paris,' at the great battle off Martinique, we read that the British Admiral 'had on board a favourite bantam-cock, which stood perched upon the poop of the "Formidable" during the whole action; its shrill voice crowing through the thunder of the broadsides.' This was an even happier omen than that of the hawk, but we do not hear that the bantam was sent to head-quarters, or even mentioned in the *Gazette*. But by

this time the omen of the bird is published to the
whole Japanese Army. The hawk has been named
by the Mikado himself, after the vessel on which
it was caught, the first syllable of the ship's name
meaning 'falcon,' and it is accepted as a 'special
manifestation of heavenly favour, and a sign of the
continued success of the Imperial arms.' The appeal
made by this omen is easily understood, for the
Japanese, if shaken in their fidelity to religion as
represented by Buddhism, are still firm in their
belief in direct communication between man and
unseen beings, whether disembodied spirits or angels.
Only recently the Mikado quieted a factious opposi-
tion in Parliament by communicating his knowledge
that the spirits of his ancestors were disturbed by
such unseemly strife ; and the common people are
not only superstitious, but steeped in symbolism, in
which birds and flowers are constantly associated.
Hawks and eagles are the favourite subjects of
much of the religious as well as secular painting ;
and it must be noted that the omen that followed
the Yaloo battle came in the form which all natural
sentiment prescribes for such manifestations.

It is the single bird that the human mind always
tends to look on as the bird of portent. It is the
οἰωνός — the lone-flying, solitary creature descending
from the sky, which was regarded as the manifest

and direct messenger from heaven. Two such birds
might occasionally appear together in particular circumstances, such as the two eagles which appeared
to the Greeks at Aulis when under the joint command of Agamemnon and Menelaus. The true
spirit of bird-augury is given in Coleridge's 'Ancient
Mariner' more completely than even in the many
passages in which Virgil treats of it. The circumstances in which the albatross appeared, were just
those in which such a sign appears to the minds of
men. The ship was 'in the land of the ice and of
fearful sounds, where no living thing was to be seen.'
Then the sailors saw the solitary bird of omen :—

> At length did cross an albatross ;
> Through the fog it came
> As if it had been a Christian soul,
> We hailed it in God's name.'

Like the Japanese hawk, it would not leave the
ship :—

> ' In mist or cloud, on mast or shroud,
> It perched for vespers nine,
> Whiles all the night through fog-smoke white,
> Glimmered the bright moonshine.'

The whole action of the poem turns on the 'accepta-
tion ' of the omen by the sailors, and their subsequent

condonation of its being killed after the nature or the omen it brought was clear to all. The criticism naturally suggested is the disproportion between the extremity of suffering endured later by the crew, and the nature of the offence committed. There Coleridge lost by the date at which he wrote. The destruction of a whole ship's crew by a Greek god for the slaughter of his winged messenger, would have been quite in keeping. But whether the crew were punished for their cruelty to the bird, or ingratitude to its sender, is not quite clear in the narrative of the 'Ancient Mariner.'

The 'auspex' who suggested the appearance of the albatross was Wordsworth, who had been reading Shelvocke's *Voyages*, though it was Coleridge who developed the omen of the bird into the leading motive of the poem. Its purely natural treatment by an English poet, though exactly in harmony with the spirit of ancient Greece, is a curious contrast to the complex and ridiculous rules for taking omens by birds invented by the Romans. The direct and simple inferences from the appearance of solitary birds were abandoned in order that a body of experts might have the monopoly of such interpretation. The oldest forms of augury from their appearance, such as that of the eagle lifting and replacing Tarquin's cap, or the flights of vultures seen at the founding of Rome, were superseded by elaborate rules of divination. The eagle still maintained its reputation as the direct messenger of Jove; but many other birds were 'scheduled' on the prophetic list, and these again were divided into voice birds and flight birds, for the purpose of augury. The raven, crow, jackdaw, and owl were among the former; and as nine different cries of the owl were distinguished for the purpose of divination, their interpretation must have been altogether confined to experts. Among the 'flight-birds,' the eagle, vulture, buzzard, and two kinds of woodpecker were the most important; and only one bird, the horned owl, seems to have been considered to be at all times a prophet of ill. But with all this apparatus of bird-divination, the omen of the single eagle seems always to have outweighed the rest in popular estimation. Among all the omens of Vespasian's greatness, on which public attention was fixed by the vague though persistent rumour that the time was ripe for a 'ruler' to appear from Judæa, it was that of the eagle perching on his tent which carried most conviction.

The complete effacement of this nervous attention to omens by birds after the conversion of the Roman world, is difficult to explain. In the whole mass of early Christian legend, these natural portents seem to have been transformed into mere fixed symbols appropriated to different holy persons. While the belief in the Sibylline books was reproduced by the Christian practice of using the works of Virgil for divination, almost every trace of belief in the omens given by birds seems to have been lost, with a single exception. The monks invented one prophetic bird—the caladrus, which was said only to appear before the death of Kings. In modern English superstition there are only two living survivals of the ancient belief. One, that the sight of a single magpie is a certain forerunner of misfortune, the other, that a bird entering a church or a house is an omen of death. Both are instances of primitive bird augury, from the appearance of a solitary individual ; for the rhymes which go on to make further divination from different numbers of magpies seen are clearly a ' gloss,' invented by the ingenious and not the ingenuous mind.

THE WILD BOY OF PINDUS

When a Greek newspaper condescends to drop the eternal discussion of the Eastern Question and chronicle the gossip of the market-place, it is apt to become intensely interesting to perverse occidental readers. Now and then in the country news there appears a reprint, in the rough rustic dialect of a local news-sheet of some tale which gives a faint echo of the old, old Hellas, and may carry the reader back in a moment to the days of Hesiod or Herodotus. Let us give, as we find it recently quoted in an Athenian paper, a tale which comes from Thessaly, of the wild boy on Mount Pindus :—'Demetriades worthy-of-honour, the warden of the king's forest on Mount Pindus, was out shooting on the mountain. Being tired, he left the chase of the deer, and turned up a path which led through a steep glen to some shepherds' huts, where he hoped to drink a cup of the milk of Pindus, milk which is famed to be the best of any. While he was walking quietly up the path, he heard a rustling in the underwood, and stayed to listen. Through the branches he saw an unknown animal moving very quickly in the same direction as himself, and made ready to fire at it— να πυροβολήση—but was stopped by shouts of the shepherds on the hill-side above, who called to him not to shoot. He then followed this strange creature, which had the form, indeed, of a man, and was wholly naked ; but ran very fast, sometimes on its feet, but more often on all-fours, and reached the sheep-cote before him. There he found it eagerly drinking the buttermilk from a trough into which it had run while the cheeses from the morning milking were being pressed. When it saw him near, it ran into the wood ; and the chief of the shepherds told him its story. "He is a boy," he said, "a Wallachian, the son of a Wallachian, who lived at Castania, on Mount Pindus. The man went back to Wallachia to seek work, and there he married. He lived there some time, but afterwards came back to Pindus. Six years he was absent, and he brought back four or five children. Then he died, and left his wife and children to the 'five roads' (*i.e.*, to fortune). The woman saw no way of keeping her children in Castania, so she distributed them among her neighbours, and went back to her own country.

But one of them ran away from the person with whom he was left, and has lived in this part of the forest for four years. He lives, even as you saw him, without clothes. In summer he lives well, and drinks our buttermilk daily. In winter he lies in the caves, and lives on roots and nuts. He has learnt no form of speech, neither has he a name." The forest warden determined not to leave him to endure another winter on the mountain ; so he bade the shepherds to catch and bind the boy, and fastened a rope to him, and took him back to Trikalæ, where he clothed him, and has done what he can to civilise him. He always keeps him with himself, or under the care of someone who can talk, because he seems unable to learn to speak any word, though he imitates the voices of many wild creatures. Nor does he learn to understand the names of things. But animal sounds he mimics well, and he has learnt to ride. As his real name is not known, his guardian has called him Sciron.'

The reference in the name to the legend of Theseus is very characteristic of modern Greek sentiment, which preserves unbroken the traditions which cling to the mountains and glens of old Hellas. But apart from its old-world setting, the story affords additional and corroborative evidence of the habits of the very curious and rare animal which, for want of a better name,

we may call Relapsed Man.   The Relapsed Man
—that is, the man who has run wild after civilisation
—is a wholly different creature from Wild or Feral
Man, who has never been tamed ; and in his degeneration seems by a sudden fall to reach a point far
lower, physically and mentally, than the Fuegians or
the Digger Indians.   As for the animals, there are
very few of the more intelligent kinds, which, whether
in work, play, or general well‑being, could not
'give points' to Relapsed Man.   Wherefore the
writer introduces him by way of contrast, the more
as Mr Rudyard Kipling's wolf boy 'Mowzli' is so
charming a boy that if he is allowed to be taken as
a type of all 'wild boys,' we shall soon have someone
trying the experiment of producing them by leaving
them in the woods as Mr Weller, senior, did Sam
in the London streets.   Unfortunately—or fortunately,
as the reader chooses—Relapsed Man can seldom be
studied with the care he deserves, because he is a
scarce and accidental product of unpleasant conditions.
War, famine, pestilence, and wolves are the most
favourable means for producing him, and an overbear-
ing civilisation has made these conditions scarce.
But there exists a body of authoritative evidence
on the subject with which we may compare the case
we have quoted, more particularly with reference to
the statement that he was a wild boy, not a wild man ;

that he went often on all-fours, and in that posture ran fast ; that he ate nuts and roots ; that he sucked up the buttermilk— *νὰ ῥοφᾷ*, the Greek word, is used of the manner in which a horse drinks water, and it will be found that it is a peculiarity of the Relapsed Man that he does not *drink* or *lap*, but sucks up milk or water in this eager, swallowing way — that he went naked ; and that he had not, and has not, learnt to talk, but can mimic animal sounds.

Relapsed Man is found in three forms—one, the most marked and least human, is that which ensues when he has, as a child, been carried off and kept—often for several years—by a wild animal. This is the acute form of relapse, and exhibits all the symptoms of the Pindus boy, with several others, among them a wholly carnivorous appetite, the voice of a wild beast, extreme ferocity, and a temper quite impossible to humanise. The second and milder form occurs when a young child has run wild or been deserted, and manages to keep itself alive without human aid, to which form the case of the Greek boy belongs. The wild boy of Hanover, found in the last century, was a similar instance. He ran on all-fours, ate nothing but roots and nuts, and was without speech. The third form, now very rare in Europe, but not uncommon in the

Ardennes, and other districts where the wolf still lives, is clearly the result of the mental malady of lycanthropy, sufferers from which are yearly brought to be touched by the Holy Stole of St Hubert, who, if less potent than his votaries imagine to drive the latent poison of hydrophobia from the tainted blood, can still minister to a mind diseased, and with mystic and consoling rites cures sufferers who exhibit beyond a doubt all the worst traits by which Relapsed Man is marked in the completist form of retrogression. What these characteristics are, may be judged from the curious and complete instances of the capture of children living in wolves' dens in the Province of Oude, collected by Colonel Sleeman, the able officer who took a leading part in the suppression of the Thugs of India. In the first case, which occurred near the Goomtee River, in a district where wolves abound, and are never killed by the natives from fear of the ill-luck which their death will bring upon the village, a native trooper saw a large she-wolf leave her den, followed by three whelps and a little boy. The boy seemed on the best possible terms with the old dam and the three whelps, and the mother-wolf seemed to guard all four with equal care. They all went down to the river and drank, after which they were chased by the trooper; but they escaped over rough ground into the den, the boy running on all-fours quite as fast as the young wolves. The man then got assistance and dug the whole party out; the wolves and boy bolted together, and the boy was caught, fastened to a rope, and led to the village. He could not speak, but growled and snarled like a young wolf, and tried to bolt into every hole or shelter that was passed. After four days he was sent to an English officer, Captain Nicholetts. Though kindly treated, he never learnt to speak, ran away from grown-up people, flew at children and tried to bite them, and ran to eat his food on all-fours. But he was friendly with a pariah-dog, and would let it share his food. He would suck up a whole pitcher of buttermilk without drawing breath apparently. He never laughed or smiled, and destroyed all clothes given him. Two and a half years after his capture he died, and just before his death spoke once or twice, saying his head ached, and pronouncing the word for water. Another child caught in a wolf's den in the same neighbour-hood was even more savage. He would only eat raw flesh, on which he put his hands as a dog puts its fore-feet. He drank in the manner mentioned before, and habitually ran on all-fours, from which his knees and knuckles were quite hard. Though reclaimed by his mother, he was quite untameable,

x

and at last lived in the village streets like a pariah-dog, going every night into the jungle. A third boy, caught near Hasanpur, could walk upright, but preferred to go on all-fours, and ran so fast in that position that no one could catch him. He could not talk, but was induced to wear clothes. But he still remained so inhuman, that few people would keep him for any time ; and for three nights in succession wolves were seen to come up and awake him. In each case the boy played with the wolves who capered round him and licked him.

We will not attempt to frame a theory from the cases we have quoted. No doubt it will be open to those who hold with the late Professor Garratt, that man was the first of the animals to stand upright, and that he has not yet learned to do this properly, or he would not be subject to spontaneous internal injuries such as rupture from which quadrupeds are generally exempt, to see in these accounts instances of a return to a primitive state. Others will fairly argue that the degradation of Relapsed Man so far transcends all known instances of man in his lowest natural state, as merely to be an example of *corruptio optimi pessima*. But, in any case, we may infer from the instances which we have quoted, that Relapsed Man walks and runs well and by preference on all-fours —cannot speak lives on raw food, fears his own species, drinks by suction, and, what is perhaps best of all, never lives to maturity ; for all the captures recorded have been those of boys, not of men.

THE END

Colston & Coy., Limited, Printers, Edinburgh.

A SELECT LIST OF BOOKS

Published by SEELEY & CO. Limited

46, 47, & 48 ESSEX STREET, STRAND

FINE-ART BOOKS

THE PRESENT STATE OF THE FINE ARTS IN FRANCE. By P. G. HAMERTON. With Etchings and other Illustrations. Cloth, gilt edges, 21*s.* Large Paper, 42*s.*
'Singularly attractive on account of its numerous and charming illustrations.'—*Times.*

SOME MINOR ARTS AS PRACTISED IN ENGLAND:— POTTERY, BOOKBINDING, EFFIGIES IN WOOD, ENAMELS, &c. With Sixteen Plates, most of them in Colour, and many other Illustrations. Cloth, 21*s.*
'Richly and beautifully illustrated in colours.'—*Times.*

ROUND ABOUT SNOWDON. Thirty Plates in Etching and Aquatint. By THOMAS HUSON, R.I. With Notes by J. J. HISSEY. Large 8vo. 21*s.* net. Large-paper Copies, 2*l.* 12*s.* 6*d.* net.
'A delightful tribute to Welsh scenery.'—*Daily Telegraph.*

ROUND ABOUT HELVELLYN. Twenty-four Plates in Etching and Aquatint. By THOMAS HUSON, R.I. With Notes by the Artist. Large 8vo. 21*s.* net. Large-paper Copies, 2*l.* 12*s.* 6*d.* net.
'Shows a true eye for landscape, both in its magnificence and its more homely beauty.'—*Daily News.*

THE RIVIERA. Twenty Etchings and Forty Vignettes by ALEXANDER ANSTED. With Notes by the Artist. Large 8vo. cloth, 21*s.* net. Large-paper Copies, 42*s.* net.
'Delicacy and care in execution are the characteristics of Mr. Ansted's work.'—*Spectator.*

DUTCH ETCHERS of the SEVENTEENTH CENTURY.
By Lawrence Binyon.
'A masterly piece of work.'—*Black and White.*
WILLIAM BLAKE, PAINTER AND POET. By Dr. Garnett.
'Of unusual interest and value.'—*Bradford Observer.*

Specimen of Illustration.

THE RENAISSANCE OF SCULPTURE IN BELGIUM.
By O. G. Destrée.
GERARD DAVID, PAINTER AND ILLUMINATOR. By
J. H. W. Weale.

**** The Numbers are bound in Quarterly Volumes. Price 10s. 6d.
Cases with Title-page, 1s. 6d. each.

THE SPECTATOR IN LONDON. Essays by ADDISON and STEELE. Illustrated by RALPH CLEAVER. Crown 8vo. cloth, with gilt edges.

THE TEMPLE : SACRED POEMS AND PRIVATE EJACULATIONS. By GEORGE HERBERT. Reprinted from the First Edition. With upwards of Sixty Illustrations. Cloth, 6*s.*

'One of the most beautiful out of the many good books we have seen.'
Church Bells.

Illustration from ' The Spectator in London.'

WESTMINSTER ABBEY. By W. J. LOFTIE. With Twelve Plates and many Minor Illustrations, chiefly by HERBERT RAILTON. Price 21*s.* Large-paper Copies, 4*l.* 4*s.*

'One of the most popular of the many books dealing with the great Abbey.'—*Guardian.*

Also a Cheap Edition. Large crown 8vo. cloth, 7*s.* 6*d.*

An Abridged Edition, with Thirty Illustrations, is published at 2*s.* 6*d.* Size, large crown 8vo.

IMAGINATION IN LANDSCAPE PAINTING. By P. G. HAMERTON. With Fourteen Copper-plates and many Vignettes. Price 21*s.* cloth, gilt edges.

Also a Cheap Edition. Large crown 8vo. cloth, 6*s.*

COUNTRY STORIES. By Mary Russell Mitford, Author of 'Our Village.' With Seventy Illustrations by George Morrow. Crown 8vo. cloth, with gilt edges, 6*s.*

ASPECTS OF MODERN OXFORD. By A. D. Godley, Fellow of Magdalen College. With many Illustrations. Price 6*s.* cloth.

'Delightful for its humour and liveliness.'—*Manchester Guardian.*

Illustration from ' Country Stories.'

GOTHIC ARCHITECTURE. From the French of E. Corroyer. Edited by Walter Armstrong, Director of the National Gallery in Ireland. With over 200 Illustrations. Large crown 8vo. 6*s.*

'To be warmly recommended.'—*National Observer.*

A WILD SHEEP CHASE. Notes of a little Philosophic Ramble in Corsica. By E. Bergerat. Translated from the French. With Illustrations. Price 6*s.* cloth.

'An exceedingly vivacious and entertaining book.'—*Yorkshire Post.*

THE LIFE OF J. M. W. TURNER, R.A. By
P. G. HAMERTON. New Edition, with an entirely fresh set
of Illustrations. Large crown 8vo. cloth, 6s.

EVENTS OF OUR OWN TIME

A Series of Volumes dealing with the more important events of
the last half-century. Cloth, 5s. Library Edition, with Proofs
of the Plates, in roxburgh, 10s. 6d.

**THE REFOUNDING OF THE GERMAN
EMPIRE.** By Colonel MALLESON, C.S.I. With Portraits
on Copper, and Maps and Plans.

'A very interesting and instructive account of the Refounding of the
German Empire.'—*Spectator*.

THE WAR IN THE CRIMEA. By SIR EDWARD
HAMLEY, K.C.B. With Portraits on Copper, and Maps and
Plans.

'A well-written historical narrative, written by a competent critic and
well-informed observer of the scenes and events it describes.'—*Times*.

THE INDIAN MUTINY OF 1857. By Colonel
MALLESON, C.S.I. With Portraits on Copper and Maps and
Plans.

'Battles, sieges, and rapid marches are described in a style spirited
and concise.'—*Saturday Review*.

***ACHIEVEMENTS IN ENGINEERING.** By
L. F. VERNON HARCOURT. With many Illustrations.

'We hope this book will find its way into the hands of all young
engineers. All the information has been carefully gathered from all the
best sources, and is therefore perfectly accurate.'—*Engineering Review*.

THE AFGHAN WARS OF 1839-42 and 1878-80.
By ARCHIBALD FORBES. With Portraits on Copper and
Maps and Plans.

'Eminently readable and spirited.'—*Saturday Review*.

***THE DEVELOPMENT OF NAVIES DURING
THE LAST HALF-CENTURY.** By Captain S. EARDLEY
WILMOT, R.N. With many Illustrations.

'A most informing and lucid book.'—*Spectator*.

***THE LIBERATION OF ITALY.** By the Countess
E. MARTINENGO CESARESCO. With Portraits on Copper.

'A noteworthy contribution to the history of Italian unity.'—*Times*.

*Of Volumes so * marked there will be no Library Edition.*

Illustration from 'The Life of Turner.'

Second Edition.

WILD ENGLAND OF TO-DAY, AND THE
WILD LIFE IN IT. By J. C. CORNISH, Author of 'Life at the Zoo.' Illustrated with Original Drawings by LANCELOT SPEED, and from Photographs. Demy 8vo. cloth, 12*s*. 6*d*.

'A more delightful book it would be hard to find.'—*National Observer.*

Third Edition.

LIFE AT THE ZOO. Notes and Traditions of the
Regent's Park Gardens. By C. J. CORNISH. Illustrated by Photographs and Sketches. Demy 8vo. cloth, 12*s*. 6*d*.

'Without a single dull page.'—*World.*

THE SYLVAN YEAR. Leaves from the Note-Book
of Raoul Dubois. By P. G. HAMERTON. With Twenty Etchings by the Author and other Artists. Post 8vo. cl. 12*s*. 6*d*.
Also a Cheap Edition, with Eight Etchings. Cloth, 5*s*.

'Few will read these pages without extreme satisfaction.'—*Athenæum.*

CHAPTERS ON ANIMALS. By P. G. HAMERTON.
With Twenty Etchings. Post 8vo. cloth, 12*s*. 6*d*.
Also a Cheap Edition, with Eight Etchings. Cloth, 5*s*.

'Few books show better or more original work.'—*Saturday Review.*

FAMOUS SCENERY

THE RIVERS OF DEVON: FROM SOURCE TO SEA.
By JOHN LL. WARDEN PAGE. With Map, Etchings, and other Illustrations. Large crown 8vo. cloth, 7*s*. 6*d*.

'A capital book to read as a preparation for a tour in Devon.'—*Scotsman.*

AN EXPLORATION OF DARTMOOR. By J. LL.
W. PAGE. With Map, Etchings, and other Illustrations. Third edition. Crown 8vo. cloth, 7*s*. 6*d*.

'The book is well written, and abounds in practical descriptions and old-world traditions.'—*Western Antiquary.*

AN EXPLORATION OF EXMOOR. By J. LL. W.
PAGE. With Map, Etchings, and other Illustrations. Third Edition. Crown 8vo. cloth, 7*s*. 6*d*.

'Mr. Page has evidently got up his subject with the care that comes of affection, and the result is that he has produced a book full of pleasant reading.'—*Graphic.*

THE PEAK OF DERBYSHIRE. By JOHN LEYLAND.
With Map, Etchings, and other Illustrations, by HERBERT RAILTON and ALFRED DAWSON. Crown 8vo. cloth, price 7*s*. 6*d*. ; roxburgh, 12*s*. 6*d*.

'A delightful book on a delightful subject.'—*Saturday Review.*

Illustration from 'Life at the Zoo'

THE YORKSHIRE COAST AND THE CLEVE-LAND HILLS AND DALES.

By JOHN LEYLAND. With Map, Etchings, and other Illustrations by ALFRED DAWSON and LANCELOT SPEED. Crown 8vo. cloth, 7s. 6d. Roxburgh, 12s. 6d.

'Written with judgment, good taste, and extensive knowledge.'—*Spectator.*

EIGHTEENTH-CENTURY WRITERS

DEAN SWIFT AND HIS WRITINGS.

By G. P. MORIARTY, Balliol College, Oxford. With Nine Portraits on Copper. Cloth, 7s. 6d. Large-paper Copies (150 only) 21s.

'An extremely sound and satisfactory little book.'—*National Observer.*

LADY MARY WORTLEY MONTAGUE.

Extracts from her Letters. Edited by A. R. ROPES, late Fellow of King's College, Cambridge. With Nine Portraits on Copper. Cloth, 7s. 6d. Large-paper Copies, 21s.

'Delightful to read.'—*Yorkshire Post.*

HORACE WALPOLE AND HIS WORLD.

Select Passages from his Letters. Edited by L. B. SEELEY. With Eight Portraits on Copper. Cloth, 6s.

'We do not often meet with a more entertaining volume.'
Pall Mall Gazette.

FANNY BURNEY AND HER FRIENDS.

Select Passages from her Diary. Edited by L. B. SEELEY, M.A., late Fellow of Trinity College, Cambridge. With Nine Portraits on Copper. Third Edition. Cloth, 7s. 6d.

'The charm of the volume is heightened by nine illustrations of some of the masterpieces of English art, and it would not be possible to find a more captivating present for any one beginning to appreciate the characters of the last century.'—*Academy.*

MRS. THRALE, AFTERWARDS MRS. PIOZZI.

By L. B. SEELEY, M.A., late Fellow of Trinity College, Cambridge. With Nine Portraits on Copper. Cloth, 7s. 6d.

'Mr. Seeley had excellent material to write upon, and he has turned it to the best advantage.'—*Pall Mall Gazette.*

SIR JOSHUA REYNOLDS AND THE ROYAL ACADEMY.

By CLAUDE PHILLIPS. With Nine Copper-plates. Cloth, 7s. 6d.

Large-paper Copies (150 only), 21s.

'Full of accurate information and very readable withal.'—*Times.*

Illustration from ' The Coast of Yorkshire.'

PICTURESQUE PLACES

EDINBURGH. PICTURESQUE NOTES. By R. L. STEVENSON. With many Illustrations. Crown 8vo. cloth, 3*s.* 6*d.*; roxburgh, 5*s.*

'Daintily and deliciously illustrated and charmingly written, they form a volume which may be described, without exaggeration, as a literary gem of the first water.'—*St. James's Gazette.*

THE BRITISH SEAS. By W. CLARK RUSSELL and Others. With upwards of Fifty Illustrations. New and cheaper edition. Cloth, 6*s.*

'A delightful volume.'—*Morning Post.*

STRATFORD-ON-AVON, from the Earliest Times to the Death of Shakespeare. By SIDNEY LEE. With many Illustrations by E. HULL. Large crown 8vo. cloth, 6*s.*

'A work of value and well illustrated.'—*Dramatic Review.*

THE RUINED ABBEYS OF YORKSHIRE. By W. CHAMBERS LEFROY. With many Illustrations. Large crown 8vo. cloth, 6*s.*

'A very charming volume.'—*Leeds Mercury.*

PARIS IN OLD AND PRESENT TIMES, with Especial Reference to Changes in its Architecture and Topography. By P. G. HAMERTON. With Seventy Illustrations. Cloth, 6*s.*

'Valuable and fascinating.'—*Courier.*

OXFORD. Chapters by A. LANG. With many Illustrations by A. Brunet-Debaines, A. Toussaint, and R. Kent Thomas. Large crown 8vo. cloth, 6*s.*

'Told in Mr. Lang's best style, and beautifully illustrated.'—*Literary Churchman.*

CAMBRIDGE. By J. W. CLARK, M.A. With Etchings and Vignettes by Brunet-Debaines and Toussaint. Crown 8vo. cloth, 6*s.*

'A thoroughly artistic work of topographical description and illustration.'—*Illustrated London News.*

THE INNS OF COURT AND CHANCERY. By W. J. LOFTIE. With Twelve Engravings and many other Illustrations, chiefly by HERBERT RAILTON. Cloth, 21*s.*

Also a Cheap Edition. Large crown 8vo. cloth, 6*s.*

'This delightful volume.'—*Daily Telegraph.*

WINDSOR. By the Rev. W. J. LOFTIE. With Sixty-seven Illustrations. Cloth, 6*s*.

'Remarkably pleasant and comprehensive.'—*Graphic.*

Illustration from 'Windsor.'

LANCASHIRE. By LEO H. GRINDON. With Fourteen Etchings and numerous Vignettes. Price 1*l.* 1*s*. Large paper Copies, with Proofs of the Plates, 3*l.* 3*s*.

Also a Cheap Edition. Cloth, 6*s*.

'Cannot fail to delight those who admire good artistic work.'—*Liverpool Daily Post.*

CHARING CROSS TO ST. PAUL'S. By JUSTIN M'CARTHY. With Twelve Copper-plates and many Minor Illustrations by JOSEPH PENNELL. Price 21*s.*
Large-paper Copies, with Proofs, 2*l.* 12*s.* 6*d.*
'Mr. Pennell's sketches are simply admirable.'—*Times.*

MADAME: Memoirs of Henrietta, daughter of Charles I. and Duchess of Orleans. By JULIA CARTWRIGHT (Mrs. Henry Ady). With Two Portraits on Copper. Demy 8vo. price 16*s.*
*** This volume contains Ninety Unpublished Letters of Charles II.
'A very attractive narrative.'—*Glasgow Herald.*

Second Edition.
SACHARISSA: Some Account of Dorothy Sidney, Countess of Sunderland, her Family and Friends. By JULIA CARTWRIGHT (Mrs. Henry Ady). With Portrait. Cloth, 12*s.* 6*d.*
'A delightful book.'—*Pall Mall Gazette.*

STUDIES IN MODERN MUSIC. Berlioz, Schumann, and Wagner. By W. H. HADOW, M.A. With Five Portraits on Copper. Cloth, 7*s.* 6*d.*
'We cordially recommend the book.'—*Church Times.*

STUDIES IN MODERN MUSIC. Chopin, Dvorak, and Brahms. By W. H. HADOW, M.A. With Four Portraits in Copper. Cloth, 7*s.* 6*d.*
'Each memoir is a literary gem of exceptional lustre and value.'
Daily Telegraph.

A SHORT HISTORY OF NAPOLEON THE FIRST. By Sir J. R. SEELEY. With Portrait. Price 5*s.* cloth.
'Within the limits which the author has set himself the essay seems to us one of singular force and brilliancy.'—*Guardian.*

GOETHE: Reviewed after Sixty Years. By Sir J. R. SEELEY. Crown 8vo. with Portrait, price 3*s.* 6*d.*
'The character and compass of Goethe's genius are admirably summed up.'—*Leeds Mercury.*

BELT AND SPUR. Stories of the Knights of Old. With Sixteen Illuminations. Cloth, price 5*s.*
'A sort of boys' Froissart, with admirable illustrations.'—*Pall Mall Gazette.*

FOREST OUTLAWS; OR, ST. HUGH AND THE KING. By the Rev. E. GILLIAT. With Sixteen Illustrations. Cloth, 6*s.*
'Distinctly one of the very best books of the season.'—*Standard.*

THE SIEGE OF NORWICH CASTLE. A Story of the Last Struggle against the Conqueror. By M. M. BLAKE. With Illustrations. Cloth, 5*s.*

FOR THE HONOUR OF THE FLAG. A Story of our Sea Fights with the Dutch. By Commander CHARLES N. ROBINSON, R.N., and JOHN LEYLAND. With Illustrations by LANCELOT SPEED. Large crown 8vo. cloth, 5s.
'A capital story.'—*Saturday Review.*

THE CAPTAIN OF THE WIGHT. By FRANK COWPER. With Illustrations by the Author. Cloth, 5s.

Illustration from 'Charing Cross to St. Paul's.'

THE CITY IN THE SEA. Stories of the Old Venetians. By the Author of 'Belt and Spur.' With Coloured Illustrations. Cloth, 5s.
'Very stirring are the tales of the long struggle between Genoa and Venice.'—*Standard.*

JOHN STANDISH; OR, THE HARROWING OF LONDON. A Story of Wat Tyler's Rebellion. By Rev. E. GILLIAT. With Illustrations. Cloth, 5s.

THE DRAGON OF THE NORTH. A Tale of the Normans in Italy. By E. J. OSWALD, Author of 'Studies in Iceland,' &c. With Illustrations. Cloth, 5s.

PROFESSOR CHURCH'S WORKS

THE STORY OF THE ILIAD. 5s.
THE STORY OF THE ODYSSEY. 5s.
THE BURNING OF ROME. 5s.
THE FALL OF ATHENS. 5s.
STORIES FROM HOMER. 5s.
STORIES FROM VIRGIL. 5s.
STORIES FROM THE GREEK TRAGEDIANS. 5s.
STORIES FROM THE GREEK COMEDIANS. 5s.
STORIES OF THE EAST FROM HERODOTUS. 5s.
THE STORY OF THE PERSIAN WAR. 5s.
ROMAN LIFE IN THE DAYS OF CICERO. 5s.
STORIES FROM LIVY. 5s.

THE COUNT OF THE SAXON SHORE. 5s.
WITH THE KING AT OXFORD. 5s.
THE CHANTRY PRIEST. 5s.
STORIES FROM THE MAGICIANS. 5s.
THE YOUNG MACEDONIAN. 5s.
THE STORY OF THE LAST DAYS OF JERUSALEM. 3s. 6d.
TO THE LIONS. 3s. 6d.
STORIES FROM ENGLISH HISTORY. Part I. 3s. 6d.
STORIES FROM ENGLISH HISTORY. Part II. 3s. 6d.
HEROES AND KINGS. 1s. 6d.
STORIES FROM THE ILIAD AND AENEID. Sewed, 1s.; cl. 1s. 6d.

VOLUMES OF POPULAR SCIENCE

With Illustrations. Price 5s. each.

THE GREAT WORLD'S FARM. By SELINA GAYE.
THE OCEAN OF AIR. By AGNES GIBERNE.
SUN, MOON, AND STARS. By AGNES GIBERNE.
THE WORLD'S FOUNDATIONS. By AGNES GIBERNE.
THE STORY OF THE HILLS. By Rev. H. N. HUTCHINSON.

WORKS by MRS. MARSHALL

A Series of Historical Romances. Illustrated, 5s. each.

THE MASTER of the MUSICIANS.
PENSHURST PLACE.
RACHEL, LADY RUSSELL.
WINIFREDE'S JOURNAL.
WINCHESTER MEADS.
UNDER SALISBURY SPIRE.
IN THE CITY OF FLOWERS.
MRS. WILLOUGHBY'S OCTAVE.
THE MISTRESS OF TAYNE COURT.

KENSINGTON PALACE.
CONSTANTIA CAREW.
DAME ALICIA CHAMBERLAYNE.
JOANNA'S INHERITANCE.
UNDER THE MENDIPS.
IN FOUR REIGNS.
ON THE BANKS OF THE OUSE.
IN THE EAST COUNTRY.
IN COLSTON'S DAYS.
LIFE'S AFTERMATH.

Cheap Edition of Earlier Works, at 3s. 6d.

VIOLET DOUGLAS.
CHRISTABEL KINGSCOTE.
HELEN'S DIARY.
BROTHERS AND SISTERS.
MILLICENT LEGH.

MRS. MAINWARING'S JOURNAL.
LADY ALICE.
HEIGHTS AND VALLEYS.
DOROTHY'S DAUGHTERS.
EDWARD'S WIFE.

London: Printed by STRANGEWAYS & SONS, Tower Street, Cambridge Circus, W.C.